THE EXTENDED EDITION

THE
PRIVATE
SERIES

Public

USA TODAY BESTSELLING AUTHOR
XAVIER NEAL

1

Public

Public: The Extended Edition (The Private Series #2)
By Xavier Neal
© Xavier Neal 2017 (Updated Extension 2024)
Cover by Dana Leah
All Rights Reserved

Subscribe to my newsletter!
http://bit.ly/XNNLSL21

Contents

Dedication:

To The Universe…Thank you for the amazing experiences I've had in private, as well as in public.

WARNING:

This novel contains **EXTREMELY** foul language (from both men and women), **EXPLICIT GRAPHIC** sexual content (including some that may differ from your own), DARKER themes (that may make a person uncomfortable) and other adult situations. Some readers may find the content/subject matter that is covered in this work to be triggering or disagree with it entirely. This novel is intended for readers over the age of 18.

This novel is also BOOK 2 in a TRILOGY and reads BEST when read in order. If you would like to start at the beginning of the trilogy the novel before this is Private (The Private Series #1).
Please keep all these things in mind and proceed at your own risk.

Thank you.

- Xavier

Playlist Selects

Here are five songs from the *Private Series* playlist!

Feel free to follow the playlist on Spotify to find more songs I felt related to the book.

1. Remedy – Adele (Soul/Pop)
2. Smile – Slim Thug (Rap)
3. The Only Exception – Paramore (Rock)
4. Don't Tell Me It's Over – Gym Class Heroes (Rap Rock/Hip-Hop)
5. The Reason – Brett Eldredge (Country)

More songs: https://bit.ly/PrivateSeriesPlaylist

Chapter 1

Wes

You would think after a year of doing these I would've gotten better at them.

I haven't.

I'm honestly concerned that I've somehow managed to get *worse*.

Which would be impressive.

Irritating.

Yet impressive.

"Uh...Mr. Wilcox?" Zaidee Khan, my personal assistant, croaks from the other end of the phone that's on speaker. "Are you...um...actually listening to me?"

"*Yes*," I acknowledge in tandem with tapping my shark pen against my pursed lips.

I am listening.

Partially.

I'm also searching this booklet.

I refuse to leave for the Morgan Brand merger press conference without being able to pass this headache back to my fiancée.

My fiancée who I barely waited six months to propose to.

They were a challenging six months, filled with work-based whirlwinds neither of us were prepared for.

While Bryn began as a tour guide at The Bower and Powell Aquatic Institute, she transitioned to Research & Rescue within her first two months, which is where she's remained and truly making a name for herself in the field.

Her change in position is what led to our physical change in location.

The *initial* acquiring of our downtown Highland penthouse was specially done to provide her with a residence closer to where she works. Her uncertain hours combined with my own sometimes resulted in us *literally* not seeing one another for days at a time.

That was unacceptable to me.

Almost as unacceptable as her crashing at the home of Calen Connelly, her colleague and newest best friend, when she didn't have enough energy for a long drive home or needed to be back at work sooner than the inconvenience of living at the estate would allow.

Purchasing this penthouse was truly done in *support* of her career.

Not in spite of the friendship I loathe her having.

J.T. would obviously beg to differ, but he won't.

Primarily because I threatened to send his Nightwing ass to Peru for four months to see firsthand which of our new beers from the Morgan merger would pair well with ceviche.

"Evie wanted me to remind you *not* to wear a tie, you look more approachable without it," Zaidee resumes reciting things from her check list.

I don't *want* to be approachable.

I don't *want* my photo taken.

Reported.

Shared and reshared again and again and again across social media.

My allowing it to happen is merely a compromise I'm making.

I want to have a life *with* Bryn, one where I can take her to dinner after a long day or accompany her to a movie on a Sunday with her friend Vanessa or go thrift shopping for vintage memorabilia, all of which means coming out of the shadows to be seen in the streets of my Gotham.

Rumors regarding me, my family, my estate, and my company all run rampant regardless of whatever official statements we make; however, they are significantly *less* when we've strategically

12

presented them with opportunities to *ask* questions as opposed to making assumptions they can be sued over for slander.

I speak to the public in press settings and attend public events to appease the public relations department along with the other shareholders of my company.

J.T. is still the *active* and *more important* face of Wilcox Enterprises, but I am beginning to share *some* of the responsibility, therefore, allowing him to have more time to work on the projects that are closer to *him*.

Like his ratings and location app idea where consumers will be able to not only rank their personal preferred flavors in their accounts, but track where it's socially available, thus putting his degree and passion of both technology integration and the alcohol business to profitable use.

And the projections of profit for it are *extremely* high.

And even more so once we add our budding library of beers to it.

"She also wanted me to remind you not to wear black on black," my assistant continues at the same time I adjust myself on the gray, L-Shaped couch. "It's not a funeral."

That's exactly what I'll be wearing.

"Julia wanted me to remind you to use *positive* buzz words such as 'welcoming' and 'family' to keep the focus on the *building* of your brand versus the destruction of others."

I use the non-ink end of the pen to diagonally follow the letters of a suspected word.

"And lastly, Mr. Hawthorne has advised me *against* allowing any more time to be scheduled with Velora until you and Bryn have scheduled time *with him* to actually sign the prenuptial agreements, the legacy asset paperwork, and your will's as well as your living wills."

Disappointment over once again failing to find something has me grumping in displeasure.

"Would you like me to go ahead and schedule that time with him now?" Zaidee politely offers. "I know Velora will be calling within the hour requesting the same."

Velora Appelbaum is one of the best wedding planners in the country.

The problem?

Her inability to understand that the woman I'm marrying isn't just an heiress with only a social calendar of obligations.

I lower my mouth in preparation to answer when movement out of the corner of my eye captures my attention instead.

The sight of my completely naked fiancée giving her dark, thick locks a lazy ruffle while unhurriedly approaching has me abandoning the word search along with the obnoxious phone call. "We'll schedule those activities at a later date."

"Was that Velora again?" Bryn quirks a curious eyebrow as I swiftly end the call. "Did I miss another one of those 'Which One of These Announcements is Not Like the Other' discussions?"

"No," my retort is attached to pulling her into my black, boxer brief covered lap, "it was Zaidee." Her arms lovingly tangle around my neck after getting into a comfortable straddling position. "Work reminders."

"*Don't tell me she's turning on the Bat signal early, Mr. Wayne.*"

I slowly trail my calloused index finger down her light mocha chest to her darker nipple. "*Not before you've touched my jewels, Ms. Kyle.*"

"Is that what I'm doing up so early?" she practically moans due to me delivering a light tug. "It's barely after six."

"It's easily past nine."

"Do you want me to use my claws for pain or pleasure?"

It's impossible not to smirk while lifting her full tit to my open mouth. "*Both.*"

Her lips move to make what I have no doubt is a snarky comeback prompting me to suck on the hardened nub, an action that provokes a heavy, heady moan instead. *"Mr. Wilcox..."* The rolling of my tongue warrants a repeat of the sound. *"Is this how you say good morning to everyone?"*

"Just my fiancée," precedes me executing the same teasing motion to her other nipple. *"Besides, I'm trying to make it a good morning, little prey."* This time the nip presented is a little toothier. Her favorite. *"We both know actions mean more than words."* A single hum of agreement is followed by me effortlessly flipping her onto her back. *"And my actions are currently telling you that I missed the chance to have you for dinner,"* the freeing of my shaft is smooth and swift, *"therefore I will not miss the chance to have you for breakfast."*

Bryn's mouth twitches again to argue yet has whatever response she conjured severed courtesy of my cock slipping inside. *"Wes..."*

"Mmm," is attached to the first bite stolen near her collarbone, *"so fucking wet for me, little prey."* Sinking my teeth deeper into the tender skin has her needily lifting her hips. Locking her ankles together right above my ass. *"Always so fucking ready."*

Impatient scratches scale their way down the nape of my neck.

Along the edges of my shoulders.

Anchor themselves into my biceps for leverage.

"Tell me missed you me," I command while harshly heaving my lower half forward. *"Tell me you're mine."*

"Make me."

The challenge is met by another hard hit, this one with enough force to cause our couch to scrape across the freshly buffed floors. Her moan over the impact combined with the rasp sound created from the furniture easily fuels me to execute an encore.

One that's slightly faster.

More ferocious.

That leads to her hungrily whining, *"More."*

15

"*No.*"

Skating my teeth upward receives a round of shivers.

Whimpers.

"*You give me what I want, little prey,*" another teasing nip is given, this time to the shell of her ear, "*and I'll give you what you need.*"

Her nails cut deeper into my arms as she surrenders. "*Yours.*"

"*Do better, baby.*" A tiny, torturous thrust is presented. "*Or we'll both be going to work hungry.*"

"*Yours, Wes.*" There's no vacillation in her voice or volume. "*All yours.*" She impatiently arches underneath me and dramatically punctuates her whispered proclamation. "*Only. Yours.*"

Growls of approval are proceeded by precise, primitive pounds.

Ones that carelessly bump her clit.

Rob her of any ability to catch a breath.

Have her soaking wet muscles swelling around my shaft again and again and again as though determined not to keep it drenched but *drowning.*

Drowning in their white-hot waves.

Diving to the darkest depths that cause the loudest screams.

Except she can't.

Not being able to gather enough air in her lungs keeps Bryn's vocal cords practically paralyzed.

Incapable of anything other than panting.

And her endless panting quickens the speed of my stroking.

Increases the pressure and consistency.

Calls to my balls to anxiously swell in anticipation every time they collide with her.

Bryn's thighs uncontrollably tremble against me while her ankles bury themselves into my back, both actions wordlessly begging me for mercy she's not going to get.

Because it's not what she needs.

16

It's *never* what my little prey needs.

"*W...*" manages to break past her lips prompting my pumps to become completely pitiless.

Feral.

Another louder, more intense attempt is made, "*W...*"

Grunt on top of grunt callously crashes into her ear.

Against the side of her face.

Between the paper-thin space separating us.

"*W...e...*"

Hearing her get closer to finishing my name has my dick incessantly thickening, desperate to paint every letter of it onto the orgasm she's barely holding onto.

"*You need to come, little prey,*" the purred promulgation is damn near instantly met. "*You need to fucking come all over my cock.*" Additional sopping wet constrictions clamor in anticipation. "*You need to show me who you fucking belong to.*"

"*Wessssss!*" rushes out of her agape mouth at the same time her pussy begins wildly pulsating, greedily sucking my shaft in deeper and deeper, until it can't resist the ravenous urge to plunge to the point of no return and release scorching hot ropes of cum. "*Wessss!*"

Inhuman huffs are attached to additional intemperate thrusts.

I mindlessly let my hips rock to the same pace as her uneven breathing and grin in complete satisfaction.

Like I said earlier, this penthouse was *initially* acquired to support her career; however, I like to believe it serves a dual purpose of providing a certain type of aid to our relationship.

Here we have actual privacy.

To talk.

To laugh.

To cook.

To fuck.

And given how much of our life has to be in the public eye nowadays, I appreciate the top floor safe haven it's become.

17

Chapter 2

Wes

"I told you no black on black," Evie Jordan, my personal publicist – well now the entire Wilcox family personal publicist – scolds, long, red hair scattering all around. "You're not Johnny Cash."

"We both knew I was going to." I casually slide my hands into my black suit pants. "I'm predictable."

"*Reliable*," she chastises with a small point in my direction. "It's all about marketability."

My best friend is the *literal* embodiment of the word.

From looks to speech to the woman of the week he finds himself photographed with, J.T. manages to demonstrate a level of relatability in the same breath as inaccessibility, which is essentially the ying and yang of the best enterprises.

Consumers appreciate his charm.

Investors admire his credibility.

I may feed the money machine to guarantee it continues to produce, but it's him who maintains the audience that wants to be fed.

Contrary to what social media likes to say, I *don't* take him for granted.

I'm absolutely aware of how much this company needs him.

I'm thoroughly aware of how much *I* need him.

Especially in moments like this.

"Your long black," an unfamiliar, slender woman cradling a tablet announces upon her arrival. "And your dry-cleaning rush order has been confirmed."

Evie accepts the beverage from the stringy haired blonde prior to introducing, "Wes meet Jenni. Jenni *officially* meet the boss."

"I thought you were my boss," squeaks the young, mousy female.

"I *am* your boss," she snips in obvious annoyance, "but this is *my* boss; therefore, by proxy, *your* boss." She lets her hazel gaze glide over the jittery individual. "Understood?"

"Mmmhmm." Jenni enthusiastically nods. "Totally! One hundred thousand percentsky!" The head bobbing continues as she extends her empty palm out to me. "I'm Jenni. Jenni Cohen. Evie's new assistant!"

We briefly shake. "Wes."

"Weston William Wilcox, sole heir and primary shareholder to Wilcox Enterprises, currently engaged to Brynley Elizabeth Winters, the only daughter to Lauren Winters Baker, the woman who runs the household department of your personal estate who is currently on her honeymoon in Switzerland."

There's no stopping my eyebrows from twitching in question.

"I study!" Her eagerness to please threatens to make me smirk. "*A lot.*"

Evie waits until my stare swings back to her to sigh, "I had to fire Dina ten days ago after I overheard her saying some very unbecoming things about your physical appearance to another employee in Julia's department."

Unsurprising.

The horrible comments and judgements regarding my disfigurement that I anticipated receiving if I ever returned to the public continuously make themselves known.

And add to the reason I decline the offers to do magazine covers or features.

I don't need pity from the public.

From anyone.

"And then Julia let me have Pruitt who was *perfect* until I caught him jerking it to Bryn's photo during a long lunch on Monday."

Low grumbles of disapproval receive an eyeroll.

20

"Yeah, yeah, yeah, I know. Gaston has already been blackballed from the village, Mr. Beast."

Jenni openly giggles at the joke despite my glaring.

"Which brings me to *Jenni* who was the only person I interviewed that didn't recoil at your photo-"

"They're just scars," she says on a casual tossing of her hand.

"-who didn't wanna bang your fiancée-"

"Total snipe but I prefer redheads."

"-or your best friend-"

"I'd rather bang one of the bunnies than the boys."

"-and understood the difference between an americano and long black." The coffee slowly creeps towards her lips. "Plus, she was willing to start immediately."

"I was taught always be ready to hit the ice."

Another twitch of my brow prompts my publicist to add, "You get used to the hockey talk."

"My big bro just got traded to Dalvegan!" Her tiny white top covered shoulders excitedly bounce. "They suck but top league is top league, right?"

I wouldn't know.

Sports aren't exactly my thing.

Getting our brands *into* sporting events, however, is on the list of goals now that this merger is officially done.

Today's signing is purely ceremonial.

"You ready?" J.T. unexpectedly inquires over my shoulder from where he's entering the spare conference room we're occupying at The Frost Luxury Hotel. "The Romulans are waiting." When no one makes a retort or smiles at his statement, he unhappily grumps, "Where's Uhura when you need her?"

"Saving seals or sea lions or something," Evie murmurs between sips.

"*Sharks*," the three of us correct in unison.

21

"And here's to hoping she doesn't get eaten by one because that's *negative press* we don't need." Evie tips her cup in a cheers like fashion before proceeding. "And speaking of your underdressed bride to be and negative press, she needs to send me over the photos of her *potential* dress choices for the Morgan merger event this weekend. I've sent her at least sixteen reminder texts and received nothing in return."

She *still* struggles to give a shit about her phone.

Where it is.

Who's calling.

While I can honestly say it's *not* a habit I typically enjoy, I appreciate that when we're together, we're *together.* She's not busy texting her friends or coworkers or scrolling social media in search of unrealistic standards to meet.

No.

She's *present.*

Purposeful.

However, when we're *not* together, it would be better – *for everyone* – if she were a tad easier to get in touch with.

Particularly when she's on a rescue dive on the other side of the fucking country.

"Where's Douglas Morgan?" Inquires our publicist, eyes scanning the fairly vacant room. "We need to go over public positioning one more time."

"It's a simple press gathering, Evie." My head tilts condescending to one side. "Not a prom photo."

"And you will be doing puff pieces for practice with private prep school pipsqueaks if you fuck this up." Her bitter smirk slides in between statements. "Find him, Jenni."

"You got it, Coach!" A tiny cringe is flashed. *"Boss."*

Once she's out of earshot, my best friend warmly states, "I like her."

"Don't," is all that leaves me.

22

"While we're on the subject of *don'ts*," our stiletto tapping leader interjects, "let me remind you, Wes, don't grit your teeth, that's not smiling. Don't fidget, that's not confident. Don't fold your arms, that's defensive. Don't hide your hands, that's not open. Don't clear your throat, don't touch your forehead, and don't volunteer *any* information about your personal life. This is strictly about showcasing the unity of this merger and the growing of the Wilcox Brand."

In spite of being overwhelmed with her notes, I force myself to nod.

I *hate* interviews.

I hate the lights.

I hate the flashes.

I hate the crowd.

I hate their voices.

I hate being the center of anyone's attention that isn't Bryn's.

"And you, Mr. Reese…"

He quirks an eyebrow in curiosity.

"Remember your left side is good," she gently taps on that side of his chin, "but your right side is better."

My best friend smugly smirks as he adjusts his dark navy blue suit jacket.

Kiss ass.

I swear his nose hasn't been this brown since college.

"*Found him!*" Jenni squawks from across the room. "He was having trouble getting past security!"

Good.

It means they're doing their job.

Rising to the increased expectations that came about after last year's shitstorm with Penny Baker, Clark's only child.

Luther's discovery regarding her true identity warranted a restructuring of his entire system. Not only did he run deeper background checks on all current estate employees, he wrote protocols that we've rolled over into the company, in which anyone I *may* have

23

physical contact with within the building is subjected to the same scrutiny. Aside from that, I – along with Bryn and J.T. – are always to be equipped with a member of my in-house security team that Luther has *personally* vetted whenever we're on property that isn't *owned* by me or my company. The extreme lengths may be viewed as overcompensation for the poisoning incident; however, I believe it's anything but.

What happened to Lauren should've *never* been possible.

Yet it was.

Ensuring that a repeat of such unfortunate events doesn't happen is needed.

Necessary.

I may have showed mercy once by sending Penny to Switzerland to receive mental help, but I will not show it again.

For anyone.

Our transition from one conference room to the other is thankfully smooth.

Hill and Hurst escort me, J.T., and Douglas to the front of the room where we pose with a ceremonial copy of the contract in the exact position Evie instructed enroute.

We allow what seems to be an endless number of photos to be taken.

We scribble rather meaningless signatures on the document.

We engage in cordial handshakes and hugs and grins to communicate to those that are witnessing the event a sense of togetherness.

This merger wasn't about the apex predator devouring the weak and swallowing it whole.

It was about aiding in someone else's dream coming true.

Assisting in them rising to higher levels.

Ranks.

It was about expanding the legacy my father left behind and venturing into new frontiers as a brand.

24

Wow.

Did I really just have a Trekkie moment all on my own?

J.T. gestures an open palm to a dark umber skinned male in the far left corner. "Justin Lakes, with Financial Investment for the *Highland Herald*." After receiving a nod of approval from me, he inquires, "Mr. Morgan, are you nervous about giving up complete control of your company to a corporation who has absolutely no current footing in the brewing industry?"

The sandy shaded man to my left gives his thick salt and peppered beard a single stroke prior to smiling widely. "Let me start by saying, I am not giving up complete control, Mr. Lakes. Mr. Wilcox and I have worked closely together during every step of this process to guarantee what we present is a collaboration of creation. While Mr. Wilcox-"

"*Wes*," I politely insist.

"*Wes*," he casually corrects further painting a friendly partnership, "may lack a specific beer-based reputation – at this time – the Wilcox brand is irrefutably one of the biggest in the alcohol industry as a whole. With that reach and level of respect, I have no doubts that they will not only make an amazing first impression into the world of brewing using Morgan Beers as their vehicle of transition, I believe they will – *we will* – rise to the top of this field as well."

I allow a natural smile to expand.

Hearing his unwavering belief in me…in the company…in what I've managed to accomplish thus far in my term at the top has my chest swelling in pride.

No.

Not all of my past choices would've made my father proud, but ones like this?

Ones where both parties can profit and benefit?

One where their brand has a chance to rise while our legacy has the chance to reach new markets?

25

These are the ones I know he would commend.

The ones I feel in an inexplicable way, he *is*.

"And was the idea to *scrap* the current logo to replace it with something that incorporates the Wilcox insignia much bigger and bolder, an *agreed* upon decision or primarily Mr. Wilcox's?" rudely questions an unidentified female somewhere in the crowd.

"Agreed upon," I retort in spite of not being able to see the attacker. "For better brand association."

J.T. quickly moves onto a peach skinned, round-faced, wavy-haired woman closer to the front who is eager to pipe in. "Courtney Peeps with Arts and Lifestyle for *Cliffsworth Chronicles*."

She's presented the same nod of approval to continue as her predecessor.

"Will there be some sort of public social event to commemorate this merger?"

"Unfortunately, not." The sympathetic smile on my face is forced. "We decided it would be more beneficial for Morgan brand employees who have stayed on through the acquisition if we hosted a private gathering in which they can meet and mingle and merge – small pun intended," light snickers from the crowd are expelled, "with those from Wilcox Enterprises who they will be working with going forward. We wanted something lowkey to allow both sides to come together like a family," another polite grin delivered, "which is what we prefer to think of ourselves as."

"Then why isn't your own *family* currently in attendance?" the voice from earlier bites back. "Your fiancée," the woman continues while my eyes scour the scene, "is nowhere in sight this morning. *In fact,* she has yet to be seen *once* at your side during this merger."

My eyes finally land on the young, fair skinned, dark-haired woman who looks uncomfortably familiar.

"Could it be because she doesn't support or agree with your hostile takeover of a defenseless brand?"

"It wasn't hostile."

26

"And we weren't defenseless!"

"Oh, then perhaps, she just doesn't believe in backing your continued monopolization of the alcohol industry."

There's no stopping myself from glaring. "*I heard no question.*"

"Yet you made no argument regarding the inference." She flashes a blindingly white tooth-filled grin. "Monica Simmons. *Global Laundry.*"

The magazine that first published my fucking face.

That changed my entire goddamn life without my permission.

Why am I not surprised they'd send someone here to what was supposed to be *local press only* to continue their campaign against me?

"Do you have an actual question, Ms. Simmons?" J.T. calmly redirects. "*About the merger?*"

"Mr. Wilcox, you are *implying* that this merger is more of an expanding family than the overthrowing of an indefensible organization, correct?"

"Correct."

"Then what does it say about your family dynamics if your own *fiancée* can't be bothered to show up in support of the expansion?"

My mouth lowers to reply despite Evie's headshakes appearing in the corner of my vision.

"What does it say about the nature of your relationship if she's willing to put *her needs* above yours?"

A single twitch is barely made.

"What does it say about *your company* when the woman marrying into it, the woman who will inevitably then have *shares in it*, can't even be bothered to take the day off of work to make a *minor* appearance at such a *major* event for your family's legacy?"

Air traps the rebuttal in my throat.

27

"Is this because – unlike Mr. Morgan – she doesn't believe in this merger's success?" The devilish smirk I'm shot stops my ability to breathe. "*In yours?*" Her face cranes villainously forward at the same time she coos, "*In. You?*"

Chapter 3

Brynley

"He shouldn't be such a giant pussy," I snip at the same time I dump the bucket of food into Steven's secluded area where he's currently being held. "*I* did his job, remember?" Shaking the stuck contents out is followed by flashing Calen Connelly, my closest colleague and one of my best friends, a smug smirk. "And you never saw me file an *official* aggression complaint when that monk seal went all *Deep Space Mine* because she thought I was standing too close to her pup."

"*True.*" A small chuckle is attached to a halfhearted shoulder shrug. "However, let me remind you – *once again* – that not everyone loves your boy Steven as much as you do."

"I understand not everyone is as incredible as me." Post my favorite water gossiping pal presenting me a fin wave of agreement, I turn to face Calen. "You know what they say. With great power comes great tits."

Another round of chortles is expelled. "That is *not* how that quote goes."

"Pretty sure it is."

"It isn't."

"Uh…which one of us is engaged to a comic book aficionado?"

"Which one of us knows that that quote you just butchered was Voltaire basically immortalized by Spiderman, not Batman?"

"Which one of us should watch more *Star Trek* and less webslinger?"

Loud laughter echoes around the room prompting me to beam brightly.

What can I say?

29

I'm gifted with words.

Backing up to add the dirty bucket to the collection that needs cleaning is accompanied by me beginning again, "The *point* I was trying to make-"

"Oh, there was one?"

He's flashed my middle finger, which sparks more snickers. "The point is Steven deserves to be loved and cared for and not bullied. It shouldn't matter if he looks a little scarier than the others-"

"He *acted* scarier than the others."

"He *acted* out of instinct."

"He tried to attack a small child."

"He tried to eat her toy!" Clamoring noises from the bucket precede me further snapping, "Those stupid neon colored squid toys were a *terrible* fucking decision."

"Kids love them."

"Yet you get your panties in a twist when Steven does."

"Because he was the one who tried to eat it!"

"If not food...why food shaped?"

Bewilderment bursts through his green gaze. *"Fucking...really, Bryn?"*

"We both know how close to feeding time it was, which is why he was so easily excited, and made the very *painful* mistake of ramming his face into the glass that child was standing next too."

"You're blaming the kid?" His head tilts sarcastically to one side. *"That's* the route you wanna take?"

"While I do like sharks more than children, *no.*" An unexpected churn to my stomach has me placing a palm on it in question. "I'm blaming our piece of shit merchandizing department." Sharp twists cause me to slightly wince in pain. "Those toys are clearly a neon-colored lawsuit waiting to happen."

Rather than focus on that statement, he kicks his chin at the other subject. "You okay?"

"I think-" my balled fist rushes to momentarily block bile from leaking out. It takes more energy and effort than I expect to force the burning back down to my stomach, yet the instant it's returned to where it rightfully belongs, I grumble, "I think *you* made a terrible choice bringing us waffles from that discount diner."

"It's not a discount diner," Calen poorly argues. "I got a discount *at* the diner because I took my car to his brother's mechanic shop, Roscoe's Wheels & Waffles."

"We should've just had sandwiches from Mo Mo's."

"We always have sandwiches from Mo Mo's!" He tosses his hands defeatedly into the air. "I thought it'd be fun to try something new!"

"Yeah, well, I'm pretty sure I'm about to say, 'Beam Me Up, Potty'."

"That's...that's *definitely* a reference I could've done without."

"And now you know how my stomach feels about your brunch poison."

My colleague rolls his eyes in exasperation while I bite my tongue from adding a line about *not* completely joking.

Sure, I know Calen would never poison me, but I'll admit. I'm still a *bit* suspicious when it comes to new food or dishes, I didn't order or weren't around when they were made.

To say I'm paranoid would be an oversell; however, I'll take somewhat *skittish*.

Not quite the nervous shark – a species of the requiem shark – around humans but nowhere near a whale shark.

That whole Raggedy Insane situation left a bad taste in my mouth – lame joke totally made on purpose. Learning the how and why she set me up, to everything about her connection to my new step-dad – Mom and Clark are currently away on their honeymoon – gave me *answers* as much as new trust issues in all things Wilcox related. And while my fiancé loves to remind me the threat has been

31

eliminated – since he literally banished her from the states for whatever remains of her *Bride of Chucky* life – I can't help the nagging thoughts that her attack was more of a first, rather than a last.

Maybe *she* won't strike again but someone else she knows or who has the same mindset just might.

Especially now that we're *constantly* in the spotlight.

I swear every week there's a new mogul or media or model out to strike.

And because of how cleverly camouflaged our last predator was, I have no choice but to be *overly* cautious of *everyone* that isn't directly Mom or Wes related.

Even Calen and Vanessa have had thorough background checks done on them since the incident.

Not sure they know.

Damn sure not gonna tell them if they don't.

"Winters and Connelly," an unseen voice says through the small corner intercom, "report to the R&R office."

My head dramatically dips backwards at the same time I childishly whine, "I don't want to."

"You never want to."

"It's never good news."

"It's not *always* bad news."

We lock eyes again so that he can see my glare. "You would *so* be one of those cadets with gross optimism during the *Kobayashi Maru* test."

Bafflement is attached to his grunted, "*Huh*?"

"Watch more *Star Trek!*"

"Watch less!"

We exchange childish expressions prior to exiting the medical tank area one behind the other.

Why Wes is worried there's something more here than friendship is truly a Riddler worthy question.

Is Calen distractingly attractive?

32

Absolutely.

He's basically a washboard ab ken doll that's found life in a full-size form.

Do we have anything outside of work in common?

A shit ton.

He swims, he surfs, he loves all things ocean-related, and lives in tank tops outside the office.

He also has a not-so-secret taste for women who typically have more melanin in their skin which would practically make me his dream chick in theory.

But the thing about theories is what happens when you test them.

Observe them in motion.

For instance, he's *never* hit on me.

From the moment we met, he could see that – despite the breakup at the time – I was off the market.

And he's always been respectful of that.

Wes.

Whenever we travel the country for work and have to share a room, whether it's somewhere far like Hawaii or somewhere closer like South Haven Island he always shares the room with whatever member of security has followed me there, so that I can have the one they've rented across the hall and enjoy a bit more privacy.

It's typically Diego Hill.

And I'm pretty sure they prefer bunking together because rather than have to endure *Star Trek* convos they can enjoy surfer ones.

Once you add those facts to how often he's had to help me get chunks of chum out of my hair, how many times I've heard him piss in a cup on a long road trip, and how often we've each played lock the windows to force the other to choke on bad burrito farts, it's *obvious* we aren't making that type of love connection.

Just a sibling one.

Which suits me.

I like the big brother vibe because *we're* friends more than the little brother vibe because I'm *fucking* your friend.

"You think it's about Fluffles?" Calen questions during our stroll for our boss's office. "You think he's healthy enough to move to a better equipped facility for rehabilitating and ultimately breeding emperor penguins?"

Regardless of my stomach deciding to churn once more, I smile widely from hearing a grown ass man have to use the name Fluffles, which was my doing. "Doubtful."

Our division in the department – the one Calen and I dominate – is directly involved with physically rescuing wounded animals, rehabilitating them at our facility, working with research to track their origins, and ultimately assessing whether it would be beneficial to our institute to maintain them for further researching and breeding or to transport them elsewhere. On the occasion, we also *assist* in the physical relocation process, which *adds* to the reasons I am sometimes literally all over the country.

And Wes hates it.

He hates it even more because he *can't* follow.

Because he *doesn't* fly.

"Could be about your bestie Steven." Calen tosses me a genuinely concerned cringe. "He's gotta be around sexual maturity age." The expression shifts to an impish one. "*Unlike you.*"

Grinning at his well-placed jab isn't stopped.

"Maybe it's time to move him to get him laid."

"He can get laid under *our* roof."

"*Really, Mom?*" sarcastically slips loose as we round the corner. "Promise you won't cock block?"

I helplessly giggle during my retort, *"Fuck you."*

"Only if I can use the gold brick Wilcox will *literally shit* to pay off my student debt." He tosses me another mirth-filled smirk. "I think my loans are taking out their own loans at this point."

New rounds of laughter circle us; however, I do my best to keep them completely sincere.

Truth is…I'm no longer drowning in debt.

Due to my Bruce Wayne living up to his nickname, I went from sympathizing with why the earliest versions of Selina Kyle had sticky claws to being someone she would absolutely try to steal *from*.

And he wasn't even remotely subtle about the whole thing.

I came home fuck early on a Tuesday from Michigan – where we had been meeting with their team to see about possibly transferring our rescued sea turtles to their facility – to discover my debt in its entirety had disappeared – including some bad living situations with lingering resentment – that I had a brand new car in my name and a penthouse apartment downtown – a whopping ten minutes from work – that was in *both* of our names.

On one fin, I thought I had just smelled too much cleaning solution in a short time frame and was hallucinating.

And on the other, I swore he was about to see Hamilton for a visit regarding how to surgically remove his balls from his belly button because I am *not* anyone's charity case.

I *have never* and *will never* be.

I can handle myself.

I can take care of things *myself.*

I didn't and *don't* need someone to toss on their heavy ass leather cape – that may occasionally now be used for sex stuff – and swoop in to damsel in distress save me.

He thought all that shit was sweet.

I thought it was controlling.

And that's how we ended up in a shouting match so loud security was called to referee.

Compromise is – to no surprise – still our biggest struggle; however, I like to believe we've made progress.

He paid off my debt, so I pay to have cookies delivered to his office weekly.

He bought me a new car, so I pay for detailing services when we're not at the estate.

He paid for our penthouse and the furnishings, so I decorated it in nerd memorabilia.

Our style could easily be labeled as chic Comic-Con.

Upon entering the office of Raquel Lane, our boss, we're immediately given a lifted index finger to instruct us to wait until her call ends to speak.

Calen immediately twitches me a glare in warning knowing there's a sarcastic snip right on the tip of my tongue.

Maybe it's rude to get lippy with the woman who decides on how many zeroes get to be on your paycheck, but I think it's rude to take a phone call when you're expecting employees that you've summoned.

"What sort of extension can you provide?" Her sun-kissed fingers fidget with the ends of her stringy hair. "No, I understand that. It's just-"

The pressing of her lips tightly together indicates *she* was the one interrupted, an action that threatens to have the corners of my lips curling upward.

I hate her.

I – honest to Spock – come in every day hoping she's been fired.

Look, I know everyone tends to hate their boss in some fashion.

I've had enough jobs, in enough places, with enough different types of individuals to know as well as understand this, but Raquel is different.

Like send her to the seventh circle of hell reserved for those that participate in shark finning and purposely make babies cry level of different.

Out of *all* the people who work for her, it's *me* she gives the most shit to.

36

Calen gets his shirt soaking wet during the day, takes it off like some sort of merman *Magic Mike,* and she praises him for his dedication to the institute.

The rescues get a little excited during playtime, my shirt gets drenched, and she chews my ass out like I was trying to start at wet t-shirt contest on the clock.

Initially, I thought it was just double standard bullshit – you know hot guy gets away with murder, hot girl gets penalized for simply existing, type of nonsense – but when I witnessed her gushing over Stephanie Edwards – a chick who can't even remember to wash out the food pails – I realized nope.

It's *just me* she hates.

Why?

Could be because I don't "need" this job like others.

Could be because I'm happily engaged and she's in the midst of a bitter divorce.

Or it could simply be because The Captain of the sky blessed me with great tits while she had to pay for hers.

"Understood," Raquel murmurs into her cell prior to ending the call. Afterwards, hazel eyes I hate looking into meet mine. "Where's Steven's daily status report?"

"In progress," I professionally reply, folding my hands politely in front of me, executing the less defensive based technique I owe Evie for teaching me.

"Why isn't it completed?"

"Protocol dictates we wait until *after* an injured creature has finished feeding," Calen swiftly explains, tone calm and even. "We are simply following procedure."

"You always do, Connelly," she coos in his direction before glaring in mine. "And if I were to ask you for a quick assessment regarding his temperament? Could you provide it, Winters?"

The answer to that is the same answer to the question "could she provide me with more reasons to despise her?".

37

Fighting the instinct to sneer is masked by a single teeth suck. "*Yes.*"

"And?" She leans back into her squeaky brown office chair. "What is it?"

"Playful."

"Not lethargic?"

"No."

"Any swimming changes due to his injury?"

"No."

"And the injury itself?" Raquel shifts her stare back to Calen. "How's it healing?"

"Well." The smile he offers is reassuring. "No permanent damage to his vision has been detected."

"Good." Her curt nodding is followed by a Lex Luthor here to scare Batman type of head tilt. "This morning a *female* scalloped hammerhead was rescued close to the coast from an attempted finning. She sustained quite a number of injuries, all of which I have been told are minor. She was brought back to the Research and Rescue division of K&T for initial assessing."

"Poor baby girl," mindlessly leaves my lips.

"They'll be assessing her *again* shortly; however, if her injuries are as minor as they believe, they would like to hold her for breeding."

Any ability to speak is severed.

"And since K&T is a larger, more equipped, and much higher funded institute that is *built* for longer term species reproduction, we're interested in transferring Steven to their facility for mating."

I swear I spot the faintest twinkle in her eyes over my inability to respond.

"Given his already isolated nature and the aggressive incident filed-"

"But that wasn't his fault!"

38

Calen places a supportive palm in the middle of my back to wordlessly encourage me to regain my composure.

"*Given* these current circumstances," Raquel hisses like the Wicked Witch of the Water that she is, "we believe a move would be beneficial for all parties involved. You two will be accompanying Eoghan to K&T to observe the female's behavior and provide any insight that may be useful in helping him during his evaluation of the potential relocation." She villainously steeples her hands together in front of her. "*You leave Friday.*"

Chapter 4

Brynley

Friday?!

I have to leave my poor, injured baby on *Friday* to go meet his possible arranged marriage bride-to-be?!

What type of trip to Murder Planet in the Hirogen star system is this?!

The slamming of the front door to our penthouse is mindless and unintentional and absolutely warrants the unhappy glower Wes is giving me, yet the new sharp stabs in my still upset stomach tell me that's not what got his Dark Knight having boxers in a twist.

"Where the fuck have you been, Brynley?!"

"Weston is using my full name," I tauntingly reply, workbag being dropped in the entryway. "This *must* be serious."

J.T. poorly hides his snicker from where he's sitting on our gray, L shaped couch with the man I'm going to marry hovering behind him.

Wes doesn't even bother glancing in his best friend's direction. *"Where?!"*

"Work!" Maintaining my far distance is done by lingering closer to the stairs. "Where the fuck else would I be?!"

"Why hasn't Holmes been able to locate you for the past two hours?"

"Must've accidentally turned the tracker in my ass off."

He aggressively curls his hands around the edge of the couch. *"I am not kidding."*

"And I know you're not being fucking serious with this impersonation Bat interrogation shit."

"Try saying that five times fast," J.T. playfully mumbles under his breath prompting me to smirk.

40

Ah.

Puppet Boy.

Our trusty shared sidekick.

Probably the *one* person in our social ocean that has any real clue how to navigate Hurricane Future Wilcoxes.

"*Brynley,*" is venomously spewed, "*I. Want. An. Answer.*"

"And I want a boss that I don't have the urge to kick in the cunt." My shoulders innocently bounce. "But like The Stones sang...'You Can't Always Get What You Want'."

"You know I met Jagger once?" Puppet Boy casually interjects, one navy suit covered leg moving to rest slightly on top of the other. "We were eating at the same restaurant."

It's impossible to resist the subject. "How hard did you fangirl?"

"Less hard than when I met Patrick Stewart but harder than when I met Simon Pegg."

"You met Stewart?!"

"*Can we fucking focus here?!*" my fiancé bellows, bringing everyone's attention back to him. "I need to know why a member of *my security team-*"

"*Our.*"

"-wasn't able to locate *my fiancée* for the past two hours." In spite of how irritated he's making me, I can't help but enjoy how delicious his heaving chest looks in his dress shirt. "*Where. Were. You?*"

"*Working.*"

His mismatched eyes that I much prefer rolling back in ecstasy rather than glaring at me harshly narrow. "*At The Institute?*"

"No." My hands slip into the back pockets of my khakis. "Calen and I met with Eoghan offsite."

"*Why?*"

"Because *unlike you* – who is his own boss – I have to do what the dreaded Sea Bitch tells me to."

"Why didn't you inform Holmes?"

"Perhaps because checking in with my fiancé appointed babysitter simply slipped my mind."

A deeper glare is thrown in my direction. *"Why didn't you take your phone?"*

"Why do I feel like you're *accusing* me of something you *clearly* don't have the balls to accuse me of?"

"Why do I feel like you don't believe in this merger you *clearly* don't seem to give two fucks about?"

"Why are you both asking rhetorical questions?" Puppet Boy intervenes for a second time. "Like an episode of *Voyager*, it *rarely* plays out well."

He has a point.

A really good one.

And one made in a language I approve of.

Lifting my palms is done in a surrendering nature while Wes lessens his grapple of the furniture.

"Pizza and beer?" he slyly suggests while lifting the latter. "I ordered a chorizo, salami, and olive one just for you."

Dry heaving thoughtlessly occurs.

"Seriously?" Puppet Boy gawks in disbelief. "I watched you put back an entire zucchini and prosciutto one like two Sundays ago, which was much crazier than what I ordered tonight."

"You mean less basic."

"I mean you are a basic *pain* in my pizza eating ass," J.T. chortles prior to indulging in a sip.

The corner of my lip twitches upward as I answer, "The combo's fine, my stomach's not."

"What's wrong, baby?" Wes instantly asks, voice riddled with concern. "Menstrual cramps? Constipation? Gas?"

"Very romantic," his best friend murmurs behind another sip.

"Bad waffles."

Amusement struggles not to appear in his expression. "You had too much sugar."

"Maybe." There's no fighting my grin. "And maybe putting caramel syrup on top of regular syrup on my banana split waffles wasn't the *best* idea I've had today."

"I wonder if maybe we should do something with notes of banana?" J.T. ponders out loud, attention momentarily dropping to the product in his grip. "The current Morgan Brand itself is pretty...average. They produce enough profit to stay in the black, which is what made it a great buy, but..." He gently rotates the glass bottle. "It's just like...*beer*, right?" His continued contemplative gazing is fascinating. "There's no *signature* to it yet. It blends in. We need it to *stand out* because *that's our brand*. That's what our legacy *represents*." When he glances back up, he's met by almost identical gazes of admiration. "What? Too idealistic?"

Wes gives his best man a gentle pat to the shoulder. *"Never."*

Their passion and enthusiasm for alcohol that they share is one I longed to have in my own field and now that I have it?

I understand and respect their bond even more.

"Should I start *Star Trek: Nemesis*?" J.T. gestures to the T.V. "Let Wes pour you a sample of..." his voice tails off while glancing at the different bottles on the low to the ground dark coffee table, "something light?"

"Pass." Heading towards them finally begins. "On the beer that is. I could never say no to a *Star Trek* movie."

"You wouldn't be the woman I can't wait to marry if you did," Wes sweetly insists during his stroll around the blockade to greet me. "The woman I'm looking forward to finally introducing to the Morgans at the event on Saturday."

There's no stopping my eyes from widening in pure panic.

Shit...

Shit.

Shit.

43

Shit!

Simply two steps away, he stops.

Stills his entire frame.

Meets my stare and states, *"You will be at the event this weekend, Brynley."*

It's impossible not to briefly cringe as a wordless rebuttal.

"That wasn't a question." Wes folds his arms firmly across his chest at the same time he adds, "It was a statement."

"Sounded like an *order* Captain Prickard." My stance swiftly matches his. "And since I'm already having to follow a *different* set of orders this weekend, I will be unable to follow yours."

"Excuse me?"

"Raquel is sending us down to The K&T Aquatic Institute this weekend to evaluate a potential mate for Steven."

Which is more likely the reason my stomach is *still* upset versus those awful waffles that tasted decent going down but disgusting coming up.

"They wanna get your boy laid?" Puppet Boy juvenilely grins. "You going down to be his wing woman?"

"Who better than *me* to pick up chicks with?"

"You escorting him or *escorting* him?" he pokes with a small laugh.

"I-"

"Cannot. Go." The man who I'm supposed to marry this winter viciously bites.

There's no hesitation to chomp back. *"Pardon?"*

"You. Cannot. Go."

"Funny, I don't remember asking for your permission to pass go and collect my two hundred dollars, Mr. Monopoly."

"This isn't a joke."

"This also isn't a discussion."

"You are *needed* at my side at this event." His entire body lengthens to its full height. "You will be there."

44

"I am *needed* to work this weekend. I will be *there*."

"This is important."

"And my fucking job suddenly isn't?"

"That's not what I said."

"That's exactly what you fucking said."

"*Do. Not. Put* words in my mouth," is growled alongside a step towards me. "I do not *appreciate* when *anyone* puts words into them."

"Fine." It's my turn to take a challenging step forward. "It's what you *heavily implied*."

"And what do you think *you're* heavily implying by constantly choosing *work* over me?" He doesn't pause for a response. "By skipping company dinners or events? By constantly being photographed laughing and frolicking with other men?"

"Did you just say frolicking?" Puppet Boy quietly gags.

"By not wearing your fucking engagement ring?"

The hiss out of the bystander in the room almost gathers my glare.

"Your job is inarguably important." Wes kicks his chin up a smidge higher. "Why am *I* not?"

"Now who's putting words into whose mouth?"

"I'm not," he smugly sneers. "It's what your actions *heavily imply*."

"Then let them *also* imply that I'm fucking done talking to you." Flashing him my middle finger is followed by making a comment to J.T. "Rein check on the flick, Riker. I think I'm gonna drown my stress in the hot tub since my stomach won't let me drown it in beer."

He simply nods and watches me dismiss myself from the room without giving my fiancé another glance.

Getting changed out of my uniform and into my black string bikini – with the extra cheeky bottoms – doesn't take much time.

And neither does strutting back through the living room where the man who sweetly asked me to marry him on a Tuesday – aka "our day" – is forced to admire my ass provocatively bent over during the retrieving of my word search booklet.

His hungry grumbles are enough on their own to spark a vindictive smirk; however, I can't resist the urge to push him *more.*

Wordlessly continue what feels like a never-ending power struggle in our relationship.

"*Oh!*" loudly precedes leaning over the edge of the couch space between them, tit purposely brushing against Wes's arm, during the stretching motion. "*There's* my pen."

An undeniable, dark gnarl rattles the piece of furniture I'm bent over prompting Puppet Boy to whisper, "*You're evil, Shinzon.*"

"*Picard started it,*" is sassily mumbled prior to popping completely back up, forcing my barely covered chest to bounce. "Enjoy the movie, boys."

Unsurprisingly, I'm not even in the steamy water, positioned over the edge beside my grabbed pool towel, searching for words for a full five minutes before I'm watching J.T. make the executive decision to leave on the other side of the glass wall.

Of course he's bailing.

Who wants to be caught in a Battle of Wolf 359 simulation?

Pretending to find something on the page masks my tracking of his cleaning actions.

His frustrated back of the neck squeezes.

His periodic pointless pacing.

It's more than apparent that something deeper than my inability to go this weekend is bothering him, but *what* it is…*isn't.*

And his obnoxious behavior of recreating the mob boss vibe from *Shark Tale* rather than just engage in an open discussion with the person he swears he wants to have a future is infuriating.

And unfair.

And the last fucking thing *I* need after learning that my finned best friend who listens to me bitch about him may be on a ticking clock I didn't see coming.

46

I wait until Wes is finally walking in my direction before theatrically wiggling out of my string bikini bottoms. Right as he opens the door, I casually toss them to one side, yet wait until he gets closer to make a bigger production out of removing my top too.

There's no denying the pained pursing of his lips that's followed by him shoving his balled fists into his black pantsuit's pockets while I dry hands on my nearby towel. *"Punishing me, little prey?"*

"Yes."

His mouth moves to speak again, and I purposely readjust my figure to ensure he almost gets a glimpse at my nipples. After deep, primal groans are barely swallowed, he gruffly asks, "If I come closer to have a conversation, are you going to make it even more difficult to have?"

"Absolutely."

Against his own volition, he smirks.

Shakes his head.

Shrugs and sighs in surrender. "Thank you for being honest."

"I'm not sure how to be anything else."

"I know." At that, Wes takes a cautious step forward. "And it is one of the many, *many* things, I love about you, Bryn."

"But?"

"No. No buts."

"It sounds like a but is coming."

"Just mine swooping down for the perching on this rooftop."

The Batman like joke receives a playful gag alongside my own head shake. "Terrible phrasing, Mr. Wayne."

"Eh, it's an off night, Ms. Kyle." Post Wes rolling up his pantlegs, he plants himself next to the word search and lets his exposed appendages slide into the heat, water immediately rushing to caress the marred flesh I love even though he still doesn't. "Do you think the Morgan merger was a mistake?"

Surprise launches my eyebrows to the night sky. *"Do you?"*

"No."

"Then why are you asking?"

"Because I want *your* opinion."

"Why?" Perplexity pierces my crystal glare. "Wilcox Enterprises is *your* company. You are the majority shareholder. You make the decisions. *Your opinion* is the only one that truly matters." My head playfully bobs left to right. "And maybe like an anal fins worth of Puppet Boy's."

He lightly chuckles. "You just wanted to say the word anal."

"Often."

Additional snickers precede his argument. "Your opinion matters as well, Bryn."

"That's why I give it when choosing takeout for dinner."

"Yes, but as the woman who is adding my last name to hers, who is signing a *legally binding document* that states *this company* will in partial become *your company*, what you think regarding this endeavor along with future ones *matters*." He folds his hands tightly together and leans slightly towards me. "It matters to the media. It matters to the other shareholders. However, it really matters *to me*." Unexpected conflict crosses his face. "I wanna know if you support the direction I'm going and the causes I'm supporting and the *risks* I'm taking. I wanna know if you hate them. Or something. Or someone. I want your...*honest opinion* when it comes to everything because you *are* my everything, Bryn."

Not melting is impossible.

And so is not tilting my lips upward to indulge in a loving kiss.

Our mouths firmly press together allowing a brushing of our tongues that's light.

Loving.

Reassuring.

When I finally slink back, I casually confess, "I guess it doesn't register to me that your company is in any way going to be *our* company. I mean...it's *yours*, ya know? It's been in *your* family

48

for generation after generation, so I just assumed it was 'our company' in the royal we sense, not the actual one."

"We are signing *literal* paperwork that indicates that it is." A small wince is flashed. "Which reminds me, we have to meet with Hawthorne before we can do anymore wedding arrangements with Velora."

"Oh no…" I sarcastically call out at the same time I pick up the pen. "How…unfortunate."

"*Bryn.*"

"The woman is a human dolphin." Letting my gaze wander the page occurs next. "You know how I feel about that."

Fuck them for being related to orcas.

"I would *like to know* how you feel about this merger."

"It seems smart." A word from the list instantly captures my circling attention. "The Morgan brand has established roots; therefore, you're not basically starting out as bottom feeders in uncharted waters and lacks a level of flare that makes it bait you can craft and cut and mold to your liking. *They* wanted global distribution and expansion. *You* wanted a new world to explore. They're winning." I scratch out the word from the bank. "*You're* winning."

"*We're winning*," he corrects during the transferring of the writing utensil from his fingers to mine.

"And the consumers are winning because they are getting new products to enjoy." My stare shifts to his. "The only losers in this merger are the ones who decided to take their severance rather than board *USS Wilcox Enterprise* to boldly go where the brand has never gone before."

"I agree."

"Yet you asked for my opinion." He's tossed a quirked eyebrow. "Which means you had doubts."

"I had…" the tugging of the booklet closer is executed to avoid eye contact, "*questions.*"

"Brought to you by the letter A, for *absent fiancée*?"

49

"You're not…*absent*."

"Not what you were arguing earlier."

"*My apologies for that.*" Wes's gorgeous brown and blue stare latches onto me. "I was out of line."

"You were definitely swimming in sleep on the couch territory."

The corner of his lip kicks upward. "And now?"

"Now depends on what happens after we wrap up *this* conversation." Waggling my eyebrows receives a small chuckle. "And also, what brought on the accusation that I'm a heartless affair having slut who cares more about her career than her future husband."

A long, uncomfortable lull presents itself prior to a deep sigh of exasperation. "I was ambushed at the press conference by *Global Laundry.*"

"That trash site that you thought I sold our picture to?!"

The picture that's framed – along with the one of him kissing my cheek – and hung at both the manor and our penthouse.

"That would be the one."

"Why were they even there?!" Bewilderment bulldozes itself through my expression. "*How* did they even get access?! It was supposed to be for *local press* only. Your way of…inviting the 'b class villains' to enjoy a panel in an 'a class' issue."

"*I'm way more turned on by that analogy than I should be,*" mutters my partner in crime while circling a word.

"Just the way I like it."

After an amused headshake, he says, "I have no idea how they got in, but Evie and Luther are both looking into it." The pen is offered to me in tandem with our gazes connecting again. "She managed to get under my skin-"

"Which is why you were trying to get under mine rather than in my pants."

"We both know I *always* wanna be in those pants, little prey."

50

A tiny lip bite is attached to the snatching of the pen. "Yeah, well, you have a greater chance of that when you're not *attacking me* for shit that I didn't even do."

"Again," he sheepishly sighs, "*apologies.*"

"And I'm sorry I have to work this weekend." Sincerity snakes through my stare. "It came up last minute. And unexpected. And honestly? I don't *want* to go. I don't *want* to possibly lose Steven. Yeah, I wanna get the dude laid and keep his species going or whatever, but…" Sadness slips into my tone, "I hate the idea of losing him."

"Isn't that the entire purpose of his time at The Institute? To heal and eventually be re-released into the wild?"

"Less logic, more emotions right now, Spock." I teasingly wave the pen in his direction. "Read the bridge."

Wes releases a round of laughter that's warmer and louder than I'm anticipating. "You know I actually *get* the reference you're making."

"Which is one more reason why *you* are the man I can't wait to marry." Tossing the drawing tool on top of the word search occurs between announcements. "Or swallow."

His jaw lowers in tandem with his gaze to where my hands are sliding up his thighs. "*I thought you weren't feeling well.*"

"Cum does the body good."

There's no delay in him smirking. "*That's milk.*"

"They're both white."

Rather than provide an opportunity for a rebuttal, I smoothly glide my hand over his swelling dick and squeeze.

Wes leans back onto his palm on a deep groan.

Widens his legs.

Grants me access to the button of his pants.

The zipper.

Groans again louder and hungrier when my fingers slip inside to tease his boxer brief covered shaft. "*Still punishing me, little prey?*"

"*Yes.*"

Wes lets his hooded glare latch onto where the tops of my tits are barely being kept under the hot water.

"Why don't *you* do the hard work?" I salaciously suggest at the same time I slink away. "And *I'll* just reap the benefits."

One deliciously slow lick to his lips is all that precedes him nodding.

Pulling out his cock.

Giving it a lasciviously long and lustful stroke.

"*Is this what you want, baby?*" Wes purrs during a repeating of the jerking motion. "*To watch how fucking hard you make me?*" Another dragged out caress is executed. "*To see how much I wanna fuck you?*"

I violently chomp down on my bottom lip to trap in a moan.

"*You want this cum?*" His tone becomes ferine and tenebrous. "*You fucking beg for it.*"

"*Come for me, Wes,*" thoughtlessly leaves my tongue as though incapable of saying anything else.

"*Show me those tits.*"

Hesitation to rise to the tips of my toes in order to do so is nonexistent.

"*Squeeze them together.*"

Once more, following an order meets no reluctance.

"*Perfect...*" he grumbles between slightly faster tugs, precum continuously being spread his entire length. "*You're the perfect fucking prey.*"

I certainly feel that way whenever he's looking at me with his sexually glossed stare.

And struggling to steady his rapid breath.

And fighting to keep his moans confined behind his gritted teeth.

"*Pull a nipple,*" is grunted alongside harsher grinding. "*Pretend it's my teeth.*"

"*Like this?*" I ask while gently executing the action.

"*Harder.*"

A slightly more forceful one is given.

"*Harder.*"

Again, I increase the strength.

"*Fucking. Harder.*" Before another attempt is made, he adds, "*Clamp down on it.*"

Yet again, as if no longer in control of my body, it does what it's told.

"*Those are my goddamn teeth, little prey,*" insists my fiancé, "*marking my territory.*"

It's impossible not to whimper and whine.

Rock my hips forward in spite of their being nothing waiting for me under the water.

"*Marking my mate.*"

Heavier and headier moans propel me closer.

Cause him to rub faster.

And faster.

Savagely snarl to the same sadistic speed of his stroking. "*I wanna mark my fucking mate, Bryn.*"

"*Mark me,*" I echo and continue to creep forward. "*Please, fucking mark me, Wes.*"

The instant I'm within reach, he snatches a fistful of my hair, yanks my head down to his thigh, and smashes the tip of his dick against my lips. "*Open.*"

Creating space is swift.

"*Wider.*"

Expanding further happens even quicker.

"*Swallow.*"

Sweltering rushes suddenly begin running rampant across my tongue in their race for the back of my throat while his animalistic bellows are barked into the star riddled sky. The feeling of my predator's legs tensing against my cheek combined with his toes lightly teasing the very edge of my nipple not only has me eagerly guzzling but greedily moaning for more.

More pain.

More pleasure.

More Wes.

Chapter 5

Wes

The writing in *Batman: The Long Halloween*?
Incredible.
Intriguing.
At the very least, enjoyable.
As for Jeph Loeb, its author?
He's a pure genius.
Worthy of every penny I spent on my collector's editions of his works.
A creator's creator.
Unlike Vihana Patel, the author – or perhaps just the lead author – on the proposal for fruit flies and genetic studies that's sitting *beside* my open hard cover book.
Is it incredible?
I'd say that's an oversell.
Is it intriguing?
Understanding genetics always is.
Is it even remotely enjoyable?
No.
It's just plain painful.
From structure to unclear goals to the seven proofreading mistakes I found in the first two pages, it's clear that once more a good idea came about yet couldn't be properly penned.
It happens.
The problem is it's been happening *too often* for me.
And I'm not sure if Newberry isn't vetting what she sends to me anymore or if these are simply the best she's discovered.
I hope like hell it isn't the latter.

An amused grunt escapes mere seconds prior to my fiancée's voice asking, "Can you zip me, please?"

Glancing upward occurs just in time to catch Bryn grasping the front of her low cut, ribbed top half during her rotating movements. Whether it's having so much of her beautiful brown skin on full display or the way her great hammerhead tattoo on her lower back appears to be wading through the water as she swivels that gets my dick's attention is relatively unclear.

Much like the direction I'm going to move the little piece of metal awaiting my grip. *"Up or down, Bryn?"*

She tosses me a sexy, taunting smirk over her shoulder. *"I think you already know the answer to that, Weston."*

"I *know* that you're not wearing a bra." Dragging my pointed digit down her spine is done slowly. "And I *think* you're not wearing any panties."

An irresistible, devilish glint grows in her crystal gaze. *"And?"*

"And I think you're going to be my first appetizer of the evening, little prey." Winding the ends of Bryn's lightly waved hair around my fingers allows me to effortlessly guide her into the bent over my desk position that I've grown a fondness for. *"You know the drill."* I use my legs to roughly widen her stance. *"Grip the edge."*

Her tiny fingertips stretch to latch onto the opposite end of the furniture while the other set of mine inch up the tight black fabric blocking the mouthwatering view of her bare ass. The instant it's exposed, a tiny hitch of anticipation echoes around the room I swear we have more sex in than our bedroom.

What can I say?

This is the perfect place for both business and pleasure.

Working my cock out of my black dress pants and into my wife to be is far from a difficult feat. In fact, the entire ease of the situation and my ability to have her whenever and however without constraints or concerns or cares spurs what began as casual stroking to transition into something more unrestrained.

56

Intemperate.

"Tell me to sign my name on this ass." One swift pop is delivered to her backside causing her slick muscles to rapaciously clamp down. *"Tell me to put Mr. Wilcox across it."* Another swat is slipped between pumps. *"Tell me to scribble that shit in white, baby."*

"Fucckkkkkkkk," is airily moaned onto the glass surface her face is squished against.

"You want that cum dripping out of this tight, little pussy?" Propelling my cock further is followed by a third slap. *"You want that shit spilling everywhere?"* And a fourth. *"You want everyone to see who you fuckin' belong to?"*

Bryn's entire body trembles underneath my hold.

Does its best to push back into the bucking.

"Who's pussy is this?" The filthy investigating is attached to even filthier fucking. *"Say it."*

"Yours…"

More ferocious thrusts result in her ankles buckling in her black stilettos.

"Say my name."

Loud gasps are given rather than what I want prompting me to pound harder.

And faster.

Crazedly carve deeper and deeper and deeper to the point I cut off her ability to scream.

Speak.

Breathe.

"Say my fucking name, little prey." The hand gripping her hair slides over to grind her face into the desk at the same time my other allows my thumb to brutishly graze against her back hole. *"Say. It."*

"Wes," meekly leaks out.

"Louder."

It grows in strength yet not in sound, *"Wes…"*

"*Fucking.*" I drive both my digit and my dick to the hilt. "*Louder.*"

Despite her seemingly pinned nature, she arches her back and shouts, "*Wessssss!*"

Knee wobbling pulsations falter my movements, leaving my cock no choice but to be laved and remorselessly drenched and desperate for my increasingly heavy balls to fulfill all the dirty proclamations I've been making.

"*Weston,*" Bryn purrs, heat from her sultry voice burning the part of my hand it can reach, "*I look so good in white...*"

"*Fuckfuckfuckkkkkkkk!*" spews out of me in tandem with me spewing into her. Blazing burst on top of burst hastily fill her past the brim forcing thick, white drops to skate across my balls during their descent to the floor. "*Keep that shit in there, baby.*" Her pussy clenches down again, pulling unsteady hisses past my gritted teeth. "*Keep it all in there for me.*"

Gluttonous moans float through the air from both of us as I carefully slide out.

Instead of rushing to clean up or help her up, I wolfishly watch the freshly cum covered area, suck more of it back in, burying it in the only depths it ever belongs.

*Lock me up in Arkham...*I really can't get enough of this woman.

The love of my life blows the strands of hair that have fallen in her face away and playfully pokes, "*You* get to explain to Calendar Girl why we're late to this event."

Teasing prods to the back of her pussy are attached to my correction. "It's *Calendar Man.*"

"Not in the cartoon."

"Which isn't always *accurate* to the comics."

Bryn good naturedly goads, "*Such a sexy nerd, Mr. Wayne.*"

"*So slippery down here, Ms. Kyle.*" I glide my finger all the way inside. "*Perhaps I should check again for my family jewels...*"

58

Girlish giggles easily fade into needy groans that smoothly guide us into going a second round in the nearby chair rather than getting ready like we should.

Our eventual arrival at the fundraising gala isn't minded by the paparazzi or the *welcomed* press; however, it *is* noted and immediately criticized by Evie who appears one wrong blink away from having a full-blown panic attack.

"Are you two *trying* to kill me?" Evie hisses under her breath, cornering us near a sparkling champagne tower. "Do you find my *misery* amusing?"

My fiancée drops her jaw to bite back prompting me to quietly murmur, "*They're rhetorical questions, Bryn.*"

"I instruct an 8:46 arrival time, I expect an 8:46 arrival time, yet it isn't 8:46, is it?"

She gestures a stern pointed finger over her shoulder which encourages Jenni to pop into the conversation. "It's 9:32."

"9:32!" airily shrieks our publicist. "9:32 Wilcoxes! Do you have any idea how much territory you are behind on covering?"

Bryn cracks her mouth open a second time, which pushes me to whisper the reminder, "*Still a rhetorical question.*"

"And why are *those* in my face?!" Evie unhappily wags a finger back and forth in front of my date's cleavage. "How many times do we have to go over *simple* not *showy?*"

"Is *that* a real question or are we still swimming in rhetorical waters?" she juvenilely asks the huffy elegantly dressed woman in front of us.

Jenni peers around her boss's arm to smoothly state, "I think you look top cheddar."

"I don't know what that means, but I like the way it sounds," confirms my favorite sparring partner on a sly smirk.

"If you try to sleep with her, I *will* fire you," Evie less than smoothly scolds.

"Jenni is Evie's new assistant," I announce as I slide my arm possessively around the small of Bryn's back.

"What happened to Dina?"

"Dina was unprofessional, Pruitt was perverted, and while Jenni may have the vocab of a frat jock-"

"*Hockey player.*"

"-she can keep up and keep going, which is exactly what I need especially on nights like this one." Evie releases an exasperated sigh and gestures an open palm towards Bryn. "Could you at least pull your dress *down?*" Her head tips condescendingly to one side. "You're currently running the risk of sharing your ass with an entire room full of people who often pay to see one that perfect." There isn't time to even consider responding. "*Seriously.* You would not believe the shit some of these politicians shell out cash for."

Intrigue darts into Bryn's wide-eyed gaze. "Sexually?"

"Sexually. Spiritually." She reaches for a flute from a passing server. "Sexual things they're passing off as spiritual."

More thrill thrums through her glare to which I have to shake my head in order to prevent her from asking additional questions.

I *don't* need to be loudly discussing other people's sex lives.

Especially not at a charity event aimed at raising funds and awareness regarding neurodivergent *children* in low-income brackets.

"Dress down." Evie insists again on a finger flick that's followed by a point to my shoulder. "Lint off." She sways her beverage closer to her lips as I remove the issue. "Rotate the room counterclockwise, putting you at the bidding area first and ending with the open bar last."

"Fine by me," Bryn unexpectedly concedes. "I have *no* interest in drinking tonight."

Her odd declaration causes me to quirk an eyebrow. "That's new. You usually need at least one glass of something to get through these. Are you ill?"

60

"Stomach is a little off *again*." She leans lovingly closer. "I couldn't even keep down my lunch from Little Soup of Horrors. Don't wanna push it."

Concern does its best to be tucked away, something that's made slightly more possible due to Evie suspiciously investigating, "And your afternoon vomiting adventures passed along by an 'inside source' were related to *that* and not the reports that's you're becoming bulimic in order to fit into your dream wedding dress, correct?"

It's impossible not to snip, "*What* inside source?"

"*What* dream wedding dress?!" Bryn scoffs in disbelief. "I haven't even started looking!"

Our publicist responds to neither question. "Your stomach being upset was caused by food poisoning?"

"More likely a stomach bug."

"Good."

"How is my fiancée having a stomach bug a *good* thing?" Swinging my disapproving glare her direction occurs next. "And if you aren't feeling well, baby, you should've stayed in. Went to the estate. Let Hamilton examine you."

"I needed to be here." The soft smile I'm presented creates an unexpected ache in my chest. "*You* needed me to here. At your side. Doing my future Mrs. Dark Knight duties."

"And I need you easier to manage, which is possible when you haven't had three whiskey sours," Evie swiftly sasses.

"I have to support our company," the woman at my side impishly argues.

"Not by drinking the entire bar's supply." Bryn's proud smirk precedes Evie's continuing, "No more than ten minutes with senators, congressman, or judges. No less than five with *anyone* hosting this event. Avoid controversial conversations. Sidestep current sports or music or film. Refrain from gossiping. And above all else do not *leave* one another's side for longer than a pee break because if I have to spend one more day countering *Global Laundry's* smear campaign about you being a 'couple in crisis' I'm gonna slash Jenni's paycheck in half and give myself an overdue vacation to Maui."

"Please, don't cut my pay," is shyly croaked in the background.

"Bright smiles for the cameras!" Evie cheerfully demands prior to spinning on her heels and exiting.

"She's like a fucking Galapagos shark," Bryn mirthfully proclaims. "Equal parts potentially friendly and dangerous."

"*Accurate*," I warmly chortle while steering us the instructed direction. "*Highly accurate.*"

Our casual strolling towards the bidding area allows for several opportunities to shake hands with other guests.

Make small talk with familiar faces.

Avoid eye contact with others.

Regardless of my brand, my status, and undeniable wealth, my mutilated appearance along with my choice in a wife – or *"first wife"* according to some of the older men I find myself around – aren't always well received.

To them, it's alright to be a monster as long as you don't physically look like one.

And it's fine to have mismatched eyes but not "mismatched" races.

Fuck, I hate having to be in public.

How my parents did this with such grace and poise is one thing I wished I would've studied a bit more.

That and cigars.

I occasionally find myself envious of a language my best friend and fiancée speak without me.

I swear learning bits of *Klingon* has been easier.

Bryn offers a polite wave goodbye during our move away from some Vlasta based child psychologist prior to inquiring, "What exactly is this shit for again?"

"Neurodivergent children in low-income brackets."

62

"Catchy." We decline the offer of champagne by a passing server. "And where are we going tomorrow?"

"A non-profit fundraiser dinner in which the proceeds go to supporting individuals with congenital heart disease that struggle to afford the extensive medical care sometimes needed."

"And on Sunday?"

"A charity brunch golf tournament-"

"You hate golf."

"*I do*," I concur upon entering the bidding table area, "however, our company *sponsors* the entire thing with Haworth Enterprises – the proceeds go to assisting military vets who are looking to start their own businesses – and J.T. gets a kick out of playing against celebrities like Pierce Wyatt and Cooper Copeland."

"The country music hottie?!"

Displeased grumbles thoughtlessly flutter through the air in response to the question.

"*Relax, Mr. Wayne,*" she saucily insists and lifts her engagement ring bearing hand upward to wiggle in my face. "I'm *happily* engaged to the man who wouldn't let me sit on his face during our limo ride here."

"*Holmes and Hurst would've seen us.*"

"And?"

"*And,*" I lean in closer and drop my volume, "*the only person I want seeing, hearing, tasting, or touching your pussy is me.*" My chin tips down to the five carat, princess cut diamond. "*If you need a reminder of that, look at your ring.*"

"*Jaws* could break all of his teeth on it."

"Which is one reason why you don't wear it to work."

Although, I wish she would.

I wish she wore it every minute of every day.

It's unfortunately not feasible given what she does and how much time she spends in the water.

Her inability to flash it all around the country while rescuing sharks and stingrays and manatees is one more reason why I look forward to the day she's less hands on and more administrative.

"Nothing good ever comes from you two that close together," J.T. unexpectedly states, encouraging us to turn to face him.

"Pretty sure *everything good* comes from us being this close together, Puppet Boy."

"Puppet Boy?" asks the petite brunette wrapped around his arm.

"An unwanted-"

"Yet totally warranted," Bryn swiftly informs.

"-nickname that my best friend's fiancée should absolutely. *Give. Up.*" His hazel eyes narrow in her direction. "Particularly in *public.*"

"Unlikely," she casually brushes off and extends her open palm forward. "Bryn."

"Shan." A brief shake is exchanged. "J.T.'s date for the weekend."

When she shifts her hand for us to connect, I introduce myself around her small recoiling, "Wes."

"Pleasure to meet you both." The honey beige skinned female sweetly expresses as she slips her grip back to her date. "I've heard *so much* about you!"

"And here we've heard literally *nothing* about you," Bryn needlessly pokes prompting me to deliver a small, playful pop to her backside.

"*You've* been busy for the past couple of weeks," he attempts to retort. "With that rescue out in Texas and the possible move of Steven-"

"Your brother?" questions the new face.

"My shark."

"You…you…um…have your own shark?"

64

Her stuttering nature seems to please the woman I'm wrapped around given her mischievous grin. "For work purposes only."

"I-I-I I thought you worked in corporate." Shan's shocked expression is shot to J.T. "Sharks aren't corporate! Did you mean *Shark Tank?!* *Shark Tank* isn't corporate!"

"Bryn has her own career *separate* from Wilcox Enterprises," my best friend rushes to explain.

"Not separate enough sometimes," is less than quietly huffed.

"And what do you do, Shan?" I politely investigate.

"I'm a second-grade teacher at a private academy in Ann Arbor."

"Michigan?" There's no stopping my brow from lifting in confusion. "What brings you to Highland?"

"This!" Small, excited claps are attached to a wiggle. "J.T. flew his plane all the way up there just to whisk me away for the weekend!"

A quirked eyebrow remains. *"His plane?"*

"It's not like you fly," my fiancée defends in a murmur.

"It was so romantic. *He's* so romantic," Shan gushes at us before turning to face him. "I'm going to go powder my nose just in case they take more photos of us."

J.T. nods in response and waits until she's completely out of earshot to explain, *"I was desperate."*

"You're always desperate," Bryn jabs with a crooked smirk. "Which makes *no fucking sense* considering how pretty you are."

Unhappy grunts are instantly expelled, a sound that have both of them shooting me sarcastic expression.

Fine.

I still have my moments when it comes to their closeness.

"Evie and Pham both advised me *not* to fly solo all weekend – evidently the rumors regarding Bryn and I having an affair are running rampant-"

"Because every article out there just *has* to paint me as some sort of unfaithful slut."

J.T. waves a hand in the air in reference to her outfit. "This isn't exactly the attire of a saint."

"Don't make me send you to the med bay for body shaming."

"*Anyway*," he continues onward after grabbing of glass of champagne, "between the issues with the app development and the coding nightmares we've been facing at one of the brewing facilities and lessons with my golf instructor, shit just got away from me and I panicked." The sip he steals is small. "Found the first woman in my phone that I've talked to in the past four months who's never been in a newspaper or magazine and went for it."

"She seems…" my voice trails off in search of the phrasing, "*nice*."

"Boring," the future Mrs. Wilcox declares. "And you deserve someone incredible and fearless and ready to be the Yates to your Sisko."

To my surprise, he tilts his head in awe like fashion. "You think I'm Sisko material?"

"Of course." Despite her complimenting of him, she presses herself tighter against me. "You've got what it takes to be a great commanding officer, human being, *and* battle star in the sack."

He shakes his head in both amusement and bafflement during his stroll away. "*So uncomfortable…*"

I let a scolding stare fall to her to which she innocently beams. "*What?*"

The two of us aren't provided with a moment to move courtesy of a familiar face taking the now vacant space. "You two look *phenomenal* per the norm."

Offering Ava Danielson, the reporter who ran my first interview since taking over Wilcox Enterprises, a warm smile is easy. "Good evening, Ava."

"Congrats on your engagement!"

66

As I have all night when someone expresses the sentiment, I politely nod, "Thank you."

"You look like you've released your inner Bond girl," compliments my fiancée. "Kudos."

"You say the sweetest things!"

Definitely the most fun.

And by far the most irresponsible.

Between the two of us Evie probably really needs that tropical vacation.

"I didn't realize local press was covering tonight's festivities." My free hand slides into my pocket. "You doing a little bit of social spying? Trying to report on who bids on what?"

"*Yes*," she swiftly admits prior to adjusting her hold on her clutch, "but I don't work local anymore. I work *global*." Pride pushes her bare shoulders completely backward. "I'm lead reporter of public figures for *Outside the Lines* magazine."

"Wow," sincerely slips out, "that is quite the career upgrade."

"Are the Lawson brothers *really* that smoking hot in person?" Bryn anxiously asks.

Ava lowers her jaw to respond only to be met by a vicious throat clearing. After a brief pause and hard swallow, she kindly announces, "I totally owe the change to the two of you." Her grin grows wider. "Writing that interview…writing that article…covering that event…it unlocked so many doors for me."

And that simply made me even happier that I had done it.

"I wish there was some way I could repay you." She lets additional warmth whirl around her expression. "Seriously. If you two ever need anything, just let me know."

An idea suddenly hitting me in the gut pushes me to ask, "How do you feel about *Global Laundry*?"

"*Hate them.*"

"Monica Simmons?"

"*Hate her.*"

"How would you like to do something productive with that hate?"

Bryn's gasp and wicked smile indicate she's onto my plan.

"How would you like to do an *eclusive* interview regarding us, our careers, and our pending wedding?"

Ava's loud squealing is attached to her throwing her hands up into the air. *"Ohmygod, I would love to!"*

Chapter 6

Brynley

First being interviewed all weekend by the media.

Now, my mom.

Does it ever stop?

Will it ever stop?

"Why aren't you eating those?" Mom's palms brace themselves on the marble countertop in her recently finished, rustic cottage home. "They're *handmade* chocolate truffles all the way from Switzerland."

Crossing my ripped jean covered ankles occurs at the same time I poke, "You sure they aren't poisoned?"

She scoldingly tilts her head to one side, dirty blonde locks shaping her face. "I bought them *near* the facility she was leaving, not *at* it."

Not smirking is almost impossible. "And how was transitioning the redheaded salt succubus from planet M-113 back into civilized society?"

"Simple." Mom picks up one of the darker chocolate pieces, wiggles it in front of my face, and then shoves it into her mouth to prove it's edible. "She seems healthy. She's on the right meds." Swallowing the contents of her mouth is followed by a sweet grin. "She's even renting a room above the floral shop she secured a job at during the reintegration process of her program. It's actually *next door* to the chocolate shop."

"Ah, you got a batch before she could sneak over and poison the supply. Smart."

"*Brynley Elizabeth.*"

It's my turn to present a toothy smile. "Just because you can forgive and fuck off, doesn't mean I can."

"Forgive and forget."

"I will *never* forgive or forget what that long lost Lethean did to you."

"She understands." Mom resumes the unpacking of the dishes from the nearby box on the floor. "However, she did give me yours and Wes's handwritten amends letters when I met them for dinner on our final night." The unwrapping of an object begins. "I'll hand them over whenever you're ready."

"Did you have someone scan them for anthrax or other Poison Ivy approved toxins?"

Another reprimanding head tilt is given.

She acts like I'm kidding.

I'm not.

Maybe that crazy cuntcake *is* healed or on the right meds or praying to a new spirit animal or whatever.

And maybe she *isn't* the chick she was a year ago.

But neither am I.

I trust *even less* than I used to.

Which says a shit ton.

"Back to you *not* eating." An odd shaped mosaic vase is revealed to be underneath the brown paper. "And I know it's not just the chocolate you haven't been having."

"How?"

"Mom instincts are tingling."

"You might wanna get those checked." I casually inspect the little brown squares in front of me. "Pretty sure there's a cream for that now."

"You haven't been eating *or* sleeping enough."

"I mean...I'm sleeping...a little...less?" Diverting my attention back to her is accompanied by a small pursing of my lips. "But like that shit is *normal* all things considered."

She quirks an argumentative eyebrow.

70

"It is! With work, traveling for work, *Wes's* work, these damn rich people parties that are *social work*, and trying to plan a wedding which is its own special brand of hellish work – seriously how many pre-nup documents do I have to read and sign – of course, I'm sleeping a little less than I was as a cigar girl living off of hopelessness and semi stale hoagies."

"What about headaches?" Mom tosses the crinkled paper into the pile on the right-hand side of the room near the fridge. "Or dizziness?"

"My fucking boss *lives* to give me headaches and Evie's compliments to criticism back to compliments gives me enough whiplash to cause the dizzy spells."

"Hm." Her contemplative hum ceases her actions once more. "Have you considered that you might be pregnant?"

"Why would you put a hex on your *only* child?!" Horror hops onto my face. "Your only *blood* child. Your new redheaded step one doesn't count."

"*Bryn.*"

"You can hex her all you want."

"*Bryn.*"

"Cast whatever spell that witch from *Beauty and the Beast* used to turn her into a mop bucket or watering can."

"*I'm serious.*"

"So am I." Finally picking up one of the milk chocolate truffles, I add, "Bippi boppiti boo that twat into a lawn table."

"Did you remember to get your last shot?"

"Of course I did!" Chomping down on the candy precedes me snipping. "It's *routine.* Hair. Nails. Wax. Shot." Another bite of the treat is taken. "I never miss *any* of those appointments."

"Right, but you do *reschedule* them."

Her accusation slows my chewing.

"And since you started working at The Institute, you've done *a lot* of rescheduling." Mom retrieves another wrapped item to resume her unloading. "Are you a hundred and ten percent sure you received or rescheduled and then received your birth control shot?"

"I'm not even a hundred and ten percent sure I brushed my fucking teeth today."

At that, she snickers, shakes her head, and starts to peel away the paper. "I'm not taking your ass to the dentist because you have eighteen cavities from covering your teeth in chocolate instead of toothpaste."

"You gave me the chocolate!"

"And I gave you the skills to brush your fucking teeth."

Laughter bounces my entire body as I finish the last bite.

"Seriously, Bryn," Mom sighs prior to finding my stare once more, "go ahead and check your schedule. We both know the last thing you need right now are any big, unexpected surprises."

Chapter 7

Wes

I click the middle option under the picture at the same time I good-naturedly chastise, "You are aware you can help, correct?"

Bryn adjusts her aquamarine "Jaws Ready to Party" tank top prior to shifting the word search in her lap around to circle a found word. "I am helping."

"*With this.*"

"With that."

Amusement dances through my gaze that's relocating to the woman sitting on our penthouse couch beside me. "*Explain, Brynley.*"

"*Say please, Weston.*"

One extended sweatpants covered leg crosses over the other alongside a chortled, "*Please.*"

"Letting you pick all the answers on our wedding test-"

"It's not a test."

"-not only guarantees that we'll pass-"

"It's not a test."

"-it also secures us a good grade."

Laughter can't be kept out of my voice during my repeating, "*It's not a test.*"

"Feels like a test," the future Mrs. Wilcox huffs prior to passing over the booklet. "Why else are there so many fucking multiple-choice questions?"

"To help our wedding design team only pitch ideas that can be considered as true candidates."

"Candidates?" She playfully pokes on a cock of her head. "Are they wedding ideas or potential employee recruits?"

Additional chuckles shake my entire frame.

"And why do we have an entire *team*? We're only two people getting married not a pair of tunas moving from hunting grounds to spawning grounds."

"The amount of aquatic knowledge that leaves your mouth on a daily basis is simply fascinating."

"Way to sweet talk your woman into doing your homework," Bryn theatrically states around the grabbing of my laptop.

"*Our homework.*" Getting the word search into a more comfortable angle is attached to providing her with the answer she's seeking, "And *Valora* has an entire team because she believes in the 'It Takes a Village' mentality."

"But like why do *we* have to be a part of that village?"

"Because it's *our* wedding."

"But-"

"Pick something," precedes me pointing to the screen. "And do not just pick the first option on each one to finish faster."

Her face slightly scrunches in mirth-filled frustration. "*You don't know me.*"

"*I do.*" Another round of light laughs accompanies me winding an arm around the back of the couch behind her. "Which is why I also know that your fondness for blue isn't simply limited to your eyeliner."

"Did Marguerite remember to order that before she left to visit her cousin in Doctenn?"

"She did." My finger slowly begins to trace letters downward. "And stocked our fridge with its weekly grocery order."

Unlike at the estate where we have staff on hand around the clock, our life at the penthouse operates a little differently.

We are responsible for the day-to-day duties of making our bed, making our coffee, making sure not to leave out leftovers that then have the entire place riddled with a foul odor. *Here* we tend to indulge in a more self-sufficient lifestyle that I know Bryn appreciates. She may not love to cook – or be the best cook at that – but whenever

74

we're at the penthouse she at least has the option to try or experiment. And I never used to think twice about having someone bring me coffee but after four or five lost battles with our espresso machine, I couldn't possibly be more grateful for those that go into the trenches for me each morning. With that said, we do still have specific staff – like Marguerite Allard – come to the penthouse for routine cleanings, maintenance, supply ordering, and the occasional Lucky hosted meal.

He was here last night along with Clark and Lauren and made *Arroz con Gandules* that Bryn threw up two hours later.

I know it wasn't food poisoning because no one else experienced any other symptoms.

And after a two-a.m. call to Hamilton – I waited until she was fast asleep – I concluded it's probably just a stomach bug she can't seem to kick.

However, if another vomit spell like it happens again, she *will* allow him to examine her.

Non-negotiable.

The last thing we need is her having some deadly parasite inside of her that we repeatedly ignored.

I'd never forgive myself if something happened to her.

And I'd make sure anyone else who could've prevented her pain never experienced forgiveness either.

"Peach and plum and cranberry," complains my fiancée loudly enough to warrant my gaze. "Are we picking colors or creating fruit salads?"

"Those wouldn't pair well together in a fruit salad."

She whips her head to face me yet lets her finger hover beside the screen. "Don't make me click terracotta as a pallet choice and really turn this shit into a fruit medley."

"You want us looking like Mr. and Mrs. Clayface?" It's impossible not to smirk. "*I'm all in.*"

An unexpected pause appears before she challenges, "You wouldn't."

"I would." A second crooked grin grows. "Whatever you want for the day is yours as long as it ends with your last name becoming mine."

"What if I want a *Star Trek* themed wedding?" The corner of her lip curls upward. "There is an 'other' option for suggestions on this questionnaire."

"I'll wear a gold shirt."

"And if I wanna walk down the aisle to the opening song?"

"We'll hire an orchestra to play it."

"And if I wanna say our vows in Klingon?"

"I'll start studying between every conference call."

Girlish giggles freely floating through the air are followed by her leaning over to plant her lips on top of mine. In tandem, they spread apart to allow light touches that almost instantly become even lighter teasing.

Teasing that leads to me abandoning the pen in my possession.

Knocking away the booklet.

Sliding the laptop onto the coffee table where my feet were just resting in order to safely lower Bryn onto her back.

Cover her body with mine.

Allow one hand to slip underneath the thin fabric to glide upwards across her silky, soft skin that feels like it's been forever since I touched.

Right as my thumb manages to brush her bra protected nipple, a familiar voice grouses, *"Come on, guys. I sit on that couch!"*

An unhappy grumble escapes as I return to my sitting position. "Why didn't you knock?"

"When have I ever knocked?" J.T. juvenilely jeers back.

"Maybe you should start."

"Or maybe you shouldn't tell me that it's alright to pop over before I head to the hanger when it clearly isn't."

The opportunity to make a rebuttal is stolen from me courtesy of Bryn rising to her feet. "We're good, Puppet Boy. There wouldn't have been time to do more than a light double tap to the bat switch."

Heat threatens to flush my face; however, my best friend openly jokes, "You're the reason I'm comfortable watching those movies now."

"And you're the reason I can't watch those *Annabelle* movies with Vanessa because you really *are* a doll come to life."

He warmly laughs, shakes his head, and gives her the finger, which she quickly returns.

As much as I may not always appreciate their closeness, I'm grateful for it.

I would rather them be on the same side than forever feuding opponents forcing me to choose between the love of my life and family.

"Speaking of Vanessa, I should probably be going." Bryn using two fingers on her left hand to flick strands of hair away from her face allows me a small glimpse of her engagement ring that's in full display. "She said ten thirty for brunch, so me showing up a couple minutes early should be fine."

J.T. slides his hands into his navy suit pockets on another amused smirk. "It's ten thirty-four."

"*Fuck*," mutters Bryn during a dart away for our bedroom, "*of course it is.*"

"You really can't tell time, can you?" taunts the other male in the room.

"And you really can't finish a whole box of trojans."

The snap back momentarily renders him speechless allowing me to call out, "*Grab your phone.*"

"On it!" she replies in the distance.

I wait until she's returned to the room, device in hand, to request more details about her day, "Why do you have your workbag?"

She gives the object on her shoulder a small push upward. "Post brunch with Vanessa, I have to meet Calen at The Institute to go over a few last-minute changes to this coming weekend's trip itinerary, which reminds me that we need to reschedule our meeting with Valora to next week because I don't know how late I'll be getting back Sunday and *reallllyyyyyy* don't wanna do champagne and chipper that early on Monday."

"*Noted.*"

"We would've done the plan changes this morning, but it was tank cleaning day with the scuba divers, and Raquel lets her merman fantasies clog her ability to communicate until they leave."

"And then you'll be home?"

"*Actually,*" her body cautiously creeps closer, "I told Calen I'd help him look into getting his marine veterinary license." She tucks her cell into her pocket. "Ever since Steven's injury, he's been really considering it."

"How is Steven?" J.T. asks the question I can't believe I haven't yet.

Hm.

Why haven't I?

Why hasn't she just gushed about him?

The situation?

Work?

Is she hiding something?

Ashamed?

Perhaps between all of our social calendar engagements she hasn't had time?

"Completely healed – thank fuck – and now into the next step of securing his move."

"That sucks," J.T. sincerely expresses.

"Doesn't rock."

Uncertain of exactly what other sentiment to add in leads to me suggesting, "Dinner?"

78

Bryn swings her crystal gaze my way.

"Can I plan on having *dinner* with my future wife?"

"With her or *on her*?" she salaciously sasses back.

"*In the room…*" mutters J.T. at the same time he lets his head fall dramatically backward.

"He won't be tonight," I promise, instantly receiving a glare from him but a round of giggles from her.

Those matter more.

"*You've got yourself a deal, Weston.*"

"*Then come sign on the dotted line, Brynley.*"

My request is quickly met; however, the chaste kiss is far from my favorite.

Particularly when she's about to spend the vast majority of a day in the presence of another man.

"Take Hill with you," I firmly insist, leaving no room for debate in my tone.

"Fine," she surrenders suspiciously easily.

Rather than turn the verbal pages to search for answers, I simply allow the conversation to end and her to peacefully exit.

Once the door is successfully closed behind Bryn, he saunters over to one of the unoccupied cushioned chairs. "You know the rumors *aren't* true, Wes." He casually flops down. "Your naughty buttons are the only ones Uhura is interested in pressing."

I lightly laugh and retrieve the laptop to finish the survey. "Tell me that's not what you stopped by to talk to me about."

"It isn't."

"Is it about you using the company plane to visit that teacher in Ann Arbor?" My finger wiggles itself across the mousepad to wake it back up. "Because as long as you conduct some sort of business before or after, there's no need to switch to one that is intended for personal use only."

"First off, *no.* I have no intent on seeing her again."

"You two looked like you had fun that weekend."

"Looks can be deceiving."

"Often."

"Aside from not being able to agree on much – including simple shit like dessert – she's got a fondness for baby talk in the sack and that's *not* the type of role playing I'm personally into."

Holding in my laughter is impossible.

"This is league week," he gingerly reminds during a crossing of his legs. "I've got introductory meetings across the country with most of the major sporting leagues to discuss sponsorship eligibility and requirements as well as an interview dinner with an app interrogation developer from Bennett Enterprises who wants to branch out of food and into alcohol."

"You're going to need a night off."

"I'm going to take one to meet an exclusive buyer named Gwendolyn Kincaid who I want to hire to procure me the *actual 3-D* chessboard and pieces they used during an episode of *Next Gen* where the crewmembers played it in Ten Forward."

"Is that the name of the episode?"

"That's the name of the *bar*," J.T. bites without remorse. "How is it you've seen entire seasons of the show and *still* don't know that?" I'm not allotted time to response. "Anyway, if she accepts the job, then I'll have Bryn's wedding gift as good as got."

Alright.

Looks like I need to begin searching for the perfect wedding present myself.

And the best, best man gift given the lengths he's gone to for her.

Me.

Us.

"The reason I wanted to stop by on my way to the hangar is because I wanted to be the one to inform you that there has been some new, unexpected digging into your past."

Clicking a silverware choice precedes me meeting his stare. "And?"

"And..." an adjustment to his lapel is made, "this isn't the typical, where was the recluse for the last ten years, type of shit. It's...*further back* than that."

"How far?"

"Your childhood."

"*Why?*" Discomfort has me pushing the device onto the couch space beside me. "What are they searching for?"

"I don't know."

"*Why* are they searching?"

"I don't know."

"How *long* have they been searching?"

"I don't know."

"*What. Do. You. Know?*"

"Other than cyber has cautious eyes on inquiries? Not much. However," two hands are offered up in a cautious manner, "Park says unknown visitors have been by your parent's mausoleum – according to the groundskeeper – and one of his sources in the historical society has contacted him regarding a series of questions regarding lineage."

"Lineage?" My brow pinches together in question. "*Why*? Is someone...trying to make a documentary about my family? A mockumentary?"

"Again..." his shoulders bounce in cluelessness, "I don't know. But I do know *you*. And keeping something like this to then blindside you later results in much bigger hysterics than had someone simply mentioned it sooner; therefore, that's what I'm doing." He gestures an open palm to me. "Mentioning it sooner."

A small nod of appreciation is presented. "Thank you."

After echoing the action, he adds, "Pham wants your focus and theirs to currently remain on cleaning up the PR nightmares from the merger hiccups, the app stumbles, the possible new brand sponsoring we may be getting in bed with, and the annual Red, White, & Blue festival, while Evie and Jenni find it to be crucial to keep your personal press showcasing you and Bryn are a power couple planning the perfect wedding around your social obligations with nothing to worry about."

I can't stop myself from scooting to the very edge of the couch. "Do *you* think I have anything to worry about?"

"With the company or Bryn?"

"Either."

"No." Whatever relief he delivers is short-lived. "But we were also taught to always be cautious of the calm."

The remainder of the wise words of my father mindlessly leave me, *"Because the calm always comes before the storm."*

Chapter 8

Brynley

I love release days.

Not only because I get to spend hours on or in the water but because they're one of the few places I get to go without supervision.

The Institute understands the magnitude of me marrying one of their biggest donors, which is why I can have my own personal security guard linger not so nonchalantly on the property. However, he is *not* cleared or permitted to be on the water during any operation.

And I love it.

I absolutely fucking love it.

"Nice rubber." A playful wink is shot in Calen's direction. "I'm proud of you for wrapping it before untrapping it."

"She always so clever?" Jacques Auclair, the new and honestly pretty hot French rescue recruit for K&T, lightly laughs while pulling his googles down from his sun kissed forehead to over his dark chocolate brown eyes. "So beautiful and clever?"

"*Down, Auclair,*" snickers Jillian Pyev, the youngest member of their team. "Winters is basically a porcupinefish. Cute in the face and deadly to the touch."

"Aw," my hand is theatrically thrown at her, "you say the darndest things."

More laughter bounces around the boat and I happily lean into it.

Accompanying other rescue teams around the country is by far my favorite part of the job. It doesn't matter if I'm the one in the water or on the ship watching the monitors. Both positions are crucial. Both benefit the creatures being rescued or returned. Both are two halves of a working whole.

83

And I *love* being part of this whole.

And I *love* having a career that's *just mine*.

Coworkers and colleagues that are *just mine*.

An entire existence separate from the one I share with Wes.

I love having a life outside of my future husband's shadow and limelight and schedule.

I love my ability to maintain some independence.

Even if it's just for a few nautical miles at a time.

"*Overbooooarddddddd*," my best friend and partner in ocean crime announces prior to wedging his oxygen mouthpiece between his lips.

His behavior is swiftly copied by Pyev and Auclair leaving me and Lance Kang to assist in lifting the plastic tank of baby stingrays over to the edge of the boat to them.

Due to this litter being larger than normal as well as our own aquatic organization ready to release some of our recently hatched, Calen and I were called in to aid in the relocation. Him being in the water is the better call – given how bad my stomach's been lately – and I truthfully don't mind screen duty.

Don't get me wrong.

The view of the ocean *in* the ocean is fucking incredible.

It just doesn't hurt my feelings to get to see it this clearly without the fuss and muss of squeezing my sexy ass into a wet suit and having to do a deep scrub and conditioning of my hair afterwards.

And I damn sure don't hate not having to dive this early when the waters are this choppy.

Kang and I move to the main part of the boat to watch the feed on the monitors. Seeing the babies eagerly disperse in various directions, anxious to eat and find their way, fills me with the same sense of pride it always does.

I *love* when creatures find their way.

Maybe because I get it.

Maybe because I know what it's like to be wading water, simply hoping you get your shit together to do more than just barely survive.

The three in the water maintain a safe space during the fish's continued departure by freely exploring the territory for other injured ocean life that may need a minor or *major* hand. Admiring the beautiful hues around them nearly hypnotizing me like normal, however, before I can completely lose myself in the moment I spot unexpected activity in the far corner.

"*There*." Tapping the left side of the screen is attached to my questioning, "*What's that?*"

Kang rotates the camera and instantly zooms in.

"Looks like a fishing net," mindlessly leaves me while surveying the scenario. "And we aren't in commercial fishing waters."

Kang grunts his irritation prior to picking up his radio to contact the authorities regarding the situation, yet I keep a visual on the situation, monitoring the area, curious to what could possibly be happening until I see it.

Red.

Streams and streams of red.

"*Finning!*" I shriek at the top of my lungs. "*They're finning!*"

Whether it's my screaming or the teams sudden shift in swimming directions that spooks them isn't certain, but the creatures that begin to be thrown overboard at a much faster speed are without a doubt sharks.

Poor defenseless, juvenile sharks.

Being left to bleed out.

Suffocate.

Die.

The team in the water darts over to see if any can be saved as Kang puts a call into the Coast Guard.

Helplessly, I watch the three, swim around, checking the dying creatures, desperately seeking survivors, pleading to themselves and whoever it is they pray to that at least one can be saved. One hand curls around my mouth at the same time the other tucks itself around my stomach, bile ruthlessly burning its way up the back of throat over the gory shambles they're sifting through. Despite my own disgust and the tears threatening to blur my vision, I assist in the process the best I can, being an extra set of eyes.

Unfortunately, I see nothing that they don't.

Not a single fucking thing.

No baby sharks to potentially preserve.

"*Anything?*" Kang questions upon ending his call to the guard. "Are *any* of them worth retrieving?"

I slowly shake my head.

"*Fuck!*" shouts the lead from K&T. "*Fuck! Fuck! Fuck!*"

My head starts to fall in remorse when I spot the same thing Calen does. "*Is that...*"

Cautious movement from my best friend continues during his approach to a wounded creature wiggling around.

"*Ohmygod...*" Both hands cup my mouth. "*Pleasebeokay. Pleasebeokay.*"

Calen scoops the wounded, little scalloped hammerhead into his grasp, not at all surprised when he doesn't put up a fight.

From first glance he has all his fins.

From the next, it's clear to the see where they had begun cutting and were interrupted.

Most likely by my shouting.

Which may have saved the little dude's life.

Rather than take a moment to relish in relief, Kang kicks his head towards the opposite side of the boat. "We need to get him into the tank."

Our rush over to help results in me slipping on a wet spot – caused by the choppy waters – and painfully twisting my ankle; however, I don't do more than release a small hiss.

Whatever is wrong with me pales in comparison to what's wrong with the baby we have a chance to save.

To help.

I'm sure the minor ache I'm experiencing can be cured with two Tylenol and a day of rest with my foot elevated.

Calen and Auclair work together to get the shark out of the water and into our waiting grasps. His wild whipping nature creates unneeded difficulties that don't stop our efforts so much as slow them, which is not something we need when fighting against a ticking clock.

And it *is* ticking.

They can't survive outside of the water that long.

Especially not this young.

In tandem, we make our way over to the built-in tank used for such on site rescues, where we manage to get him secured and Kang a better view of his injuries.

"They look cosmetic," he promptly informs during his scanning, "but we need to get him to K&T for further inspection."

My nods of agreement barely precede Calen hoisting himself over the side. The second he rips his mask off, he urgently inquires, *"Is he gonna make it?!"*

"We think so!" Excitement leads to me moving towards him. "But-"

Where the end of sentence lands is unknown due to the combination of the rocking and my suffering of another slip courtesy of my hurt ankle buckling under the weight.

"Bryn!"

My entire body brutally falls backwards with a loud thud sound being the last thing I hear before everything goes completely black.

Chapter 9

Wes

I prefer working at home – the estate or the penthouse – rather than our main headquarters building.

I get more done there.

I am interrupted significantly less.

While being here, I am somehow magically always needed significantly *more.*

My being here – according to J.T. – is good for office morale.

I'm not entirely sure that's true and not something he's simply concocted to guarantee that I don't backtrack into my preferred reclusive lifestyle.

Especially when he's not here to properly monitor that I'm getting enough "in public" time.

Tugs of frustration are delivered to my black tie at the same time I bite into my cell, "So, *another* rejection?"

"Individual venues are allowed to carry our beer per their own respective policies, but at this time, we cannot make a bid for national sponsorship for the *major* leagues. However, the Wilcox brand-"

"I don't *want* our whiskey for sporting events. I want our *beer.*"

"I'm aware," my second in command grumbles back, "but *at this time, Wes,* it's not an option. This is one of the drawbacks to any new endeavor."

An unhappy grunt is all he's given.

"I've got calls in to get meetings with minor league organizations and internationals. We may just need to start *there* until one of the majors becomes available for doing business. We need to have patience."

"We need to have *reach.*"

"You need to get laid."

The accusation cracks my jaw.

"You only get this...*non-understanding* when you haven't heard the cat *purr* in a while."

Airy croaks are all that manage to escape prompting him to arrogantly chuckle.

"*Exactly.*"

"Mr. Wilcox!" Hasty knocks on my office door across the room suddenly occur. "*Mr. Wilcox!*"

"Go find the Morgan brand a viable home." Ending the call precedes me replying, "*Yes?*"

Zaidee peers her panicking face around the blockade. "Um...you have an *emergency* call from Hill on line one."

My brow furrows. "Did *he* use the word emergency or are *you?*"

"He did."

The transition from sitting on my light gray office couch to hovering over the nearby matching desk on the phone is damn near instant. "*Wilcox.*"

"There's been an accident," Hill professionally states causing me to drop my cell. "Involving Bryn."

"*What?!*" Gripping the office device tighter in my hand occurs at the same time I growl, "*What type of accident?!*"

"According to Connelly-"

"What the fuck do you mean according to Connelly?! Were you not there?"

"I-"

"Why the fuck weren't you there?!"

"I-"

"You are *paid* to fucking be there, Hill!"

"I am not allowed on the water transport vehicles, Sir."

"It happened while she was working?!"

"According to Connelly, she slipped and hit her head resulting in what the attending physician believes may be a concussion."

"What do you mean *may* believe?! How do they not know?!"

"They-"

"Why do they not know!?"

"They-"

"When the fuck was this?!"

"We rushed Bryn straight here to the Tellman Medical Center after the boat docked."

Indecipherable roars reverberate throughout the room.

"She is currently being examined further by the doctor who may want her to get an MRI."

Additional growls rattle my teeth as I struggle not to snap the receiver in half.

"Connelly is currently the only one allowed in the room-"

"*Why?!*" Lunging pointlessly further is attached to me barking, "*You* are a member of her security team! *You* should be in that room until I can be!"

"Connelly-"

New rumbles of disapproval effortlessly seep loose.

"-is her coworker and according to The Institutes policy listed as an onsite contact during emergencies."

"*What?!*"

"It's policy for each member of the pairing to have that direct point of contact according to Connelly. I haven't had a chance to verify that information but-"

"*I will get that fucking verified. You get your ass outside that fucking room and give me constant information until my arrival. Understood?*"

"Yes, Sir."

The second I slam the phone down, I shout, "*Zaideeeeee!*"

My assistant scrambles into the room, clearly ready to take whatever action is necessary. "Yes, Mr. Wilcox?"

90

"Contact personal transport. Tell them I need a vehicle and emergency assistance from here to South Haven."

"Vehicle?" Her brows scrunch together in surprise. "Not a plane?"

"*What did I say?*"

I still don't fly.

I can't.

I can hardly even *look* at the ones we have in our hangar without hyperventilating.

Do I need to get to Bryn?

Yes.

Am I desperate?

Fuck. Yes.

Will me having a goddamn heart attack or stroke benefit the situation?

No.

But donating *generously* to emergency departments such as police, fire, and medical permits me such liberties that will allow me to get there in remarkable timing.

"Vehicle!" squeaks Zaidee. "Got it!"

She spins on her heels to exit damn near bumping into a pair of women on their way in.

"Is it true?!" Pham forcefully questions. "Has there really been an accident? Is Bryn really on life support?"

Outrage bumps into bewilderment. "*How the fu-*"

"Tell me it *was* an accident and not a botched abortion of an affair child," Evie demands pushing her sunglasses into her untamed hair. "Tell me I am not canceling my day of dying and waxes to deal with something worthy of a telenovela."

Irateness reaches my vocal cords yet isn't presented with the opportunity to be released.

"The press is *somehow* all over this already," Pham huffs in indignation. "They're supposedly reporting from outside the hospital

91

she was brought to *if* she was brought to one. Was she? And if she was, how did they know before we did?! Who told them?! Who is leaking inside information?! And if you knew when they did, why didn't you immediately call me and the team to get ahead of this?!"

"*Is she pregnant?*" Evie investigates again. "Do these reports that claim this may be history repeating itself with her having a secret child hold *any* sort of weight?! Even a pea sized amount?! I mean…when did your father have an affair? Or an affair child? Why don't I have any documentation of that? *Where* is the documentation for it?!"

"*Enough!*" rushes out of me upon the arrival of Hurst and Holmes who were stationed in the lobby prior to my yelling. "*Not. Another. Word.*"

Both women clamp their mouths shut.

"*I need to get to my fiancée.*" The only thing I pick up off the desk is my cell. "I *do not* have time to deal with vicious lies or slander. That is what *both of you* are paid to do." Moving their direction occurs next. "So, I *heavily suggest*, you get the hell out of my way, and go do *your* jobs before you no longer have jobs to do."

Chapter 10

Brynley

I wanna say all these conditions are being caused by my fall.

That that's why my head throbs.

And stomach churns.

And why I wanna punch Doogie Houser here in the middle of his can't grow facial pubes covered face.

It has nothing to do with the information he just read to me off his corner computer.

It can't.

It's impossible.

"You're wrong," I effortlessly argue while attempting to sit up a little higher. "I'm not pregnant."

The young, blond doctor whose real name I can't quite remember – another sign of having a concussion not being knocked up – sympathetically tips his head to the side. "Miss Winters-"

"*Bryn.*"

"*Bryn,*" he corrects at the same time he angles himself to completely face me. "According to your blood test results, you are in fact pregnant."

"But like I can't be."

"You're a virgin?"

"No."

"Celibate?"

"No."

"Then...?" The polite hand gesture indicates it's my turn to fill in the answer.

"Because I took one of those piss on a stick things that says right on the box – in big bold print – that the results were ninety-nine percent accurate!"

93

"Ninety-nine percent does leave a one percent margin for era, Miss Winters."

"*Bryn!*"

"*Bryn.*" His maroon covered torso leans slightly forward. "There is a possibility that you and your test fell into that very thin exception percentage."

Frustrated squeaks are attached to me curling my fingers like claws yet all the extra movement results in sharp pains reappearing in my head.

Fuck.

Can't move like that again.

Or that fast.

Or maybe at all for a minute.

Two.

Seven.

I momentarily shut my eyes and release a deep exhale.

His test has to be wrong.

If the piss one I took at work earlier this week can be wrong, then so can his!

Unless...unless the one I took in the bathroom *wasn't* wrong so much as wasn't done processing?

I mean I did chuck it the second I saw one line appear because Raquel and Heidi were entering, and I didn't want them to see me waiting for results.

But like...there weren't *two* lines on that test, were there?

There just...couldn't have been.

"Bryn?" cautiously questions the male in the room forcing my attention back over to him. "How have you been feeling lately? Nasuea?"

"I thought it was a stomach bug."

"Lightheadedness?"

"I forget to eat."

"Fatigue?"

"Who doesn't get that way when they haven't had a vacation in the last decade?"

"Tender breasts?"

"I bump into shit." A comedic point to head is attached to a snarky, "*Obviously.*"

"Moodiness?"

"Born this way."

He let's the corner of his lip kick upward prior to stating, "You have all the early indicators; however, if you would like us to run your blood sample to double check your pregnancy results then-"

"*Pregnant?*" Wes's deep voice unexpectedly rattles the room. "*You're pregnant?*"

Fuck. Fuck. Fuck.

"Are you family?" Doctor Can't Remember His Name politely inquires. "Those are the only individuals allowed in the room at this time."

His cut jaw throbs during his proclaiming, "*I'm. Her. Fiancé.*"

"Dr. Wallace Markman." He extends an open palm in his direction. "Her attending physician."

Wes crosses over to shake while Calen cringes and shuts the door with himself on the other side.

Great.

Now, *he* knows too.

Just what I *didn't* need.

"As I was just expressing to Bryn," the doctor resumes speaking while Wes plants a protective palm on my thigh, "I *can* rerun the blood test to verify the pregnancy if you're truly concerned it's a mistake; however, I can also run a different test that would be able to tell us about how far along you are. If the other test you took was *too soon-*"

"*What* other test?" Wes snips at the same time he snaps his attention to me. "*When* did you take another test, Brynley?"

Oooo.

95

Yeah.

No.

Not ready to take the bait off that hook yet.

I gently flick my finger back at the doctor. "Let's um…let Doctor Wahlberg-"

"*Wallace.*"

"-finish talking, first."

The glare I'm shot barely precedes our eyes returning to medical professional in the room.

"If the over-the-counter test you took was *too soon* that could've also been why the test gave you a negative read rather than a positive." He uses one hand to wake his computer back up. "I'll reorder that while we're waiting on the results from your MRI. Due to the severity of the hit and its location, it was marked a rush order, which can still take up to twenty-four hours depending on how many other patients are a head of you." His fingers begin to get to work. "From your initial exam and reviewing your chart, I believe you're experiencing a mild TBI."

"TB…what?" The wrinkling of my forehead is instant. "Is that better than a concussion? Worse?"

"One in the same," Wes calmly replies to my surprise. "It stands for traumatic brain injury, which is any physical disruption to normal brain function."

Doctor Marky Mark pauses his typing and shoots my fiancé an arched eyebrow. "Doctor?"

"No, I've simply spent years with one at my estate." After the announcement, he relocates his stare to me to make another. "Who *will* be tending to your follow up and insuring you follow *any* recommended regimen for recovery and any for…proper…*pregnancy*…care…as well."

Additional throbbing to no real shock appears.

"Having a doctor on hand will be quite useful during the three Rs and prenatal care," informs the male at the computer. "With a mild

96

TBI you're going to rest – both physically and mentally – rehabilitate – some minor exercises to gage and/or improve cognitive responses – and lastly a return to regular activities such as *work*. Considering what you *do* for a living according to your paperwork, it may be in your best interest to avoid diving as well as potentially hazardous areas where a repeat injury could occur. With that said…if you are indeed pregnant, you are still being advised not to do diving – particularly scuba – to avoid areas that increase the possibility for a fall and any heavy lifting." A pause in typing is taken once more for him to make eye contact with me. "Monitoring you overnight is protocol; however, if there are no major issues with your MRI or blood tests, we should be able to get you out of here by late tomorrow morning."

I nod my understanding.

"I'm gonna finish putting in these orders and then have Nurse Anita come draw some more blood. After that, additional visitors are welcome, but let's keep their time *in the room* to a minimum." He resumes his clicking. "Rest really should begin now."

No one says another word until the scrub covered man is preparing to exit.

At that moment, we both politely thank him and properly say goodbye.

The instant the door is shut the man I'm surprised got to me as quickly as he did – considering he didn't fly – quietly seethes, "*Why didn't you tell me you were pregnant?*"

"I didn't think that I really was."

"Yet the thought *crossed* your mind if you took a fucking pregnancy test, Brynley."

More pounds to the head have me groaning under my breath. "Am I supposed to tell you *every* thought I have, Weston?" The sneer he's presented is bitter. "*Neither of us wants that.*"

"This is not a joke."

"And you do not see 'ha-ha' thought bubbles surrounding my face."

97

He folds his arms firmly on top of the black dress shirt and tie combination that's admittedly one of my favorites. "How long have you known?"

"Since about two minutes before you walked into the room."

"How long have you *considered* this to be a possibility?"

"I don't know…like…" my shoulders innocently bounce. "Couple weeks maybe?"

"*Weeks?!*"

"I thought it was just shit I kept eating and then my mom reminded me that maybe it was time for my birth control shot and then when I checked about my appointment, I saw I had meant to move it and then never did and then the next thing I know I'm getting me a pregnancy test and Calen an orange soda so it's not the only thing on the receipt."

"Wait," a single finger of objection is lifted up, "*he knew* you might be pregnant before I did?"

"*No.*" Another attempt to sit up higher is made. "*He knew* I needed to stop at the corner store and because I can't so much as scratch my left tit without someone reporting on it, I thought buying something extra would help cover up what I was really buying."

Relief settles on Wes's shoulders upon his approach. "So, all the media speculating about your pregnancy was just that? Speculation? Not someone selling them your personal information?"

"If you're implying that one of my only best friends *outside of you,* the person who apparently *carried me* to Hill, tried *calling you* on our way to here, collected all the information to *give to you* that he possibly could when you didn't answer, is secretly *betraying me* then I suggest you go back to your *Batman: Year One* roots and fresh up on your investigation skills."

Guilt grossly covers every crevice of his complexion.

As it should.

Just because he doesn't love my relationship with Calen doesn't mean he gets to blame him for every little leak the press and blogs receive.

Calen – like Vanessa – signed an NDA early into our friendship.

And *like Vanessa* he didn't hesitate.

Didn't think twice.

Couldn't have cared less because *that's* not what our friendship is about.

What it'll *ever* be about.

It's the same reason he doesn't expect me to always pay for lunch or dinner or movies or bowling or whatever activity it is we decide to do.

It's not about money.

And it'd be nice if the most important man in my life could fucking swallow *that* versus taking a bite out of my best friend's ass every chance he gets.

"*My apologies,*" Wes quietly states at the same time he sits on the edge of my bed, facing me. "*You're right.*"

"I know. I'm basically the *captain* of the *USS Righterprise.*"

Light laughter is attached to a good-natured headshaking. "Letting you pilot that seems like a bit of a reach."

"A reach *around* maybe." The waggling of my eyebrows receives snickers from us both, but unfortunately for me, it hurts. "*Ou...*"

Wes immediately scoots closer to cup my cheek. "*You okay?*"

"You mean other than having an unexpected concussion and pregnancy?"

"I mean..." his hand falls down to grip mine, "*with* the unexpected concussion and pregnancy, *little prey?*"

There's no stopping the corner of my lip from twitching. "Not really."

His mouth opens yet instantly closes, clearly not wanting to cause me pain again.

Which is really *not* what I want from him.

I don't need to be further protected and tanked in like *I'm* the hurt hammerhead and he's the sexy beauty randomly saving me from the dangers of the unknown waters.

I need him to let me *breathe*.

Let me *be*.

A gentle thumb stroke is delivered to the area he's cradling. "Shall we discuss one and then the other?"

"Shall we not?"

"*Brynley.*"

An unhappy huff escapes prior to me caving. "Accidents are always a risk in and on the water. That's part of the job."

"Then maybe you need a *different* job."

"And maybe I'm going to pretend you didn't just ask me to give up the *first* and *only* real career I've ever had because I got a tiny bump to the head."

"*You blacked out.*"

"I was knocked out."

"They're the same thing!"

"By a tiny technicality."

"Be serious."

"I am." Snatching my hand away occurs out of spite. "*I'm not giving up my job because of a fluke accident, Weston. That's non-negotiable.*"

"*And I'm not losing my wife and child because you're too stubborn or selfish or both.*" He leans forcefully closer. "*That's non-negotiable, Brynley.*"

"I didn't *know* I was pregnant."

"Now, you do."

"No," it's my turn to lift a finger, "that's still *pending* another test."

100

Wes sarcastically cocks his head.

"Fine! I'm *most likely* pregnant!"

"And?"

"And I will refrain from falling to the best of my ability! Kind of like I already was!"

A simple lifting of his dark brows is all he presents.

"I will proceed with *additional* caution, Mr. Wayne."

Hearing the nickname has him fighting a smirk.

"*I promise.*" Our fingers find their way back together. "I'll do whatever it takes to keep our mini caped crusader safe."

For the first time since his arrival, joy successfully spreads itself through his stare. "*We're really gonna have a baby.*"

"That's what I'm told." His excitement tries its best to trample my nervousness. "And you...seem...excited."

"You don't."

My head thoughtlessly sways back and forth for a moment. "It's not...the most...*ideal* timing."

"Is that all?" Hurt struggles not to be heard in his tone. "Is that the only reason you're not excited?"

"You're concerned I've changed my mind about wanting kids."

"Yes."

"*Well, I haven't.*" The firmness in my voice seems to melt his shifting demeanor. "I just...didn't want one right *now*." Another shrug bounces my sore shoulders. "And considering I got my job *because* the woman before me was *pregnant*, I can't exactly pretend I'm not worried that I'm about to meet the same fate."

"*You won't, little prey.*" Wes's proclamation precedes him planting a gentle kiss to the back of my hand. "*I promise.*"

Chapter 11

Brynley

You know I'm starting to fully understand the reason why juvenile sharks probably don't mind being abandoned by their mother.

It beats the fuck out of constantly being smothered.

"You *sure* you don't need anything?" Mom asks again for the fourth time since entering Wes's comic book room in the estate where I thought I would be safe from the household's suffocating ways. "*Anything at all?*" She lifts my chin up to meet her gaze. "How about a sandwich? You hungry? You're probably hungry. You need to eat again? Have you been consuming enough calories? Hydrating? Do you need me to get you some more water?"

"Mom, I'm not an invalid. Just pregnant."

Her hand falls back to her side on a scowl.

"And I'm *fine.*" Adjusting the comic book in my lap occurs between statements. "The only thing I need right now is a little bit of space."

Which is the same fucking thing I've needed for the past ten days and *still* not been lucky to receive.

Sex either.

It *just* became a "doctor approved" activity after my gyno visit yesterday.

Unlike swimming.

And heavy lifting.

And drinking coffee.

I can't even have fucking *coffee* in the morning!

A suggestion was made about ginger lemon tea, and I may have Klingoned out.

Mom lifts both hands in a surrendering nature prior to bowing her head. "I'll return to work then. You know how to use the intercom if you need me."

She swiftly shuffles out of the room, but unfortunately for me, her exit becomes Wes's entrance. "Need anything?"

"To find out what happens next in *Batman: Year Two*." The turning of the page is dramatically done. "Particularly *in peace*."

"It gets darker," Wes absentmindedly announces at the same time he parks himself on the arm of the couch at the opposite end and continues to text. "And is not *technically* considered part of the canon in which *Year One* came from." Rather than look up, he lets his fingers fly across the screen while he continues to ramble, "Still an excellent read."

"I wouldn't know," I sassily snip. "No one will give me five minutes alone to read it."

Finally, my fiancé meets my gaze. *"Problem?"*

"With what?" Sarcastically folding my hands in my lap is executed. "Having Hamilton hover? Or Clark? Or Mom? Or J.T.? Or you?" The angling of my head is done for additional emphasis. "Or having to be supervised when hanging out with Calen? Or Vanessa?" I let my shoulders bounce. "Or the fact I'm on *admin* duty, which is just mindless amounts of paperwork and reading research notes, rather than being hands on with the creatures in our care? Or having to write Steven's diary notes for his transfer but not getting to see him and feed him? Or not knowing when I get to return to the water? Or *if* I'll get to return?"

Wes's mouth begins to lower in spite of the fact I'm not done.

"Or are you asking me do I have problem with the fact regardless of me getting the approval from *my licensed physician* about attending the annual Red, White, and Blue event where Evie is already planning for us to officially announce our pregnancy as 'Red, White, and Due' that you *still* want us to cancel once more leaving me *trapped* in this castle like Belle before the village people stormed the gates to try to prison break her out?"

Responding to me isn't done due to him answering his phone. "*Wilcox.*"

It's like getting pregnant is a literal crime with my sentence to be served out in the world's nicest brig.

I mean am I *excited* about being pregnant?

No.

The mood swings, the tender tits, the food aversions and the prenatal meds are all *not* big sellers of the experience.

Not to mention the seemingly ceaseless fight to keep my position in the R&R department in which I keep having to remind my boss that while I may not be able to dive, I *am* able to ship assess.

Tend to creatures on the spot.

Identify their breed and species and whether they're on the endangered list or not.

However, being *pregnant* – even barely pregnant – is not a liability The Institute wants to take; therefore, my hours are becoming more limited.

My tasks more restricted.

My purpose more narrowed.

Part of me believes that if it weren't for my husband's company – soon to be *our company* – signing the biggest donation checks, I wouldn't even have a job anymore.

And that?

That I *really* fucking hate.

"I understand the Morgan merger is about *beer* but that's global. I want us to look into local. Craft. I want the company to be willing to invest in businesses that we believe in that are right here in our own backyard so to speak," Wes describes to someone on the other end of his phone. "*That's* really the whole purpose of you walking the beer booths at the upcoming festival, J.T."

"You have a hundred and eleven rooms in Wayne Manor," I unhappily turn the page backward, "could you *please* take your convo elsewhere?"

"I'll call you back." The ending of his conversation is followed by a gentle touch to my stretched-out leg. "Hungry?"

"Why?" My stare momentarily moves to find his. "Do you wanna spoon feed me like a Gerber Baby?"

"That's…an unsettling image."

"This is an unsettling way to live."

"Your future husband taking care of you is an unsettling way to live?"

"Holding your future wife hostage like Khan in *Into Darkness* most certainly fucking is."

"Just like your mother wasn't a prisoner while being taken care of neither are you."

"Then why can't I so much as wipe my own ass without someone from on the other side of the door waiting to offer me a towel when I've finished washing my hands?!"

Against his better judgment, Wes inquires, *"Hormones?"*

"Ohmygod, everything is not my hormones!"

Though this might be.

At least a little bit.

Defeat drops onto his shoulder propelling him up onto his feet. "What do you want to me do, Brynley? Pretend like nothing fucking happened? Like you didn't suffer from a life altering injury?! Like you're *not* carrying around our child?!"

"I want you to remember that I may be *carrying* your child, but I am not one!"

"I-"

"I can get my own bottle of water. I can drive myself to work. And I can damn sure decide if I'm up for reading or visitors or walking around a 4th of July festival!"

"I just don't want anything to happen to you again! I don't wanna lose you! I *can't* lose you!"

"I get that, Wes." An unexpected sigh shakes my short, yellow summer dress cloaked figure. "But if you don't let me sit in my own chair on the deck versus your lap, we're not gonna be able to pilot our ship much longer."

The words send him sulking back onto the leather sofa closer to me.

"I *appreciate* how much you love me and wanna take care of me and the little superhero growing inside of me, but I kind of need to breathe some non-Wes infused air once in a while."

It appears to pain him to hear the declaration; however, he nods in submission. "*Understood.*"

"Good." Leaning slightly forward precedes me smirking. "Because I would like that right after you do *something* that takes my breath away."

His eyes drop to where my bottom lip endures a bite.

"All the swelling in my ankle is *completely* gone."

"It is."

"Yet I don't think I should push it." I abandon the comic book on the nearby table and crawl into his sweatpants covered lap. "Meaning…" The winding of my arms around his neck allows for him to rest his hands on my hips. "*I'm just gonna sit here and enjoy the ride, Weston.*"

A low, bestial growl I haven't heard in what feels like eons vibrates his chest as much as mine. "*Is that what you want, baby?*" One set of fingers slips underneath the edge of my dress and inches over to my thong covered ass. "*To be taken?*" He delivers a gentle nudge to the space between my thighs. "*To be broken?*" The light prodding grows harder. "*To be my prey?*"

"*Always,*" airily leaves me at the same time I needily rock forward.

106

"The door is open," Wes lasciviously reminds. *"Give me something to help keep you quiet."*

Before I inquire what, he snaps the string to my panties and presents a devilish grin.

And it's that exact grin that gets me onto my feet.

Wiggling the delicate fabric off while he slides himself out of his sweats.

I display it like a dangling offering from the tip of my index finger.

His effortless snatching of it is followed by him harshly yanking me forward and stuffing the material in the open space created by my gasp.

"I wanna be the only one to hear you fucking scream, little prey." He rubs the edge of the material that didn't fit inside across my bottom lip. *"And you will fucking scream."*

There's no time for agreement.

Or objection.

Or anything that isn't me spread wide in his lap with my knees borrowing deep into the couch cushions on each side of him.

Hisses sparked by the roughness of his initial invasion almost instantaneously become louder, headier whimpers.

Having the wet, underworked muscles mercilessly stretched to the point where both ends of me are screaming is enough on its own to warrant my shuddering yet it's the short, barbaric, pounding that increases the speed at which I do it.

The consistency.

Intensity.

Wes's palms possessively grip my ass to keep me pinned in place, providing him with the leverage needed not only for every pump to be deeply felt, but to guarantee that each one results in a teasing brush of my clit.

"This is what you really needed, isn't it?" He purrs against the side of my tit that's popping out of my dress. *"To be fucked?"* His teeth

107

fiercely sink into the exposed skin causing me to arch into him. *"To take that hard dick?"*

My body helplessly bucks into the slamming.

Trembles fiercely when he widens his thighs for a deeper angle.

Another round of biting begins prompting my hands to curl around the back of the leather couch as he growls, *"Is that a yes, little prey?"*

Moaning my answer is attached to my head falling back in ecstasy.

The dangling of my locks becomes too tempting for my future husband not to touch.

Tangle.

Tug.

Jerking me into his increasingly frantic thrusting has my bare ass jiggling uncontrollably.

Bumping into his balls.

Having his balls slap back against me.

Wetness is steadily smeared and slathered along my inner thighs while the friction from my clit constantly being rubbed causes my pussy to ceaselessly constrict around his cock.

Clamp down.

Cry for it to come and come and keep coming until cum is what we're both covered in.

Wes pulls my ass apart further prompting shivers to run along my spine from the unexpected added sensation, a set of actions that leads to him groaning, *"Fuckkkk, baby. You really want that cum, don't you?"*

His question receives a throaty scream that's instantly absorbed by the fabric.

"You want me to remind you that I'm the fucking apex."

The proclamation is punctuated with hard pulls.

Harder heaves.

108

"That it's me you fucking belong to."

Whimpers and whines fight to drip down my elongated neck alongside the tiny bits of drool.

"That this is my pussy."

It's impossible to keep my eyes open.

To stop my nails from trying to tear into the couch.

"That this will always be fucking mine."

Sopping wet throbs begin to occur more consistently around his dick, warning him how close I am to going over the edge.

How desperate I am to feel him join me.

"That you will always be fucking mine." His sharp, piston-like motions, pound the promise into me one undeniable word at a time. *"Only. Mine."*

On a high-pitched, muted scream, my arms carelessly curl around his neck, smashing him into my chest, smothering his savage roars between my tits as I do my best to withstand the unstoppable withering that's invading my system. Wes barely manages to execute two more thrusts before my pussy mercilessly milks from him exactly what he's ripping out of me. Our carnal cries incessantly fuse together to the same relentless rhythm of our orgasms until we've merged into one, sweaty, breathless, mixture of twitches and murmurs.

I really am *only* Weston Wilcox's.

And no matter what lies ahead…I always will be.

Chapter 12

Wes

"This is a terrible idea. We should've just left her and her headaches in the idle threats to ignore file," Evie bitterly snips underneath her breath from the seat to my left. *"I do not condone this course of action."*

"I don't either," Pham hisses from the chair beside her. *"And neither does legal."*

"Noted," I casually announce while tightening the black tie that's resting on top of my black dress shirt.

"Did you have to wear black on black like we're attending a supervillain's funeral?" chastises my personal publicist in her continued hushed volume. *"You couldn't have picked a lighter color shirt with a power tie like J.T.?"* She shoots him a small air kiss. *"You look like perfection."*

Like the kiss ass head of the class he is, he sits a little taller in the cushiony conference room chair.

I don't need her praise.

Just like I don't *technically* need her approval or her presence.

It's my name on the company.

Therefore, it's my decision.

And my decision to engage in a *civilized* sit-down with Monica Simmons is one they'll all be grateful for later.

After all, it was *this* or fucking buy the magazine she works for to fire her as well as everyone else that works there.

This is more cost efficient.

All of a sudden, the conference room doors are opened by Zaidee who then gestures her warm sienna skinned hand inward. "Mr. Wilcox and his team have been expecting you."

The pain in my ass that has made it her personal mission to print personal information – that unfortunately *aren't* lies – barely flashes my assistant a grin of gratitude.

That's the real reason why I can't let this go.

I need to know her source.

I need to know who has broken their NDA.

I need to know who is busy betraying me and my family for a measly payday before my son or daughter is born.

I want them safe.

Protected.

Guarded long before they've even taken their first breath.

Which isn't possible until I know *who* needs to be removed and from where.

Who can't be trusted.

And despite Park's thorough searching, he can't find any suspicious activity to make such a connection.

Hence the decision to take a more direct approach.

"Ms. Simmons," I professionally greet. "Thank you for agreeing to meet with me and my team."

Her overly bronzed face doesn't bother fighting the thrill running through her system. "My editor didn't exactly present me with a *choice*, Mr. Wilcox." She lets her brown gaze glide around the room. "Although, I must admit. I do feel rather outnumbered."

"I have asked my publicists as well as one of our company's higher ups to be in attendance."

"J.T." He stands and politely extends an open palm at her approaching frame. "J.T. Reese."

"I'm aware of who you are, Mr. Reese." She less than kindly shakes. "I'm also aware of your long-standing relationship and dedication to the Wilcox family, including how they took you in like a second son when your own mother could no longer care for you."

My best friend is instantly taken back. "H-h-how did you-"

"*I'm a journalist, Mr. Reese.*" A vicious smile slips onto her face during her descent into the closest chair. "*I do my research.*"

Clearly uncomfortable, he tugs at his collar.

Clears his throat.

Sits down and shoots me a cautious glance.

And here's *another* reason to put a stop to her nonsense.

She's not only upsetting my pregnant fiancée but my best man too.

"Ms. Simmons," I casually proceed on a folding of my hands, "I have brought you here today because I want information that you have."

Boredom is the only expression she presents.

"*You* have a 'source' that's handfeeding you information that has no business being in the general public."

"Then you shouldn't be a *public* figure," she swiftly snaps back.

"*That* wasn't my choice as you might recall." The darkening of my tone can't be helped. "*You* were the one who ran the exclusive. Who posted *my* photo. Who invaded my privacy without permission."

"*Actually*," the snark in her voice is unmistakable, "I didn't invade anything. You unfortunately had an information leak, which given the things I'm still capable of printing without a need for retraction, you *still* have."

It takes otherworldly strength to maintain my calm disposition. "I want the name of your source."

"No."

"They are in *legal* violation by leaking that information to you."

"Only if they've spoken *directly* about conversations or incidents, they've had with you or your fiancée or a member of your team. There is *no line* in this person's contract that says they can't discuss things they've *witnessed* or *found* or are simply *speculating* about." She victoriously smiles prematurely. "There's also no

112

violation in them *informing me* of the *other people* who may have spoken to one of you and following those leads." An amused hand spin is executed. *"Aka journalism."*

Unhappy rumbles rattle my frame as I tighten my grasp. "I want the name of your source, Ms. Simmons and I'm willing to negotiate the information for a respectable price."

"Why am I not surprised another Wilcox is just willing and ready to *buy* more silence?"

The statement furrows my eyebrows. *"Excuse me?"*

"You have *a lot* in common with the man you inherited the company from."

"Careful how you speak of those that came before me, Ms. Simmons."

"Careful how you threaten me in a conversation I *am* recording, Mr. Wilcox." She pulls a tube of lipstick out of her pocket. "Guess security missed one."

Deeper grumbles reverberate around the room.

"As I mentioned, Mr. Wilcox, I do my research." The recording device is gingerly placed on the table. "Which doesn't *just* include reporting on your fiancée's desire to get a little Batman tattoo on her hip to honor you or how many times her work partner has had to retie her bikini top while they were surfing between assignments or even how she'll pretend to work late just to get some space away from *you*."

Rage rolls around the pit of my stomach.

"It includes so many very *intriguing* details regarding *your* lineage. Details that I get the sense you know *nothing* about." Her red painted lips twist upward again. "Details *I* am willing to negotiate to *you* for a *respectable* price."

Pham quickly objects, *"Wes-"*

"I know everything there is to know about where I've come from."

113

"Not everything." She leans back in her seat at the same time she asks, "Were you aware that your mother, Arabella, was actually married *once* before your father?"

The new information pinches my brow.

"It's where her well known Parisian obsession stemmed from."

Uneasiness momentarily clogs my vocal cords. "That could easily be an unsubstantiated claim."

"The decoration obsession or the marriage? Because *either way*," Monica twirls her finger around for theatrics, "I *can* prove it. I *can* send you a copy of the marriage certificate they had public records erase from existence. And I can do that *because* Aloïs – despite their divorce and being happy with his partner Lyam for the past twenty years – has a *copy* of their license and their wedding photo."

Disbelief drops my jaw into a bobbing nature.

"*See.*" She arrogantly winks. "*You don't know everything.*"

It's Evie's turn to interrupt, "*Wes, I think-*"

"However, you can know *more*," she tempts like the wicked adversary she is proving worthy to be. "*For. The. Right. Price.*"

J.T. swiftly interjects, "*Wes, you should-*"

"What else do you have?" I desperately inquire on a lean forward. "What else do you know?"

"It's less of a question of what…and more of a question of *who*," Monica obnoxiously goads. "And I will give you *that* as well as *all* of my research involving it in exchange for a measly television interview one month from now."

Both publicists rush to speak only to be hushed by a lifted hand. "One interview?"

"One interview in which you *publicly* acknowledge the information, openly discuss your family's coverup, take a test to further verify information, *and* generously offer shares of your company as compensation *for* this longstanding secrecy that has destroyed the life of this young individual."

"Those are quite the accusations, Ms. Simmons."

"And it is *quite* the scandal, Mr. Wilcox."

"*No*," my best friend practically barks, summoning my attention. "*Do. Not. Do. This.*"

A small tilt of my head is mindlessly given.

"Whatever it is she *thinks* she has, whatever it is she's *convincing* you she has, is *not* worth dragging our company's name through the mud." The sight of my mouth twitching pushes him to add, "It is not worth tarnishing your family's legacy."

"A legacy filled with *secrets, and scandals, and lies, ohmy,*" taunts the female at the opposite end of table from me.

"I am advising you against this for the sake of the *company,*" Pham manages to proclaim.

"And I am advising you against this for the sake of your *brand,*" Evie echoes.

"And *legal,*" my second in command reminds.

"Something tells me your father received a similar talk from his advisers or at the very least *Clark.*" The particular naming of him regains my full attention. "After all, this is the type of person that even your *best friend* would help keep hidden."

J.T. once more wisely tries to intervene, "*Wes, don't-*"

"I agree to *one* television interview one month from now. I agree to publicly acknowledge the *person* and the *situation* on behalf of my family. I agree to said test for verification purposes. I also agree to financial compensation to the aforementioned individual *if* your information is proven to be irrefutable and *only* irrefutable."

"Wes!" both women hiss in outrage.

"*However,* if your information *is* proven to be inaccurate, this person will receive *nothing* and *you* will publicly resign from the field of journalism, *permanently.*"

"Wes!" barks my best friend.

"*Do we have an agreement, Ms. Simmons?*"

"*We do, Mr. Wilcox.*"

"Wes!" shouts my entire team.

"It's on record." An open palm gestures to her recording device. "And I will have legal draw up paperwork for us both to sign."

"Perfect."

"Now," I menacingly lean forward, "*who* is this individual?"

"*Your. Half. Sister.*"

Chapter 13

Brynley

I know the real focus here should be on the *insanely* gorgeous wedding gowns taunting me from every fucking angle in this *Pretty Woman* approved boutique; however, *McCoyhavemercy* this cupcake that I got from Yasmine's Yummies across the street is giving me an orgasm that rivals the one Wes gave me before he went into the office for a PR meeting.

This shit is so good I cried when I ate my first one.

Cried and begged the owner to cater our wedding.

And then cried again when she immediately agreed.

I'm not *entirely* sure all of those tears were joy based.

They could've just been the hormones.

And also fuck hormones.

All of them.

I lean back against the cushioned light gray couch near the full-length modeling mirrors, pull the Andes mint I'd been saving off the top of my second mint chocolate cupcake and prepare to shove it in my mouth. "It doesn't matter what I wear. I'm gonna end up looking like a fucking beached whale shark."

"Is that what you *want* to look like, Bryn?" Kristal Riesgraf, one of the owners, cautiously asks upon her return. "Because our *only goals* here at Weardeville are to make the bride look and feel the way *she* wants." Her caramel beige hand politely extends my mom the glass of champagne she retrieved while I finally push the candy past my lips. "We understand the importance of being surrounded by those who want to love and support you on your special day, but the day is about *you* and *your fiancé*. And the dress?" She lets a wide smile slide onto her thin lips. "*That's all about just you.*"

"As it should be," echoes her identical twin, Kristine Riesgraf, during her reappearance with a bottle of water for me and Holmes who is positioned silently near the locked shop door. "Wear what you wanna wear. Make the statement you wanna make. Be whoever you wanna be. Give yourself that gift on your wedding day of all days."

"That's a helluva sales pitch," I compliment prior to having another bite of my crumbly mess. "I see why Velora insisted I come here."

"Less of a pitch and more of a family policy," Kristal informs as she pulls her long, black hair to one side of her face. "Our parents were both married twice – to other people – before finding each other, and each of those wedding days were disasters focused on everyone but them – something that isn't too hard when you're from small towns like Applecourt and Middlebrook – so when they finally decided to tie the knot to one another, they insisted it be about *them*. And that empowering moment inspired them to want *others* to be inspired. They claimed that it was their ability to get married on their own terms that led them to have a marriage on their own terms which is what has kept them together for all these years."

"Mom says it starts with the dress hence why she quit her job to pursue her passion of wedding dresses."

"And why dad didn't mind working an extra part-time gig to help get this place off the ground."

"And why our dress up time was spent playing *here.*"

"And why we got our prom gowns *here.*"

"And why we will get our wedding dresses *here*," Kristine states at the same time she positions herself beside her sibling, hands folding together in the front of her black dress. "Assuming we ever *get* married."

"Turns out men are actually a lot more intimidated by women who work *in* the wedding industry than other fields."

"Like just because we work with brides all day, we're *dying* to be one."

"It's quite the opposite, actually," Kristal insists. "After being around this much tulle and lace and beading and fighting and meltdowns and crying, weddings are basically *the furthest* thing from our minds when we step foot out of this place."

"I'd rather talk about rock climbing and Harleys-"

"Kristine *so* has a thing for those Misfit bikers," whispers Kristal from behind her hand.

"And Kristal would rather do shots of Torrez while talking about basketball or hockey."

"Go Dragons!"

"*The point is*," she sighs as I shift the remainder of the treat into my mouth, "we always pour all of our wedding thoughts and enthusiasm into *the bride* we're helping rather than worrying about what we think, or their wedding party thinks because the dress should be about *them*."

"And we are ready to serve *you*, Bryn," Kristal sweetly announces on a folding of her hands together. "And only you. Mr. Wilcox rented out the shop for the entire day. He wanted you to be our only client and have the privacy to shop at your own pace."

"However, if you feel you need a break from dresses, we can switch to shoes or accessories or even shift our focus to the lovely *mother* of the bride." Krstine shoots my mom a wink. "We have quite a selection for her as well as bridesmaids in the back rooms."

"Main floor is only about the *bride*."

Kristine politely inquires, "Will others be joining you today?"

"I'm not even sure I have others that will be joining me on *the* day," I absentmindedly confess prior to having a sip of water. "I um…I don't exactly have a lot of friends."

"I'm sure Vanessa and Calen will both say yes when you ask."

It's impossible to not shoot her a sarcastic stare. "Yeah, because Wes just *loves* my off the bridge relationship with Scotty. I can only imagine how *excited* he would be to see him standing beside me on *our* wedding day."

119

"Is Scotty another friend?" Kristal inquisitively investigates.

"It's simply a *Star Trek* reference she's making in relation to Calen, her best friend," Mom retorts before I can. "My daughter is a Trekkie."

"*Seriously?!*" Kristine enthusiastically exclaims. "I have *just* the dress to show you!"

There's no stopping my head from angling in curiosity. "You have my attention."

"We just got in a shipment of 'fandom' inspired gowns with nods to their *original* creations. Like Princess Leia-"

"That's *Star Wars.*"

"Samantha Carter."

"*Stargate.*"

"And T'Pring."

"*That*," my finger feistily points in her direction, "is me. *That one* is my *Star Trek* shit."

"Eeeek!" squeaks Kristine. "Let me go get it!"

Her swift disappearance threatens to make me smirk.

Is it just *luck* that my future husband rented out a space that had something related to my favorite franchise or did he make sure to mention that to Valora during one of their conference calls I couldn't make courtesy of a bitchy boss that doesn't believe in love.

Or personal phone call breaks.

Or personal space considering how much she's been hovering since my injury.

Which is *healed* by the way.

So, I don't know why the fuck she's still breathing down the back of my neck like a goddamn megamouth shark.

"While my sister grabs that, why don't I get an idea of what else you're looking for?" Kristal invested demeanor remains. "Long? Short? Tight? Flowy?"

The latter causes my brow to furrow in contemplation.

Just exactly *how* pregnant will I be when our wedding day hits?

Do I want that to be seen in all our photos?

Do I want *that* to be the focus?

Can we move it up sooner?

Can we move it up *a lot* sooner to the point people probably can't even tell?

Sure, we made the formal announcement a couple weeks back during the 4th of July celebration, but that doesn't mean I want it to be the focus on the day.

"Did I overwhelm you?" Kristal uncomfortably cringes. "It wasn't my intent! I swear! I just…I was just looking for a direction to go or avoid or-"

"*I don't know,*" comes out in more of a whispered confession than intended. "I…I didn't think I'd be pregnant during this time so…I don't know what to wear. Or what I *should* wear."

"You wear whatever you want," she declares at the same time she lowers herself to be eyelevel with me. "You want something flowy to hide your curves. Let's do it! You want a bump to be what people see, we can tie that shit up with a red bow! Something in the middle sound better? We'll arrange it. Whatever *you want*, Bryn, is the only thing *we* want to deliver." A gentle, encouraging palm lands on top of my chocolate crumb covered lap. "All you have to do is communicate with us what that is. We're here to serve you."

Being served whatever you want sounds wonderful.

Except of course when you have *no clue at all* what that is.

Chapter 14

Wes

It's not possible.

Monica Simmons cannot be *my* half-sister.

She just can't be.

"First floor personal office," I practically bark at Hurst who is leading the box toting parade. "I want. *Every. Single. Box.* In that fucking room." Firmly pointing occurs mindlessly. "*No exceptions.*"

"Yes, sir," mutters one of the housekeeping attendees that's assisting.

"Where the fuck is Park?!" is shouted to the guard that's opening the door. "I told him to meet me immediately!"

"He's on his way," my best friend informs as he steps into the entry way, fingers moving quickly across the screen.

"And Clark?!"

"Idontknow," J.T. mumbles out the answer prior to commanding into his device, "Hawthorne tell me what we can do." Tugging at his collar is done in tandem with him marching forward. "Tell me what clauses we have in place to deal with the possibility of an unknown heir." He snaps his fingers multiple times at a member of the staff that was headed to help unload. "*Cuban. Trinidad. Reyes.*" He grumps into the phone. "Yes, I'm deadly fucking serious, Hawthorne." Once more he meets the servant's stare. "Two fingers. Neat. Aged. Nothing less than ten years. Got it?"

"Make that two," leaves me without a second thought.

His stride stumbles, clearly preparing to question my remark, when head of legal snaps, "*Start at the beginning, Mr. Reese!*"

Grumbles from him precede additional ones from me.

That's what I should've done.

I should've had Monica start at the very beginning versus letting myself get baited.

Trapped.

Exploited.

The very thing journalist like her are trained to fucking do.

Low rumbles echo throughout the opening space as the convoy of property continues to make its way into my personal downstairs office. "*Where. Is. Clark?!*"

"Your summoning is steeped in impatience," the man I'm not even sure I can trust anymore mirthfully states upon his arrival at the bottom of the stairs. "This does not typically bode well for what remains of the evening."

"Does the name Aloïs mean anything to you?" There's no hesitation to interrogate. "Is it of *any* familiarness?"

He politely folds his hands behind his back. "Perhaps."

"I am not looking for perhaps and perhaps nots, Clark. I am looking for *certainties.*" Stepping towards him blocks his view of the items being hauled inside. "And I expect to receive them. Is that understood?"

The smallest twitched stare is attached to his agreement, "*Understood, Sir.*"

"Does the name Aloïs mean *anything* to you?"

"He was your mother's first husband." Clark's neck noticeably tightens. "They were young. Eighteen or nineteen when the marriage occurred. It lasted less than six months."

"Why is there *no* mention or record of it anywhere?"

"It was concealed. Per your father's request."

"*Why?*"

"To protect your mother from slanderer's claims."

"Such as?"

"Her *only* being interested in your father's wealth."

"And is that the *only* reason for his concealment?" Rage rolls its way down my spine. "Did it have *anything* to do with the fact that

123

he was worried it might embarrass him or the brand or the family or our legacy?"

His lack of responding merely fuels my resentment.

"You needed to see me, sir?" Park suddenly asks, appearing near our situation, redirecting our attention to him. "You expressed it was urgent."

"I need you to run the name *Will Cox*."

Ignoring Clark's slight attire adjustment is impossible.

"Will Cox. Owned a sizeable ranch in Stovlen Springs, Texas a few miles south of Sunshine Bend about twenty-five years ago."

More nervous fidgeting.

"He might've signed the property over to a woman named Marzia Simmons at some point."

And more.

"Find out *everything* you possibly can about him, her, and their relationship." A sharp finger is stabbed in his direction. "*And I mean fucking everything*. Down to how often they bought fucking toilet paper and condoms. Am I clear?"

"Yes, sir." Park promptly nods. "I'll get cyber digging and have Soni reach out to one of our P.I. contacts for actual footwork."

"*No one sleeps until I have the answers I want*," I unhappily seethe. "*The clock is ticking.*"

He nods a second time and hastily rushes away to get to work leaving me alone once more with the man I *know* has answers even if he wished he didn't.

"Do those names mean anything to you, Clark?" Folding my arms firmly across my chest precedes me invading his space further. "*Either* of them?"

Thankfully, he doesn't deny what we are both already aware of. "*Yes.*"

"What?" It's a struggle to keep my tone and volume steady. "*What* do they mean to you?"

"I'm not at liberty to say."

124

"What the hell do you mean you're not at liberty to say?!"

"I am *legally* not at liberty to say, sir."

"He's dead!"

"I am aware."

"Any legal documents or agreements at this point involved in the subject matter at hand are null and void!"

"They are not, Mr. Wilcox."

"Do not call me that!"

"There is a contingency clause in the aforementioned documents that prevents me from speaking on the topic you are currently inquiring about *regardless* of their life status."

"That's. Asinine!"

"That is the *legally binding* agreement I signed."

"Then send it to fucking legal for review!"

"Yes, sir."

New waves of frustration not only lead to my jaw throbbing but me barking, *"I cannot believe you never told me my father had an affair!"*

"I cannot speak on the subject."

"That he cheated on my mother!"

"I cannot speak on the subject."

"She was supposed to be your friend too! How could you let him get away with it?!"

Clark's mouth twitches in what appears to be agony, yet he repeats, "I cannot speak on the subject."

"How could you let him hide a fucking child from her?!"

"I cannot speak on the subject."

"From me?!"

Finally, his stoic demeanor along with the repeated robotic phrasing cracks, *"Weston, I am begging you on behalf of them both...on behalf of this family...to let them as well as this subject lie in peace."*

125

"*No.*" The viciousness of my bite buttons his lips. "*Now, get that document to Hawthorne by morning or me your resignation letter.*"

Without another word, he politely moves past me, hopefully to retrieve the former rather than write the latter.

Because its existence has to be the only reason, he would've kept this from me.

That *anyone* would've kept this from me.

Could've.

But why?

Why have no record of it in *any* document, *anywhere*?

Not even a secret file?

Why live under an alias?

Why cheat to fucking begin with?!

Why wasn't my mother enough?!

Why weren't *we* enough?!

Why did he need a second family before he could appreciate his fucking first?!

Roars rip from my chest as I storm into the office right after the last of the materials has been left behind.

I guide myself around the seemingly endless collection of belongings from Simmons family, gawking at the boxes.

Glaring at the possibilities that may be found inside.

The hidden truths.

The hidden *lies*.

Bitterness burns up the back of my throat during my continued surveying.

How much of my legacy *is* a lie?

How much of *me*?

"Your glass," speaks a member of the kitchen staff, holding up the item for display.

"*Desk.*" The second it's placed down, I growl, "*Leave.*"

126

Sounds of their feet scurrying away barely precede my fiancée's displeased voice, *"Redecorating, Weston?"*

I reluctantly force myself to turn and face her. *"No."* Bryn attempts to come further into the room prompting me to bite again, *"No."*

"No, what?"

"Do not come in here."

Confusion and consternation alike collide in her complexion. "Excuse me?"

Uncertainty regarding what exactly I'm going to tell her along with when, pushes me to proclaim, "This area is off limits for now."

"To me?"

"To. Everyone."

Additional unhappiness appears in her tone, *"Why?"*

"I cannot speak on the subject," mockingly leaves me.

"Okay."

Her surrendering is easy.

Too easy.

"How about you speak on the subject of *standing me the fuck up* at the opening of Maxximum Effort?" Bryn's scowl instantly deepens in tandem with her vision narrowing. "You know the new fucking *comic bookstore* you personally promised the owner *we'd* be at?"

Guilt tries to claw its way under my skin yet fails.

Because there's no room.

No room for anything that isn't hostility.

Frustration.

"Care to comment on where you were or why I waited there for *two hours* for you to show or fucking call?!"

Against my better judgement, I sneer, "How would you know? Your phone was probably stashed under the seat in the SUV or between the cushions in the aquarium room or behind a box of Cinnamon Toast Crunch."

127

Her jaw cracks just enough to remind me of the *terrible* mistake I just made.

How I'm directing my irateness at the wrong person.

For the wrong reasons.

"Where. Were. You?"

My hands shove themselves into my black pants pockets at the same time I announce, "Something came up."

And by something, I mean a meltdown of epic proportions that resulted in Zaidee having to schedule repairs for the conference room.

Post my very *physical* response to the news that came from following Monica to her storage unit.

Seeing the reveal.

Watching carefully as everything was loaded.

While she smugly smirked.

Giggled.

Made plans to publicly harangue me as my best friend tried to swim through the deep end of the social hell I selfishly threw us into.

Except I'm not the only selfish one here.

My so-called father was selfish.

And a fucking cheater.

And liar.

And left me a house of cards to build an entire brand on.

Concern carves itself into her gaze in spite of my demeanor. "Would you like to tell me what?"

"No."

"Fine." Understanding struggles to slide into her expression. "Would you like to have dinner?"

"No."

"Would you like to talk about our wedding?"

Our wedding?

Would I like to talk about love and commitment and what's supposed to be the most significant and monumental moment of our

128

relationship on the same day I discover it didn't mean shit to the man I've spent my entire existence looking up to?

"*No.*"

"Would you like to tell me about your meeting from earlier?"

"*No.*"

"Would you like to spend time with me at all?"

"*No.*"

The bluntness stumbles her backward; however, rather than verbally retaliate, something I can usually count on, she surrenders.

Again.

Suspiciously.

"Okay." Bryn tosses the tiny black bag she's holding into my empty nearby chair. "There's the Foes of DC wordsearch I had custom made to surprise you at the opening." Her Batman crop top covered shoulders slightly bounce. "Hope you like it."

Being unsure of what hurts more, the irony or the thoughtfulness, is what leads to me remaining silent.

Pressing my lips tightly together.

Not even *thanking* her.

"Enjoy your space. Perhaps Puppet Boy can spare some time for me."

"*He. Can't.*"

My curtness receives an instant arched eyebrow.

"He is also currently unavailable for the foreseeable future."

"I'm sorry, you're *both* unavailable for the *foreseeable* future?"

"Yes."

"Foreseeable as in you don't know when you'll step out of your bat cave here? The bat cave I'm *not* allowed in?" She lets her head cock to one side, disbelief deepening. "You're basically saying you don't know when you'll see *me* again? Me, your *pregnant fiancée.*"

"*I just need...*" one hand lifts to give the side of my face a sobering scrub. "*Some...time, Brynley.*"

"*Then I guess I'll just go find someone who can spare some for me, Weston.*"

Unbridled ire savagely spews past my lips, "*What are you gonna do? Run away to another state? Go have an affair? Become exactly like my fucking father?*"

Shock sends her mouth to the ground. "What?!"

"*Just. Go.*" Kicking my chin to the open door she's near occurs before another word can leave her mouth. "*Close it behind you.*"

"*No.*" Familiar defiance is attached to her exiting movement. "Close it your goddamn self."

Her stomps away are echoed by mine crossing the room.

Reaching the desk.

Lifting the glass of aged liquid up to my lips.

I shouldn't do this.

I shouldn't have a sip.

I shouldn't start down this path.

Nothing good will come of it.

Nothing good every fucking does.

Glancing over my shoulder at the sprawling packages containing only Commissioner Gordon knows what evidence convinces me to concede.

To cave.

To give into the darkest and dirtiest temptation I can fathom.

Just like my father did.

Chapter 15

Brynley

Valora: What are the new potential dates?
Valora: We may need to reevaluate mood and color boards again.

I hate every word of that sentence.

Seriously.

Particularly the *we* portion considering I don't even know who "we" is.

Does it include the supposed groom?

No clue.

And why don't I have a clue?

Because he hasn't left one.

Things are worse than they were when we first met.

Back then, I may not have had his face, but I had his voice.

His written words.

His *presence.*

Now?

This will be the first time I've *seen* him since he found out the giant family secret his parents *clearly* hoped would stay buried.

He hasn't left that bat basement *once* to my knowledge.

Not to eat.

Not to sleep.

Not to shower or shit, although there is a small ensuite bathroom I imagine he's using for those chores.

And the only people who have been allowed in?

Luther with security reports.

J.T. with business ones.

Even the idiots who have been supplying him with bottles and bottles of alcohol around the clock are told to just leave it at his door.

That he'll grab them when he needs them.

Clark has done everything he possibly can to reassure me that this bump will pass, that Wes just needs a little more time to digest the truths he never expected to receive, that I'm more important than anything he may have discovered in those boxes he's building the world's worst fort with, but I'm having a hard time believing him.

Maybe because the last two events for *his company* that we were supposed to attend together, I magically attended *alone.*

Maybe because we haven't slept under the same roof in the past eight days?

Or maybe because I haven't received more than ten words – *via text at that* – from him in the last ten?

I exit out of the text from Valora and open the conversation thread with my fiancé.

The same thread that has me keeping my phone glued to my palm in hopes of seeing new words in.

I've been feeling this dull, gnawing pain in my gut lately that I'm begging Bones is just like preggers indigestion and not an annoying warning buzzer that my ship has been critically hit.

"There." Hill casually points at the same time he leans over from his chair to my right. "C-H-E-E-T-A-H."

"Circle it," I instruct on an offering of the pen.

"You sure?"

"Your word. Your circle."

A small amount of excitement thrums through his gaze as he transfers the writing tool into his possession.

A lot like Lurch and Frankensuck, he's started to have a fondness for participating in doing these whenever possible.

None of them got the appeal at first.

But like so many great things…time helped reveal the true magic of playing "Where's Waldo" with words.

Hitting the call button on my device for Wes is followed by me handing Hill the booklet to continue playing without me. I press the receiver tightly to my ear and unconsciously suck in a deep breath of anticipation that I hold.

And hold.

And hold while it rings.

And rings.

And rings.

And keeps ringing until his voicemail message begins.

Hope that he simply just didn't get a chance to see or hear the device because he was momentarily occupied is what prompts me into repeating the call.

Once.

Twice.

A third time.

Rather than try a fourth, I redirect my efforts to someone else, someone who can probably reach him despite that I can't.

Two rings are all J.T. allows to occur before chiperly answering, "*Catwoman.*"

"*Puppet Boy.*"

Small laughter leaves us both and for a minor moment a flicker of hope returns.

Perhaps just because I'm losing Wes, doesn't mean I have to lose him too.

"Busy?" I nervously inquire.

"Headed to an acquisition meeting with the owner of Runt's Beer, then a meeting with Faulk who wants to turn that Fire & Ash event you helped make into a mega success an *annual* event, then early drinks with Morgan to break the news about needing to fire the current head brewer he vouched for before having late drinks with Sully to off the books explain to him why pickle is not an unusual whiskey flavor but an abomination that should never see the light of day."

133

It's impossible not to snicker, "*So...yes?*"

"Eh," he chuckles back, "I'm not *not* busy." More chortles precede an unexpected proclamation, "But I've always got time for you Uhura."

Pressing my lips tightly together is done to stop the tears that are threatening to expose themselves.

"Need something?"

"My fiancé to be more like you" is definitely *not* the answer I should say.

Even if it's the one I *want* to.

"Um..." a small clearing of my throat is given to buy myself time, "do you happen to know where Wes is?"

"Shouldn't he be there with you?"

Yes.

Yes, he sure fucking should.

"Isn't it your baby doctor day?" The concern in his voice increases. "Aren't you supposed to be going twice a month because of your concussion?"

Right again.

Why my future husband's best friend seems to remember more about this situation than the actual man I'm signing up to marry isn't helping kill that ache in the pit of my stomach so much as causing it to fucking grow.

Bigger.

Stronger.

Blatantly more painful.

"Is he really not fucking answering?!" I swear his movements completely cease. "Not a video? Not a call? Not even a fucking *text?*"

It grows more difficult to hide the heartache. "No."

His sudden shock is presented in silence.

Unbearable.

Bile stirring.

Silence.

And when he finally speaks again, it's in an almost stutter like fashion. "Do you…uh…do you…um…want me to…um come there?" J.T. diligently works to steady his voice. "You want me to reschedule all of this shit, Bryn? I can be there in…" A brief pause is taken. "Twenty, twenty-two minutes tops."

"No, I'm fine, Puppet Boy." Tears clumping together in my vocal cords prove otherwise. "I can do this shit."

"But-"

"I can do it on my own."

"Yes, but-"

"Get to your meeting," I quickly insist. "We can talk later."

"We *will* talk later." His correction is forceful and irrefutable. "Text me after your appointment. Let me know everything went fine, alright?"

An almost bashful nod he can't see is given. "Sure thing, J.T."

Ending the call occurs before he can inquire about my choice in using his name or can second guess that I'm really fine.

Because I *am* fine.

Er.

I'll *be* fine.

I'm like the hammerhead species.

Endangered but made of what it takes to fucking survive.

I prepare to dial Wes again when I spot a word out of the corner of my eye, "I see snow leopard."

"Fuck, really?!" Hill enthusiastically exclaims. "Where?!"

"Nope." Good natured giggles help mask the sniffles. "You gotta find it yourself."

His long-shaped face somehow falls further. "Seriously?"

"You won't get better if I just *circle* the answers for you."

He lightly laughs; however, the opportunity to join him is cut short by the door to my left, the door that patients use to enter the facility, opening.

135

Hope swiftly swoops into my stare as I hold my breath in anticipation of seeing my fiancé finally walk inside to join me.

Probably rushing Pham or Evie off the phone in the process.

Or maybe finally giving Valora the greenlight for moving our wedding date.

A hooded male walks in, but unfortunately, it's instantly revealed not to be mine. He flicks the gray coverage down, shakes away whatever water droplets have managed to drop down, and grins brightly at his waiting partner who probably isn't that much further along than me.

The sight of him embracing her pushes my attention back down to make another phone call, truthfully not wanting to do this alone, yet don't know who to dial.

J.T. is *extremely* busy with work.

Vanessa's out of town for *Avó's* – her Portuguese grandmother's – ninetieth birthday.

And Mom is helping Clark assemble a small Justice League approved care package for the ecoterrorist that happened to try to kill her.

Hesitation regarding the one option I have left isn't surprising.

Maybe I should just go in there alone.

Get used to what my future is going to consist of at this rate.

Letting my finger hover over the call button continues for just a moment more before I hit the key and lift the device to my ear.

Much like Puppet Boy, there are merely two rings prior to an answer. "I already agreed to be your Groom of Honor," Calen lightly chuckles. "Please don't make me regret that decision by telling me I have to find a Pine lookalike stripper or wear a Trekkie uniform or give my toast speech in fucking Klingon, dude."

"None of that crossed my mind."

"Good."

"But now that it has..."

136

"Not good," he laughs a bit louder as I fidget with my airplane necklace. *"Totally not good."*

I don't bother fighting the small smile doing its best to wash away the sorrow.

What can I say?

Giving each other shit always shifts my mood.

"And like *actual* not good. Not the not good I used when we were weighing different marine veterinary program options, which were relatively speaking all good, just not good for my great, great grandchildren who'll be stuck paying off the mountain of debt I'll have accumulated in lifetimes before theirs."

Additional snickers seep free.

"You're not calling to give me more responsibilities, are you? 'Cause Nes and I were pretty good with the fifty/fifty split we agreed on. It definitely has us stacked for the least amount of dings."

"You surfin' today?"

"Bout to head down to test my new twin fin." A happy hum warmly escapes. *"Best. Be my groom of Honor. Gift. Ever."*

After trying on dresses and being stood up by Wes, I spent that night searching for fun and weird ways to "pop the question" to them. I made sure to do something that fit them each separately before getting us all together for pizza, laughs, and very, *very* light wedding talk.

Like we talked more about government conspiracies than we did about my pending nuptials.

"Need something?" Calen quickly investigates. "Your voice has that weird rasp to it."

"What rasp?"

"The same one you always get when you've got chick feelings you don't wanna cope with."

"That's not…a thing."

"It is."

"Isn't."

137

"*Is.*"

"*Isn't.*"

"Yeah, dude, it's like you're trying not to cry, even though you could cry, but you don't wanna cry, because you hate people knowing you're capable of crying. Kind of like the way great whites can spy hop like fucking orcas but would rather get eaten alive inside out by a parasite than admit to it."

"The accuracy of that comparison is horrifying."

"You're welcome."

Laughter passes between us yet again dissipating additional grief.

Clearing the air.

Reminding me that regardless of how alone I feel in this very moment, I'm not.

I'm *very* far from it.

That I'll *always* be far from it with friends like him around.

"So," Calen casually proceeds, "what do you need, Bryn? A toothbrush? A kidney? An alibi?"

"A best friend?"

"You've got that."

"Any chance that best friend could postpone surfing for a little bit and be here with me at the doctor?"

"You're *alone* at the fucking lady doctor?!"

Reluctance rears its ugly head. "Yeah."

"Where the fuck is Mega Millions?"

"Billions."

"Worse."

"Better."

"*Bryn.*"

"Idontknow," comes out in a whispered jumble. "Not here."

"He fucking *should* be there."

Agreed.

"He fucking shouldn't be anywhere else *but* there."

138

Double agreed.

"And I'm gonna be *right there* to tell him that shit to his fucking face." Calen doesn't wait for any type of rebuttal or rejection of his declaration. *"Text me the address, Bryn. I'm on my way."*

Chapter 16

Wes

I don't know this man.

Yes, at first glance he *looks* like my father.

In every single one of these photos.

He has his same build.

Eye color.

Hair.

However, his style is *wrong*.

There are no designer suits or shoes.

Just jeans.

And boots.

And belt buckles.

Fuck, *this man* had more belt buckles in his possession than the one who named me had ties.

And the man I called my father had a ton of ties.

I carelessly toss the photo of him happily holding a pregnant woman off to the left to join the others in the pile.

Or fall to the floor.

Doesn't matter.

There's no need to preserve this shit.

It's mostly just copies.

Why?

Because his other child – which is what all of this evidence is pointing out to be true – is *smart*.

And cunning.

But me?

I'm fucking clueless.

Useless.

Not the one who should've ascended the throne of lies I had no idea he sat so comfortably on.

Mindlessly reaching for the nearest whiskey bottle to top off my glass is done in tandem with me beginning to review his financial records again.

Correction.

Will Cox's financial records.

He couldn't even be bothered to create a better goddamn alias to fuck around on my mother with!

It was almost as if giving us the finger.

Saying I care that this may hurt you but not enough.

Not enough to completely hide it.

Damn sure not enough *not* to do it.

Splashes of liquid fall on the photocopied journal entries they're closest to during my drunken disregarding of another empty bottle.

I've read and reread and reread every single line Marzia Simmons, Monica's mother, wrote about him.

When they met.

How they met.

What she called him.

What he called her.

Their first hug.

Hand hold.

Hug.

Kiss.

Fuck.

Tossing back a mouthful of the dark liquid is slipped in between thumbing through the next page of offshore documents used to properly fund his second life.

The one where he owned a fucking ranch that took up most of the property in some no nothing town.

And in that town, everyone or anyone who worked for him, crossed paths with him, had any sort of contact for longer than the time it took to shake his hand signed a fucking NDA swearing silence.

Allegiance.

Protection to this fucking stranger who staggered into their godforsaken piece of shit spot on the map and invested in it, in *them*, simply to maintain his anonymity during his shady secret scandal.

A scandal that I'm sure he kept quiet not to lose shareholders or investors or other backroom business deals that would've never been possible had his face been plastered in the *wrong* magazines.

Attached to the *wrong* interviews.

Had history put him in the lying, cheating, prick category instead of the saintly one.

Another mouthful burns its way across my tongue in an attempt to summon solace.

This bastard was *far* from the upstanding man I looked up to.

What kind of *real man* goes to the lengths he did to keep this a secret?

To create coverups?

Destroy evidence?

Finnegan, the P.I. Park hired, worked every person possible in that dusty watermelon town, even threatened to have official's badges and attorney's disbarred, yet no one would talk.

No one would hand anything over.

Even the fucking town's public records had been tampered with.

It's as if the only proof my father and Will Cox were even the same person was the one woman who knew it to be true.

The woman he would eventually knock up.

Have a secret child with.

Abandon, but keep in a comfortable living situation literally until her death.

Something funneled through our company – *my fucking company* – without my knowledge!

I thought I knew everything we touched.

Handled.

Considered.

All the fine print and the fine print's fine print and the loopholes.

I didn't.

I don't.

And not knowing…knowing *he's* the reason for my not knowing…only makes me hate him more.

Which is impressive given how much I hope he's rotting in hell now.

One final gulp empties the glass and convinces me to visually scour the cluttered room for reinforcements. Despite my somewhat blurry gaze, I do my best to find the tiniest glimmer of hope I haven't run out of alcohol again.

I'm told our household supply is low; however, I know that's a lie.

Because that's what everyone does.

Especially around here.

They lie.

And keep lies.

And create more fucking lies.

Rising to my feet to conduct a more hands on search is not only a terrible call, it's one that leads to me stumbling into the edge of the desk, knocking all the air out of me. My backward movements have me thumping into the nearest wall and that collision causes me to veer to the side to experience another with the door, ultimately resulting in me cascading to the ground where I sprawl myself out on my stomach.

Mmmm.

This shit feels amazing against my face.

143

"Wes...?" calls out a voice from the other side of the blockade. *"You in there?"*

I think that's my best friend.

And your best friend is evidently supposed to have *your back* even in death.

Like Clark apparently.

He knew.

He's *known*.

He's known this entire fucking time and never said a word.

Not. A. Single. Fucking. Word.

How can I ever look at him again the same?

How could he ever look at my father like he once had?

J.T. delivers two sharp knocks prior to investigating, *"You alive?"*

"Relatively," reverberates off the unclean floor I'm nestled against.

"Can I come in?"

"No."

"Has *anyone* been in there today?"

"No."

"Is anyone *allowed* in there today?"

I shut my eyes at the same time I grunt, *"No."*

"You...um...find anything new?"

"Finnegan couldn't find the doctor who *delivered* Monica but found the nurse that was on duty for it at a luxury elderly home paid for by *Will Cox's Watermelons*, which is a *Wilcox* company, which is. *My. Fucking. Company.*"

"Did she...have...anything to offer?"

"She claimed that she remembered them but that she couldn't talk about it. All she could say was the same fucking shit Monica's mother wrote. The holding of her hand. And the pushing her hair out of her face. And holding the newborn like he had his whole world in his hands."

144

"W-"

"Where was his *old* world?" Sneering has my face scraping against the ground. "Were we skiing with *his* parents? Was mom having cucumber sandwiches *alone* with royalty? Was I falling off my fucking bike that I was learning to ride forcing his *best friend* to bandage up my knee?"

"W-"

"*My knee! He couldn't even help me learn to ride a bike because he was there with her!*"

"W-"

"I spoke to you as a courtesy." The small breath I suck in is a struggle. "I'm done."

"But-"

"*Done!*"

When he doesn't attempt to speak further, I consider getting up to resume my booze search yet find my legs incapable of moving.

Perhaps I'm paralyzed.

Perhaps being disfigured *and* permanently unable to move would be the appropriate penance for shunning a sibling I never knew.

Denying her access to our resources.

Our reach.

Having her live a partial truth simply because my family refused to live a full one.

She deserves more than the funds that had been deposited into her mother's account.

More than the hush money that put her through college.

And she wants more.

And she's gonna get it.

On. Live. Fucking. Television.

All of a sudden there's a sharp pounding on my office door that shoots my eyes back open. "*Weston fucking Wilcox you open this goddamn door right now!*"

Fuck, she's loud.

145

Too loud.

An unexpected hit is delivered to the locked door. *"Now!"*

Too loud and too fucking angry.

"You open this goddamn door and tell me how you could stand me up at the fucking doctor!"

Doctor?

What doctor?

Why was she at the doctor?

"How could you not be there for your child?!"

No.

That's not right.

That appointment is for…

Well it shouldn't have been until…

Huh.

What day is it?

What *time* is it?

"How could you not even answer my fucking phone call?!" Another hit lands on the barrier, although I'm not sure if it's from her hand or foot. "How could you not text me back?!" More banging. Pounding. "How can you treat me *worse* as your fiancée than you did when I was a fucking stranger here just to make sure you didn't kill my mom!?"

Her accusations spark unwanted aches in my head.

Push me to close my eyes.

Squeeze them tight.

"Stop ignoring me!" she fiercely screeches between strikes. *"Stop treating me like I'm the fucking problem!"* More flinch worthy noise occurs. *"Stop hiding from me before I'm no longer here to fucking hide from!"*

The tiniest twitch occurs in my lips; however, I remain completely silent.

Perhaps she should go away.

Perhaps that's what's best.

146

Perhaps I'm not the man *she* thought I was.
Perhaps I'm not the man *I* thought I was.
Perhaps that's exactly why all this shit hurts.
Because I'm exactly like the man in these boxes.
A monster.

Chapter 17

Brynley

Being shoulder checked by the door frame during my storming inside the breakroom area of The Institute instantly pulls a loud, high-pitched, screeching sound out of me.

"Rough morning?" Calen cautiously questions from the round table he's stationed at.

"*Fuck this day.*"

"Ouch."

"*Fuck this day right in the ass.*"

"Hm." He pauses all fork movement. "Without or without lube?"

"*Without.*"

"Painful."

"Fuck this day right in the ass without lube and may a great white feast on its dangling nut sack."

"Flat brain coral colorful as always, Bryn." This time he stabs a piece of melon in his mixture. "But fucking brutal." Calen keeps his attention planted on me. "Wanna talk about it?"

"No."

"Wanna scream about it?"

"Yes." Another heavy huff escapes blowing a piece of damp hair away from my eyes. "But that is inappropriate conduct in the workplace."

"Is it really any more inappropriate than you chanting at the giant otters to 'get some' during copulation yesterday?"

"First off, be professional."

"I am being professional."

"Professionals would use their names."

"Fine." Humoring me occurs between bites of his honey dew. "Is screaming your *human* frustrations any more inappropriate than you cheering on Peanut Butter and Jelly during their copulation time yesterday?"

"Why can't you just say during their bang time?"

"How is *that* professional?"

"It's not, but every time you say copulation, I basically get PTSD style flashbacks of Intro to Marine Biology with Professor Stojan and wanna start dry heaving from the inexplicable wafts of tuna and term papers that seemed to seep from the pores of that Cardassian looking bitch."

"You had a professor that looked like a Kardashian?"

"*Cardassian.*" Dropping my bag near my locker space proceeds me glaring. "*Star Trek* not reality star."

"But you *hear* how confusing that is, right?"

"What I *hear* is you need more time binging and less time booging."

"We both know I prefer surfing."

"We both know you prefer surfing when the bikini bottoms are low, and the waves are high."

Calen chuckles to himself at the same time I shove my key into my work locker. Almost immediately after opening, I release another unhappy huff over the sight inside.

"We also both know you don't have a spare shirt in there, so you're going to need to grab one out of mine."

He's immediately tossed a tiny glare to which he responds to by smugly shoving the last bite on his fork into his mouth.

Asshole.

But like the *good* kind.

The kind I actually *need* in my life unlike the bad kind I'm engaged to.

Though, I'm not sure for how long at the rate he keeps disappointing me.

149

And fucking *ignoring* me.

I didn't think it was fucking possible to be ghosted by your own fucking fiancé yet here we are.

Calen waits until I shift over a step to open his locker with the spare key, he gave me to claim, "You're pissed off about more than just the unexpected rainstorm here to usher away your man in style."

There's no stopping my shoulders from dropping as I meet his gaze. "Palaemon is literally fucking *weeping* for him, bro."

"Greek God of Sharks?"

"And harbors and sailors in danger and ships with fucking problems and really just shit in that category."

"Isn't that Poseidon?"

"That's the big dick of *all* of water." Grabbing a spare work shirt from his locker is effortlessly executed. "Palaemon is just the big dick of *marine* shit."

"Won't *literally* scream at work due to the handbook's ruling about appropriate voice volumes yet has no problem saying the word dick with impunity every chance provided."

"What can I say?" The ripping off of my damp tank top is swift. "*I'm gifted.*"

"*You're exhausting.*"

"I'm *exhausted*," I chomp during an adjustment of my gray sports bra that's wedged on top of my regular bra for extra support. "I honestly don't know if we were interviewing wedding vendors or future possible vice presidents."

Hope hops into my best friend's expression. "Wilcox finally came out of hiding?"

"*No.*" Carelessly throwing the wet article into the bottom of my open locker is followed by me yanking on the dry one. "And the only thing worse than wedding planning for 'the wedding of the century' is doing said wedding planning *alone*." I slam his locker closed. "Not that I'm even sure there is going to be a wedding at this fucking point."

150

"You don't wanna marry him anymore?"

"I don't even know if I wanna be *with him* anymore."

Calen's mouth drops to retort when Raquel unexpectedly interjects, "Connelly, Winters, transport is about an hour out."

Her surprise appearance forces a more professional demeanor to appear during my step back away from the lockers to make eye contact. "Understood."

The fact she's barely put more than her head in the room indicates this was simply an unplanned pitstop on her way to destroy other people's happiness.

Lucky us.

"Winters due to your…current status you are on verbal prep, evaluation, and paperwork transferring *only*. You may not drive the escort vehicle. You may not be *in* the transport vehicle with the creature. And you may not have any direct contact in which you are required to be in unsafe surface areas."

Forfuckssake, slipping *once* during your whole career shouldn't you get banned for life from wet territories.

"Connelly, you'll be *hands-on* overseeing each portion of the transition as well as responsible for driving the escort vehicle for you and Winters. The transition of care from us to K&T is likely to expand what's left of the day; therefore, I went ahead and had a room booked for the two at the usual hotel."

"Yes ma'am," Calen politely acknowledges only to instantly receive a girlish grin.

"You know better than to ma'am me," she practically coos. "I'm not *that* much older than you."

Older enough.

He's damn near the exact halfway mark between her and her preteen daughter.

A much less kind expression is abruptly presented to me. "I expect your pre-evals in my inbox in the next twenty minutes."

151

Rather than wait for me to respond, she slips back into the hallway with the same ease she poked into the room with leaving me the perfect opportunity to grumble, "It's like Picard having to report to Armus every day."

"That doesn't sound good."

My face shoots him a sardonic smirk, "That's because it's not, Spock."

"Yeah, well, neither is you ending your relationship with The Billionaire Kahuna because he skipped out on a couple scheduled wedding planning dates and a few social cal events."

"How about because he *missed* the OB/GYN appointment?" Securing his lock in place occurs prior to me sliding back in front of my own locker. "How about because for the past two weeks I've been talking to his voicemail more than him?" I squat down to rummage around in my bag for my blue eyeliner. "How about because I've been having a more intimate relationship with our text thread than him?"

"Intimate relationship?" Calen promptly teases, warranting my glare. "Being preggers is seriously making you more chicklike."

"And more irrational." The snatching up of the object precedes me pointing at him. "So, be careful before I use this tube to create a different type of blue balls than you're used to."

"They rarely get *that* blue."

"But it *has* happened."

"And thanks to you being the wing woman you are, it probably *won't* happen again." His compliment receives a crooked grin that he encourages me to stick around with bribery. "Lock up your shit and come eat my pineapple."

"God, I love it when you talk fruity to me."

My theatrical winking gets him snickering and shaking his head in amusement. "It's like you *want* your Bruce Wayne wannabe to have to shell out for a sexual harassment lawsuit."

"It's like I no longer *care* what my Bruce Wayne willneverbe does in general."

152

Calen waits for me to complete the task of stuffing my bag away and locking up to counter, "Except that you do."

"Okay, but I don't *want* to."

"Yeah, but it doesn't change the fact that you *do.*"

"Don't training mission test me right now," I grouse during my crossing over to the table. "I need more cheat codes, less no-win scenarios."

He pushes the container of fruit to the shared space between us. "You're gonna name my god kid after something from that show, aren't you?"

"*Franchise.*"

"Fuck you," Calen lightly laughs on a shake of the head.

"Only if you promise to hold me afterwards."

My best friend's grin slightly fades prior to him inquiring, "Wilcox really hasn't been around?"

Shaking my head occurs before viciously chomping down on the yellow cube.

"You haven't had dinner together?"

The action is repeated.

"Lunch?"

Yet again I execute the movement.

"Breakfast?"

"I have been on more dates with *Nes* at this point than him."

"*Fuckten,*" grumbles the man beside me as I stuff another piece of food into my starving mouth. "Although, her Fed boyfriend doesn't strike me like the type of dude who would object to her dating other women."

"Dating? *Yes.* Occasionally banging? No."

"*Really?*" Curiosity creeps into his gaze. "*No shit?*"

"Can we *not* talk about my other best friend's thriving sex life and maybe focus on the demise of mine? How *I* haven't been fucked in weeks? Or touched?" I shove more fruit into my mouth. "Who doesn't hug their pregnant fiancée?!" Another square finds its way inside despite the fact that I haven't even chewed the other. "Who doesn't hold them when they're crying?!"

Additional chunks are jammed against the others

"Whodoesnttellthemotheroftheirchildtheylovethem?!"

The jumbled mess of the last claim is what prompts Calen to stand and wind his arms around me.

To no surprise, there's no hesitation for the tears I had previously banished to begin pouring from my eyes, coating his work shirt in wetness, whatever flakes of mascara haven't rubbed off yet, and tiny specs of fruit littered spit. Through incoherent sobbing, I thoughtlessly confess everything that's been eating away at me since I physically lost sight of the man I love.

I cry angrily over the media.

Their latest lies.

Their latest highlights of our notable failures as a couple.

I bawl about them blowing this possible sibling thing out to the Andromeda Galaxy.

Turning Monica's well-planned ambush into a war with no possible winner.

Destroying Wes to the point he'll miss *his* chance to be a father because trying to defend the one he had is all he can fathom.

And it's that blubbering that leads me to the ugliest, scariest fear I actually have.

The one that's festering on my ocean floor.

Being. A. Single. Parent.

How and when I go from basically using my partner in crime's shirt as a tissue, to clinging onto it with two hands like that bitch does that door in the movie *Titanic,* is a mystery, much like the exact amount of time that passes during my whispered confession about not wanting to be alone.

To go through any of this alone.

To wanting my child to have what it is I didn't.

Two present parents.

154

Eventually, Calen pulls back just enough to use the pads of his thumbs to gingerly brush away the tears that he can. *"You are not a great hammerhead, Bryn."*

"Because I won't eat my own baby?"

"Because you *are not* a solitary creature." More swipes at my cheeks are delivered. "You are the largest and most fit and most fierce shark that has formed her own school that consists of others who will play and love and protect you as much as your little pup." An undeniably soft smile slides into place on his face. "You may hunt alone. You may occasionally separate and swim alone. But you are *never* actually alone." His hands gently plop onto my shoulders. "We're all here for you, babe. You just gotta move your body to communicate that you need us."

It's impossible not to tease, "Pretty sure *that's* against the rules in the handbook."

"You make me wanna migrate to another group."

"And you make me grateful that you can't."

A small chuckle precedes a gentle kiss to the middle of my forehead. "I love you too, Amphitrite."

"I *so would* be the head bitch of the sea."

"How about you be the head bitch of the tank and get Steven's pre-evals over to Raquel before she returns to hang ten on another wave of ass chewing?"

Seeing his point – his very valid point – is what pushes me to give my face a quick wash in the sink, reapply some mascara, and hustle to the office area to send our boss the requested documentation while he begins his portion of the transition process.

As much as I tend to hate paperwork – and I really fucking do – today is different.

Today it provides me with a much-needed distraction.

Allows me to focus on Steven's safety versus his sorrow.

My sorrow.

155

It forces me to keep my attention on the crucial protocols regarding the transport tank, the forklift, and the transfer trailer rather than my heart wrenching horror of losing my favorite creature.

In a way…my first born.

I mean he was the first being in this building I bonded with, and according to many of the aquatics in The Institute, I was the first one he developed any sort of relationship with.

Yet instead of obsessing over the ache of having to let go, having to let him grow up, and move on, I oversee our team along with K&T's to insure he becomes properly sedated.

Secured in the netting.

That the harnesses are tight, and the safety straps are latched as well as reinforced once he's in the exhibit tank.

Triple checking paperwork and lists prevents me from acknowledging the lump of grief lingering in my throat and gathering signatures from various employees that have to sign off on having done what's requested of them aid in distracting me from the hopelessness heavily weighing on my shoulders, threating to crumple me to my knees.

Unlike the father of my child, I can't simply crumble under this pressure.

I have to keep going.

I have to keep moving.

I have to get my gear and my ass in that transport vehicle to finish escorting Steven to his new home because it's my job.

Because *he's* counting on me.

The same way I know I can no longer count on Wes.

Chapter 18

Wes

I don't like westerns.

I never have.

I never will.

Fuck, I didn't even know *he* did until I started looking through the collection Monica bestowed upon me, claiming to have no place for such dribble in the home she inherited.

Letting the glass linger near the edge of my lips, I continue glaring at the disgusting photo *haunting* me.

Taunting me.

Torturing. Me.

I hate how much I fucking look like him.

In fact...I'm actually *grateful* for the scars.

The burns.

The leathery patches.

It makes me look *less* like this pathetic excuse for a person I praised most of life and more like who he truly was.

Who I'm destined to be.

Crumpling the photo reveals to me another, although this one is worse.

Far.

Worse.

Seeing him lovingly tangled around a round stomach, dark-haired woman that's damn near identical to the one who brought all of this to light results in me guzzling down the remainder of what's in my cup.

Filling it to the brim again.

Chugging back gulp after gulp after gulp after gulp, no longer tasting.

Simply erasing.

Numbing.

Removing the ability to feel.

Care.

Think.

Unexpected jangling sounds part the fugue fog I'm trying to head into summoning my attention to my right where the handle to the door plummets to the ground. The loud clank causes me to loudly groan in displeasure, yet the careless swinging of it open, letting in unwelcome light, prompts a much louder grumble to reverberate around the room.

"I am glad to see you are indeed alive, sir," Clark cheekily states upon crossing the threshold. "I will report my findings to Hamilton."

"*Out*," leaves me at the same time I tip the glass towards my lips for another drink. "*Now.*"

"I am afraid not, sir."

Post another slurp, I sneer, "*It wasn't a request.*"

"And it is not an order I will be following."

His refusal pokes at my ribs.

Does its best to spark life into my chest.

Whispers to my senses to sneak away from being paralyzed to begin processing everything liquor has so lovingly prevented.

No.

I don't *wanna* process shit.

Or protest it.

Or make peace.

I wanna remain just like I am.

In a copper liquid prison of pacification.

"I'll fire you," I threaten between slightly smaller swallows. "For insubordination."

158

"Then fire me." He politely folds his hands in front of him as I slouch down further into my seat. "However, I cannot simply allow this to continue."

"*What* to continue, Alfred?" The snarky retort is followed by guzzling down what remains. "Why don't you do that thing you haven't done enough of in my life and be fucking specific?" Slamming the glass down occurs while I search for a non-empty bottle. "A straight shooter." One stack of files gets knocked onto the floor during my reach for what's left in the nearest container. "You know that shit the old lying, cheating, dick of the house apparently loved." Twisting off the lid is done in tandem with locking eyes. "Another fucking secret he kept." I carelessly toss the object at his feet. "Cause you know he didn't have enough of those."

He doesn't allow my drinking straight from the bottle to deter him, "Your drinking is out of control again, Weston."

"No," I shake my head and wedge the bottle between my open legs, "my drinking is the only thing *in* control."

"You've missed work."

"Yet money was still made."

"You've missed events."

"Yet money was still spent."

"You've missed wedding plans."

"Yet I'm still getting married."

"*Are you?*" The challenged question cuts deeper than it should, indicating a need for more alcohol. "I'm not entirely sure Miss Bryn has any interest in marrying someone who has not only blatantly ignored her for over two weeks but also missed her prenatal appointment."

It's difficult to present indifference but not impossible. "She has nothing to worry about. I'll pay for knocking her up just like the bastard who raised me did."

Clark swallows one comment to spew another. "She deserves more than that."

159

"And Marzia didn't?"

Simply hearing her name has him shifting his weight.

Tugging at his tie.

Directing his gaze anywhere but into mine.

"What's wrong, *Baker*?" I callously croak prior to sending the container towards my lips. "Can't stomach hearing her name?"

His green glare gravitates back in my direction.

"How about looking at her face?" My free hand snatches up the nearest photo and shoves it forward. "Can you fucking handle that?! Can you sleep at night knowing you helped him hide this woman for fucking *decades?!*"

There's no response out of the man I once admired.

Respected.

Trusted more than anyone else in my household.

"Can you sleep at night knowing she wasted away practically *alone* from pancreatic cancer?"

Still nothing.

"Can you sleep at night knowing she *died* being his dirty little secret?"

Not a word.

"Was it easy for you?" Smug bitterness encourages me to jeer. "Maybe because while he was out bangin' some backwoods bar bitch out in Texas, *you* were busy fucking his wife in *his* bed." Demented laughter bounces my unwashed frame. "Is that it? Is *that* how he kept you quiet? Let you fuck his wife while he fucks around on her?" Waggling the bottle damn near causes me to drop it. "You two were some slippery fucks, huh?" All of a sudden, an idea launches me onto my wobbly feet. "Let's go ask him!"

"*Weston-*"

"Better yet, let me go piss on his grave and give him the same fucked up treatment he gave to me and my mother."

"*Enough.*"

"N-"

160

"*Enough!*" The rattling volume as much as the impact damn near shoves me back into my seat. "*That. Is. Enough!*"

"It's not enough!"

"Why?" He viciously bites. "Because the drunken petulant toddler in front of me can't handle not getting his way?!"

"Well…" a small drunken shrug leaves me. "Yeah."

"*Grow. Up. Weston.*" Clark steps uncomfortably closer. "You are *not* the same eighteen-year-old child you were when he died!"

"I-"

"I am tired of having to pretend this behavior is acceptable!"

"I-"

"I am tired of having to allow you room to wallow in self-pity and worthlessness."

"I-"

"I am tired of having to watch you throw your own life away simply because you just now realized the man you idealized was not perfect!"

"He was a liar!"

"He did what was necessary to protect his family! To protect you!"

"That's what you call disowning your own child?!"

"He had his reasonings for doing what he did when it came to the Simmons even if you don't understand them," Clark defends without reluctance. "However, what's *yours*?" Another step forward has me fumbling into my desk. "What are *your* reasons for abandoning *your* own child?"

"My father-"

"*Your father is gone, Weston!*"

The proclamation prompts my grip around the bottle to tighten.

"*He* made his choices! He made his mistakes! He lived his life! And now *you* must figure out how to do the same!"

Plopping into the chair is mindlessly done.

161

"Stop wasting all this time wallowing about what he did or didn't do or what you did or didn't know about him! *Accept* that the man you admired, the man you looked up to, was far from perfect." An almost unbearably heavy breath leaves him. "He was arrogant. And argumentative. And obnoxiously stubborn. He drank too much. He drove too fast. He was shitty at rowing, polo and could barely swing a fucking golf club yet if you asked him or anyone around him, he was a fucking Olympic champion. Your father *boasted* and *bragged* and overcompensated like *that* was the actual sport he was good at."

Confusion crinkles my forehead and stirs the senses I was trying to keep inactive.

"He missed birthdays and anniversaries and first steps and dates and graduations and a million other things because he *chose* to put the Wilcox legacy – and all that that entailed – above all else. And *that* was his choice. Just like it was *mine* to put *you* first."

Throbbing aches begin at my temple.

Travel downward towards my ear.

"I spent more time raising you than I ever did Penny and that was *my choice.* That is *my burden* to bear. Just like having to process and deal with what she did *to you* because of that choice. We all have demons we have to face, Weston." Unimaginable pain flashes briefly on his face. "Deals with the devil we didn't see coming. Mountains of mistakes we have to figure out how to climb or conquer or demolish. To be less than perfect...to...not measure up to someone else's standards, doesn't make us monsters." The side of his frame rests against the edge of my desk. "*It makes us human.*"

Absentmindedly, my grasp on the bottle slightly loosens.

"And no matter how much you drink to forget that," the object is smoothly shifted out of my possession, "or drink to disprove that," it lands beside him on a thud, "or drink in hopes of changing that, it doesn't." His hands once more fold in front of him. "*You are human, Weston.*" He allows his head to angle itself to one side. "*Just like your father was.*"

I wish the words escaping weren't so weak, *"How could he do that to Mom?"*

"How can you do *this* to Bryn?"

My jaw drops to retort when the truth gets lodged in my throat.

Because I'm selfish.

Because the only shit that mattered to me was *me*.

Not my best friend.

Not my family.

Not the love of my life.

Not even our unborn child.

The only fuck I gave was about my pain and confusion and betrayal.

Mine and only mine.

And there's this nauseating sensation in the pit of my stomach that tells me my father did the same.

At least I think that's what that shit is.

It could be I've simply given myself alcohol poisoning again.

"How could she forgive him?" is whispered out prior to bile burning up the back of my throat. *"How can I?"*

"Forgiveness is a powerful tool." In an almost effortless motion, he uses the tip of his foot to scoot the trashcan closer to me. *"How* you wield it…and what or *who* you wield it *for*…all lies with you." The bottle filled bucket knocks into my bare toes prompting me to lean forward to begin heaving. *"Just. Like. Acceptance."*

Chapter 19

Wes

The problems with drinking in excess are obvious.

Balance struggles.

Slurred speech.

Blurry vision.

Nausea.

However, the problems that occur when the pendulum swings the other direction aren't exactly much better.

Shakes and tremors.

Racing pulse and colds sweats.

Hallucinations.

Vomiting.

Gordonknows, the human body isn't meant to endure expelling this much fucking bile.

I use the back of my hand to wipe away the bit of spit that was left behind from my latest round of heaving as Lauren finishes covering the bed in the estate medical suite I've been occupying for the past three days. "*Thank you.*"

"Of course," she sweetly hums while smoothing out the wrinkles. "It's my job."

"It is *not* your job." Reaching for the cool washcloth lingering on the bedside table is accompanied by clarification. "Your job is budgeting. Scheduling. Disciplining. Managing." A gentle dab is delivered across my forehead. "Not changing sheets."

"Changing sheets is *part* of the managing process better known as *mothering.*" At that, she shoots me a scolding stare. "Now, you let me do my job while you focus on doing yours."

"Which I'll be doing as soon as J.T. brings me a tablet."

"*Detoxing, Weston.*" One hand lands disapprovingly on her hip. "*That* is your primary focus."

Not by choice.

Withdrawal doesn't exactly allow room for much else.

Interestingly, it behaves quite similarly to the substance I am distancing myself from.

It slinks in.

It overthrows your senses.

It captures your sanity and stability.

It's ruthless.

And unforgiving.

And painful.

It's everything I fucking deserve.

Every penance I need to pay.

"*Bed.*" Lauren tips her head towards the piece of furniture. "Hamilton should be back from lunch to check your vitals shortly."

Just the thought of food conjures a deep groan of disgust.

"Still no appetite?"

Shaking my head precedes putting the small towel down and sliding back onto the mattress.

"I'll inform Lucky to maintain the smaller portions." Her fingers wind around the end of the blanket to pull it up. "How do eggs sound for lunch?"

"Like a punishment."

"Perfect!"

The sassy retort doesn't fail to make me smirk.

It's no mystery where Bryn's sass stems from.

Although, having Lauren's does remind me that I don't have hers.

That I haven't had hers.

That I don't *deserve* to have hers for what I've put her through.

"How's Bryn?" meekly leaves me as I reach for the washcloth a second time. "Our baby?"

165

"Alive," she announces in such a way I know that's the best answer I'm going to get, which is honestly more than I deserve.

Instinct to pry for more rears its ugly head, unfortunately for me, detoxing is *uglier.*

Ruder.

More relentless.

Puke abruptly propels itself upward forcing me to curl sideways in hopes of spewing into the nearby trashcan rather than my freshly changed sheets. One round easily becomes two that transitions to three and four and five, further purging any nutrients that had somehow managed to take hold in my system. Cramps from the endless stomach tensing cause guttural groans to grow in numbers yet the added vibrations amplify the pain ultimately prompting more grumbles to appear and continue an agony filled cycle.

I should've never picked up that first glass.

I should've never downed that first shot.

That first sip.

Heaving after a short period transforms into dry heaving, an action I hate more than vomiting itself.

When you actually throw up, there's action.

Purpose.

An accomplishment.

When you dry heave, there's all the suffering, but none of the relief.

None of the reprieve.

Again.

Not that I deserve any.

"How about some tea?" Lauren politely suggests, prompting my lids to lift, revealing my tear-ridden gaze. "Maybe some hibiscus? Get your electrolytes back up?" She lifts the laundry basket upward at the same time she teases, "Don't worry. I'll hold the poison."

The playful remark regarding what had her in this bed over a year ago has me trying to smile. "I appreciate that."

166

She lovingly winks, turns, and exits, leaving me alone once more to brush away the spit from my lips.

Wipe down my face with the cool rag.

My neck.

Press the cloth firmly against my eyes in hopes of relieving the throbbing that seems incapable of ending.

Having to work through this shit episode the first time was miserable.

Why did I think a sequel wouldn't be worse?

"You look like that scene in *The Dark Knight Rises* where Bruce is recovering in the pit," my best friend unexpectedly states causing me to lower the towel to lock stares. "Post Bane breaking his back and taunting him but pre that old dude beating him like a piñata and using his ancient chiropractic degree."

I grunt in agreement. "Feel like it too."

He winces and adjusts the sky-blue collar to his dress shirt. "Progress?"

"I'm no longer vomiting every other hour."

"Sweats?"

"Still soaking the bed."

"Sleep?"

"Nightmares."

"Mood?"

"Dour."

"But less hostile?"

"Yeah." Tossing the rag back into the bowl it's being kept in precedes bracing my back against the pillows. "I'm past the need for a sedative to prevent me from irrationally screaming at everyone."

A half-hearted grin is given. "And that my injured cape-crusader is my least favorite phase of this shit."

"At least I didn't throw anything this time."

"Only because you were handcuffed."

167

"And who am I to thank for sparing me their hot pink fuzzy handcuffs?"

"That would be the future Mrs. Wilcox."

It's impossible to keep hope out of my expression.

"They were a bridal brunch gift from Vanessa. Along with cupcake flavored lube and a fox mask I was afraid to ask questions about."

Despite the desire to dive deeper into those details, I soar around them to investigate something much more pressing. "When was that?"

"Couple days after she asked her to be a bridesmaid."

When did that happen?

When did she make that decision?

Did she tell me?

Did she mention it and I simply can't remember?

"I've requested to walk down the aisle with her versus Calen," J.T. playfully adds. "Assuming there's still going to be a wedding."

"Fuck, I hope so." Watching him slowly stroll inside is done in tandem with me asking, "Has she mentioned *not* wanting one?"

"Not to me." His positioning in the room is at the foot of my bed. "But I haven't exactly spoken to her much."

"Why?"

"You mean aside from reporting to the other board members about the possibility of *your shares decreasing*, dealing with app development issues, delays in distribution, juggling multiple press events – alone – and Nightwinging my ass here to assist in your recovery?" J.T. shoves his tablet free hand into his pocket. "She hasn't been answering me." He doesn't wait for me to counter with the obvious. "And I don't mean normal Bryn not replying to a text because her cell has magically found a new home in a box of tampons or whatever. I mean phone turned completely *off* level of not speaking."

It's impossible to ignore the tightness in my chest increasing.

168

"She's also distanced herself from Hill after informing him his services for her wellbeing were no longer required."

Shit.

Is there going to be a wedding?

Do I even still have a fiancée?

The other half of my heart?

My soul?

"Hill, however, has been maintaining a casual visual on her whereabouts at all times to ensure her safety continues per Park's orders. Given that Hill is employed by the personal security department of the Wilcox Estate, the only people who can 'relieve him of his duty' are the *head* of security – Park – the 'face' of the company – me – and those that *legally* bear the last name Wilcox, which she *technically* doesn't yet."

"*A technicality?*" Another grin threatens my face. "You think a bullshit *technicality* is going to save you from *The Wrath of Khan*?"

"I think she'll *appreciate* the effort."

"She won't."

"*I know*," my right hand instantly caves, entire body sulking forward, "but I need to know she's okay. I need to know our Uhura is okay."

Silence momentarily slithers itself along my spine stirring up vomit in the process. "*...is she?*" I force myself to swallow the expanding lump back down. "*Is she okay?*"

"Physically?" He tosses the tablet on the bed beside my thigh. "From what Hill's mentioned she seems fine. No lingering cognitive issues. No developing pregnancy problems. And her single overnight trip for work, did *not* have her on or near the water."

That's gotta be driving my little prey insane.

"Emotionally?" An uncomfortable cringe is shot. "All Calen says is that she's moody." J.T. leans his side against the furniture. "He doesn't know if it's from lack of beer or lack of pizza or lack of the Batarang."

169

"*Do not call my dick the Batarang.*"

"Come on, dude, that's like a perfect nickname!"

Whether it's hearing his mirth or simply hearing news on the woman I love that gets me smiling is unknown.

It also doesn't matter.

Feeling something other than disgust and spite is welcomed.

"He planned them a beach date to see if it would help."

The word choice sparks outrage in spite of me doing my best to hold it back. "*They're dating?*"

No.

That's impossible.

She belongs to me.

And only me.

It's *my* last name that's to become hers.

My cape she borrows.

My family jewels she loves to keep her hands on.

That *has not* changed.

That is *not* going to fucking change.

Not now.

Not ever.

"According to Monica – your half-sister maybe – 'Calen and Bryn's relationship is developing'. Between the dinners – mostly to Mo Mo's – the outings – like the beach – and her sleeping at his apartment – instead of the penthouse – proving her inference isn't difficult."

"She's not even staying at our place anymore?"

"Not according to Hill. Or Monica for that matter."

"How the fuck does she know that?!" New waves of rage ripple throughout my voice. "How the fuck does she know anything?! *Everything?!*"

"You're probably not looking for the answer that she's a real-life comic book villain, are you?"

"*No.*"

"Fine." His voice lowers to needlessly mumble, "Although, she has *a lot* in common with that creepy flower power zombie thing."

"Mister Bloom."

"Was not a fan of those comics."

Neither was Bryn.

However, it's not because of the villains or storylines or artists.

It's just that she prefers the simpler, more familiar arcs.

Claims to be a "basic bat cannon bitch", which is almost impressively articulate in a strange way.

In what I can only classify to be the Bryn way.

"Pham and Evie believe we have a leak," J.T. unenthusiastically announces. "*Again.*"

Low rumbles rattle my raw throat, effortlessly amplifying the lingering aches.

"Park's looked and been looking and there are no red flags. His team hasn't found any bank accounts with suspicious activity. No questionable visitors, meetings, or phone calls for those with direct access to the two of you. He has no idea how Monica is getting her information."

"He sweep the building for bugs?"

"*Weekly.*"

"Our vehicles?"

"*Daily.*"

Groans of frustration precede me slamming my head backwards.

I momentarily squeeze my eyes shut, instantly wincing over the pain it ignites.

"His plan is to extend his search parameters outward a bit, but hey," a small nudge at my leg forces my attention back to the man that's always been at my side, "let *him* worry about security." My dry mouth twitches to argue only to be met by an all-knowing headshake. "And *Hawthorne* legal. He's been diligently searching for technicalities and strategies to minimize the amount of financial as

171

well as public damage this Monica stunt is causing the company. He'll be by tomorrow to touch base."

Good.

Because I've come to a very important conclusion.

I want Monica to have what she rightfully deserves.

In spite of the Joker worthy circus she's turned my life into, she deserves a portion of our company.

Perhaps our father didn't want the masses to know that; however, that was *his* choice.

It doesn't have to be mine.

I refuse to not acknowledge a portion of my family, of my bloodline, simply because *he chose* not to.

Simply because rather than publicly acknowledge his mistakes or imperfections, he went to extreme lengths to hide and erase them.

Monica mostly likely is this…bitter…and vengeful *because* of the rejection she's lived with her entire existence.

I can't fault her for that.

And I don't have to.

I will give her what she's requesting – both in word and financial compensation – and then offer to buy out her portion.

I don't wanna work with her.

I don't want her anywhere *near* our branding or what *I've* built.

I want her to have what she's entitled to and the opportunity to create or build what it is that fills her with passion exactly like I have.

While I followed in the footsteps of my father and grandfather and all the Wilcoxes that came before me, I've found my own calling within our legacy. A love for whiskey above all else, and it's *that devotion, that dedication* I think Monica needs in her own life.

It'll help her heal.

Move forward.

Realize what it took cases of aged booze for me to understand.

We do not have to bear the weight of other's mistakes.

Only our own.

J.T. offers me a small grin, "You just worry about getting better, okay?"

"I concur," Lauren sweetly interjects at the same time she reenters the room with a mug in hand. "And you can continue that process by drinking this cup of tea before Dr. Sawyer arrives for your session."

"And how is Dr. Feelings enjoying his time back in Gotham?" my best friend mirthfully teases.

"He's not complaining." I transfer the hot beverage from her possession to mine. "And neither is his bank account."

Having your therapist – that is technically a psychiatrist – move into one of the guesthouses on your property in order to provide steady round the clock sessions isn't cheap, especially when you have to fly him in on your private jet from where he's vacationing with his girlfriend in Italy as well as her back to Mistletoe, Montana, the place she's trying to convince him to move to.

Expensive doesn't even begin to cover it.

However, getting the help I know I need is worth it.

Getting the help, I know others need me to have is worth it.

I want to get things back on track and in order.

I want to be there for my brand.

My company.

My family.

I understand I can't do this shit alone.

And thanks to Clark, Lauren, Hamilton, and J.T. I know I don't have to.

"Homework yet?" investigates the other male in the room prior to Lauren offering him a lemon shortbread cookie.

"Just the amends list."

173

"That's where you write the person you wronged on the left, what aspect of your relationship was damaged in the middle, and actions you can take to begin to repair it on the right?"

Finding myself impressed by the fact that he remembers the activity from my first rehabilitation stretch is what prompts me to simply nod and use the back of my free hand to wipe away the building perspiration on my forehead.

"Tell me Bryn's at the top of that list."

There's no hesitation to nod again.

"*Good.*" Firmness in his expression isn't surprising nor unwarranted. "*It's definitely time you put 'The Cat' first, Mr. Wayne.*"

Chapter 20

Brynley

"I look like a pregnant yellow seahorse." Dramatically pausing in the middle of my penthouse living room for Mom, Evie, and Jenni is accompanied by a sneer. "Which is *the male* by the way." Pointing to the area in front of me where the two-tone yellow evening dress is poorly framing my stomach precedes another jeer. "In nature, this pouch would be on the dude, and *he* would be the one having to deal with pregnancy problems like trying to make it from breakfast to lunch without puking or through an episode of *Deep Space Nine* without bawling away his mascara." Both hands fall defiantly onto my hips. "I don't wanna be a seahorse!"

"Gah, you say the most top-cheddar shit," Jenni dreamily swoons under her breath. "You're such a fuckin' beauty."

"Let's *not* hit on the boss's pregnant fiancée," Evie instantly reprimands. "I like you on payroll. Plus, finding your replacement is simply something I do not have time for in this phase of our PR strategy." Her fingers deliver an exasperated ruffle to her long red locks prior to sighing at me, "And can you give me *something* to work with here? You were the one who *refused* to meet with Taylor for styling this week."

No shit.

First and foremost, who the fuck wants to meet with a recently retired Swedish supermodel *especially* when you're pregnant and agonizing over how much longer you're going to be able to wear your favorite tank tops?

Second – and almost equally as important – why would I wanna be styled by Runway Barbie when I'm *actively* trying to avoid the limelight?

I don't know the status of my relationship, let alone if I'll ever walk a red carpet or gala stage with him again.

I didn't wanna meet to play dress up when I'm over here basically drowning in unknown waters.

What if we're over?

Really over?

Wouldn't engaging in a real-world game of *Pretty Pretty Princess* be a waste of everyone's time?

His money I could happily waste.

We'd just call it asshole tax and that would be that.

However, my time?

Not so much.

Between proving to the wanna be queen of Atlantica I still have valuable *purpose* at The Institute in spite of being pregnant and skimming through what to expect while pregnant books during less beloved episodes of my favorite franchise, I don't have minutes to waste on unnecessary shit such as being properly clothed by the long lost Skarsgård sister.

That was a priority when being there for *Wes* was a priority.

When showing up as the future Mrs. Wilcox was a priority.

When I was learning to be queen of an empire, I'm *highly* underqualified to even be a townsperson in.

My world?

It's the one under the waves.

The one I'll never have to wear something *this* ridiculous in order to rule.

Wet and dry suits are definitely my favorite black-tie attire.

"You wanna try the green one on again?" Evie politely suggests. "Perhaps if we keep your hair down it'll *redirect* focus up to your chest – where we both know you like it – and away from your stomach area – where we both know you don't."

"*No.*" Folding my arms firmly under the uneven cut of the gown is attached to a sardonic smirk. "I'd rather not wear The

176

Spearmint Gum gown to the gala for the Global Society of Pathological Liars."

"*Pathological Outliers*," Mom swiftly corrects.

"That's what I said."

"No, what *you* described would be a charity event to support con artists…" the woman who gave birth to me does her best not to grin. "This is a charity event to support an organization that's committed to better public health, medicine, and awareness on a global scale."

"*God, that sounds so boring*," is thoughtlessly mumbled. "And I can't even fucking drink to make it interesting."

"Or…really…eat," Jenni adds on an uncomfortable cringe. "They're doing a whole app night-"

"*Hors d'oeuvres*," her boss revises to imply more class.

"-to go with the open bar thing and it's *all* shit you're not supposed to eat according to the pregnancy blogs I've been reading for you."

"For me?"

"Like for me to help you, help you through this whole pregnancy team change." For some reason, her sports metaphor captures my interest rather than repels it. "You're the head coach – obvs – and Wes is the assistant couch – double obvs – and your mom is like the equipment manager – really obvs – and like Evie is clearly somewhere in operations-"

"Don't say obvs again," the latter instantly grouses.

"Which kind of leaves me to be like the rando that has to be ready for whatever assist is ness, so that's what I'm doin'." Her baby pink blouse covered shoulders innocently bounce. "Reading things and making sure I have answers when answers are needed about things that maybe you might have questions over like what types of foods you can't eat at these events such as raw oysters or mango tuna tartare-"

"I don't like either of those *not* pregnant."

177

"Goat cheese and salami stuffed dates-"

"I like *two* of those things."

"And bananas foster bites."

"But those are so fucking good!"

"Pregnant women shouldn't have too many bananas because it can cause high pulse rate, dizziness, or vomiting."

"I'm already vomiting all the time!"

Jenni shrinks back into herself prompting Mom to deliver a loving pat to her lap as if reassuring the poor girl, it's not her I'm pissed at.

And it's not.

She's actually...*helpful.*

Much more fucking helpful than the person I am actually pissed at which is the person who knocked me up to begin with!

Who climbed on top of me or behind me in our bed or over the balcony one lunch break or two a.m. conference call time and recharted my entire existence before abandoning me out in the middle of the ocean to survive on my own.

ForFederationsake, where is the emotional equivalent to the Coast Guard when you need them?!

All of a sudden, the doorbell rings, buying me an overdue moment of reprieve.

Knowing it's probably Calen – who I bribed to attend the event with me by ordering him some very expensive surfboard wax – I helplessly grin over the reinforcement I know he's going to be for team "No Pregnant Seahorse".

The guy has my back.

Whether we're on the water or on the shore, I know he's here for me.

Where his allegiance lies.

It's why he hasn't complained once about the media implying that we're together and why he hasn't told me his thoughts on the father of my child.

That's not what I need right now.

So, that's not what he's giving me.

Which is exactly what makes him a better bestie than J.T., who considers space to only be a thing of the final frontier.

Casually opening the door immediately reveals to me a not so casual sight.

In fact, it's a sight I haven't seen in what feels like forever.

Rather than rush to say anything, Wes allows me a moment in silence to drink in his signature, designer black suit.

The fitted black tee underneath.

It's impossible to ignore his crisp white shoes that are making his matching pocket square pop.

His freshly cut hair and even fresher scented cologne both inform me of exactly how recent his transformation from unreachable alcoholic to apologetic asshole truly is.

And he *is* an asshole.

Regardless of the tears I can see struggling not to form in his mismatched gaze.

Gah, is it wrong to hope our son has that?

I say son because there's no fucking way I'm having a girl.

I can't have a girl.

I can barely have me.

Wes pushes his shoulders slightly back, the same direction his hands appear to be folded. "May I please come in?"

Retreating occurs in tandem with emotionlessly retorting, "Your name's on the lease too, so do whatever you want."

"Yes; however, it's *your name* on the building."

"Wait," abruptly stopping precedes a quirked eyebrow, "we own the *building*?"

"*You.*" He remains in place. "*You* own the building."

"Since when?!"

"Since yesterday."

"What?!"

179

"This is your home and the home of our child regardless of whatever happens between us."

Conflicting emotions don't hesitate to go to war, and the strife leaves me speechless.

And anxious.

And annoyed.

And wishing there were no consequences to have a shot or four while pregnant.

After clearing his throat, Wes repeats his question, "May I please come in?"

I opt out of verbally answering with a wave of my hand once I'm stationed back in the middle of the room near the coffee table.

"Why aren't you *appropriately* dressed?" Our favorite redhead unhappily grumbles as he enters the penthouse, shutting the door behind him. "*You* know better. *You* are not my headache without a cause to deal with."

"I have causes," playfully leaves me in the middle of her tangent.

"*You* – may derive pleasure from my irritation over you not wearing a color – but you *know* the difference between black tie and formal. Formal and business casual. Business casual and business pleasure. Business pleasure and recreational."

"There cannot possibly be that many different options," I whisper to my mom.

"*Right?*" she quietly replies.

"You *know* your attire doesn't have enough buttons but too few stitches to make a public appearance at the type of event you're attending tonight, so explain to me – in the least amount of words possible because we clearly do not have time to spare – why on Desiree Gruber's green earth you are not dressed for the press."

"You will have your answer in three..." he travels into the room but wisely not closer to me, "two..." his figure stops near the couch, "one..."

Evie's cell suddenly rings prompting all of us to redirect our attention to her.

Her lack of answering isn't surprising nor are the hums of agreement she repeatedly makes.

Woman is few of words on the phone.

Likely because she saves them all for when she's seen in person.

The conversation lasts about a minute before she ends the call to announce, "The Pathological Outliers Gala is being rescheduled due to unforeseen security concerns." Her suspicious glare swiftly finds her boss's. "They will be in contact within a week with a rescheduled date."

Wes's expression remains stoic. "Sounds like you're now free for the evening."

"It does."

"Why don't you and your lovely assistant go enjoy dinner on the company?" A tiny flicker of mirth flashes in his gaze. "You've put in so many long and hard hours lately, you certainly deserve a bit of downtime."

"Can we get Japanese?!" Jenni excitedly squeaks. "Ever since I read about Bryn not being able to eat it – pregnancy suck –"

"*Pregnancy does suck,*" I unhappily hiss at him.

"I've totally had a craving for sashimi."

"You can dine wherever you like," the male in the room informs. "And *drink* whatever you like. On me."

"There is a particular champagne that the Charming Chef recommends to go with the multi-course dinner at Adachi's," Evie gushes to Jenni in an almost giddy tone. "I've been *dying* to go there ever since."

"*GetoutGreatOne,* I've been dying to try that place!"

"*Go,*" Wes warmly encourages with a small nod. "Book a table with my name. Get dressed up. Eat and drink and tip freely."

"That sounds so bardownsky!"

181

"I don't know what the means," our publicist sighs at the same time she stands. "However, I'm willing to learn over something that sparkles." What appears to be an almost flirtatious smile shifts onto her face as she tips her head towards the door, "Shall we?"

"Let's fuckin' wheel!" exclaims her assistant during the jumping to her feet.

Their exit is accompanied by tiny finger waves and the man that's keeping his distance asking, "How was your day off, Lauren?"

"I don't know if I would label holding my daughter's hair back while she pukes and fighting over takeout menus and celebrity word searches as a day *off*, but all things considered, I was happy to finally spend some time with her." She offers me a sweet smile. "I think we both needed it."

We did.

But we *didn't* need for her to lecture me about the lack of nutrition in my diet.

Or vitamins.

Or why I should consider playing the baby a little more Beethoven and a little less Bon Jovi.

My suggestion to split the difference and play the tiny thing a bit of Biggie was not welcomed nor well received.

"I absolutely agree." His head tilts slightly to the side. "I also agree with the notion of you spending the evening with your husband who happens to be waiting in a limo downstairs." The corner of his lip kicks upward. "I think he mentioned something about Abuela's Kitchen and salsa dancing?"

Seeing her blue eyes widen ten times their size narrows my stare.

Sneaky, slippery, bastard.

He's a fucking horn shark!

Slow mover.

Only leaving the shelter to hunt.

And that's exactly what he did.

Bit down on their shells with force and precision so powerful and accurate they didn't see it coming.

"We haven't been there in ages," Mom swoons as she shifts to a standing position while I drop to a sitting one. "I don't even know if I have heels for that anymore."

"Buy some," my more powerful opponent nonchalantly declares. "*On me.*"

Of course she doesn't object.

Or argue.

Or insist otherwise.

She simply squeals like the others, cups his cheeks in motherly fashion during her passing by, and lovingly wags a finger at me prior to exiting.

I don't know why she's scolding me.

She's the traitor.

Clearly part of this Khitomer like cabal against me.

Once the door is securely shut, leaving us completely alone, I look up at the saboteur and sneer, "Amazing how you managed to sweep everyone off their feet *except* me." Wiggling around in the uncomfortable evening gown fabric is attached to another jeer. "Guess having someone gift me real estate just isn't that romantic to me."

An unpredicted collection of syllables clumsily leaves him.

Certain I misheard him is what pushes me to snip, "*What?*"

Wes sucks in a deep breath.

Crosses the short distance over to me.

Lowers himself to his knees directly in front of me and reveals a single red rose alongside the repeating of his gibberish.

Yet it's *not* gibberish.

And it's not a mixture of butchered Russian and French.

It's an actual language.

Just one he's not speaking very well.

Against my own volition, I adoringly coo, "Your *Klingonaase* is terrible."

183

"And that's after six consecutive hours of practicing."

Not giggling is impossible.

"I honestly thought J.T. was going to insist on us having a strictly business relationship going forward."

Additional snickers seep free as my bare shoulders mindlessly melt towards the floor.

"I don't think I've ever studied something so hard in my entire fucking life."

"*Well played.*" Letting a small smile linger on my face is accompanied by transferring the offering into my possession. "*I accept your surrender, Mr. Wilcox.*"

"*Can you accept my love, Miss Winters?*"

In spite of the sincerity in his tone – and it is undeniably there – I bitterly bite, "Why? Did the whiskey bottles finally stop putting out?"

Hurt glosses over his grim gaze at the same time he concedes, "I deserve that."

"You deserve castration served by *Jaws*."

Discomfort of epic proportion begins building around us.

Between us.

Prompts me to push him away.

Amble elsewhere.

Anywhere that isn't directly in his presence.

That isn't making me feel suffocated.

And alienated.

Eventually, I arrive in our bedroom – with him trailing behind – and am exposed to the other dress options, a view that leads to me investigating, "Did you call and *cancel* Calen coming over tonight?"

Wes leans his shoulder against the doorframe during his declaration, "His presence is no longer required."

"*Excuse. You,*" I viciously chomp and chuck the flower onto the bed. "That is *not* your fucking call."

"I think it is."

184

"I think what *you think* when it comes to me and my life doesn't fucking matter, Weston." Impatience to get out of the scratchy material increases with an unsurpassable vengeance. "Kind of like what I think doesn't fucking matter when it comes to *yours.*"

"It *does* matter, Brynley."

"Does it?" Mockingly escapes in a high-pitched tone. "That's why during your daddy drama episode you shut *me* out of your life?" Trying to reach the back zipper becomes my new task. "That's why you wouldn't let *me* be there for *you*?" More awkward twisting is executed. "That's why you didn't answer my calls? My texts?!" Frustration filled swiveling continues. "That's why you missed my fucking doctor's appointment?!" I can't stop the fury filled fidgeting. "That's why I went into that appointment with *Hill*, sobbing like a nerd in the 90s that just found out they cancelled *Next Gen*?! Because what I *think* or *do* or *feel* matters to you?!!"

Rather than touch a single word of my accusations, he softly proposes his assistance, "May I unzip you?"

"Why?!" defiantly leaves me. "I've been learning to do pretty much everything else on my fucking own! Why not this too?!"

"*Because you don't have to,*" he replies without reluctance. "*Because you never should've had to.*"

"You're damn right I shouldn't have!"

"*I made mistakes-*"

"*Several.*"

"*And. I. Am. So. Fucking. Sorry.*" His lower half twitches like it's considering moving closer, yet he stays put. Maintains the distance I've created. "*Klingonaase* doesn't exactly have that phrase-"

"It's really not something you should say when you're part of a warrior clan."

"-so I substituted it for the one I learned because it was the most fitting."

My squirming completely ceases.

"However, I am *so, so sorry,* Bryn." I watch his Adam's Apple nervously bob. "And I understand that saying those words is not enough. That saying those words does not undo the damage that I've caused."

"Not by a longshot."

"But they still needed to be said."

Sardonically nodding precedes a wave of the hand. "You've said them. You can go now."

"No."

"My building, my choice."

"My fuck up, my fix."

It's difficult to hide the impressed smirk the words conjure.

"I respect that I am no longer someone you can rely on, that that trust has been broken. That's why you call *Calen* and *Lauren.* I respect that I am no longer someone you can talk to you. That's why you text *Calen* and *Vanessa.* I respect that I am no longer someone you believe will protect you. That's why you let *Calen* and *Hill* know your whereabouts. I *respect* your decisions no matter how much I fucking hate them."

There's no stopping my eyebrow from quirking.

"And I fucking hate them, Brynley." He shoves a hand into his pants suit pocket. "Yet the thing I hate the most isn't that you've turned to other men to fulfill your needs – which is surprising considering my high loathing of it – it's that *I* didn't keep up my end of our agreement. You agreed to be mine and then *I* abandoned *you.*"

Surprise over the statement lowers my jaw.

"You agreed to belong to me *and only me* under the pretense that I would be there to belong to." Another hard swallow is taken. *"And I wasn't."*

Speechlessness – a rarity for me – continues to rule my system.

"I breeched this contract, Miss Winters." A small sniffle presents itself. "Therefore…if you choose to consider this relationship null and void, I will respect that." Tears can't be kept out of his tone.

"*I'll fucking hate it*...but I'll respect it." The trembling in his frame threatens to create one in my own. "*You.*"

In a voice that's more air than anything else, I cautiously investigate, "And if I don't?"

"Then I will prove you to every day why not dissolving this partnership was the second-best choice you ever made."

"The first being the agreement to be together to begin with?"

"*Yes.*"

Not smirking doesn't cross my mind.

"You *deserve* a better partnership, Brynley. One where you don't have to feel guilty for choosing your career over mine at times. One where you don't have to justify not wanting to put on your 'Fiancée Face' or play press puppet-"

"J.T.'s job."

"-simply for the shareholders benefits. One where your significant other holds out his open arms for whatever bullshit you need him to after a long a day. One where...he will turn to *you* rather than a bottle for solace when his world is completely turned upside down without his permission."

"And what exactly is to stop him from reaching for the company brand whenever the waters get a little too choppy or a shit storm hits our coastline?"

"His rather strict substance abuse regimen created by his physician and psychiatrist, backed by his best friend and honorary godfather."

Intrigue cocks my head.

Inches me closer.

Inspires me to insist, "*Go on.*"

"I am on the *other side* of the physical detox," Wes openly confesses. "It was uglier than the first time by vast portions. I was properly monitored around the clock and while I'm grateful you weren't there to see the vomiting or the shaking or the hallucinations, you were the person I wanted there the most. And the only reason I didn't reach for you *then* was because it would've been a selfish prick move to not be there for you when you needed me then expect you to be there for me when I wanted you."

"*Extremely,*" I whisper out and close the gap slightly more. "*But I still would've been.*"

Because I love him.

Because in spite of all the bullshit he's put me through for the past few weeks, I still care about him.

Give *all the fucks*.

Especially when it comes to his health.

His sobriety.

I know it was the alcohol putting the divide between us – a divide I will not stand for again – but that doesn't mean I wanted him to suffer through trying to get out of its hold without me.

If I learned anything from my father's gambling addiction, it's that not having support always leads to a greater fall.

"For the next few weeks, I'm still on a heavily supervised diet – that Lucky is doing his best to be creative with – to ensure my system receives the right increase of good and the best decrease of bad. I'm allowed to begin running in a couple days. Lifting weights next week. I am no longer allowed *any* alcohol – not even sampling for work which J.T. understands as well as supports – and all alcohol currently on the estate premises is locked up in a single cellar to which Clark and Lauren possess the only key."

The new information successfully gets me creeping closer.

And closer.

"Dr. Sawyer – my psychiatrist – is currently taking up residence in one of the guesthouses to aid in recovery counseling, coaching, and management. I currently see him three times a day to discuss my progress, my actions, and my personal self-villains."

"Three times a day?!"

"*Yes.*" For the first time since this conversation started, he takes a step towards me. "And I will continue to see him three times

188

a day until I only need to see him for two. And then until I only need to see him once. And then once a week, which is when he can move out. And then I'll see him once a month – still in person. And then once every six weeks – still in person. And then whatever it is we come to the conclusion that I need regarding what I'm now accepting is a lifelong journey."

Awe drops my voice to a hushed volume. "*Seriously?*"

"*Seriously, baby.*" His frame arrives in the space directly in front of mine. "The only thing I'm more committed to than my sobriety is my relationship *with you.*" Wes's white sneaker covered toes innocently brush against my bare ones, stealing a breath out of my lungs. "So...if that means we need to start at the very beginning again with crossword dates and driving you to work, then we will. If that means sleeping in separate homes until our baby arrives, I accept that. If it means sleeping on the couch in the other room once he or she is born, then I'll upgrade to a more comfortable one. If it means you not wearing your engagement ring again until they're three, then I'll make sure to keep it locked in my comic book vault. And it means you not being willing to marry me until they're seven and asking can they go away for their slumber party, then so be it. I'll keep Valora on retainer, so we have first priority when the day finally comes."

Words rush to come out yet are out paced by a swoon courtesy of his hand gently cupping the nape of my neck.

"*Say you're mine again, Bryn, and I swear you'll never regret it.*"

"*Yours,*" barely manages to leave my lips before he's smashing his on top.

The initial impact is familiar yet foreign.

Intense but inviting.

Rough and soft and strong and light all in the same breath.

Our tongues tumultuously tangle, each taking unpredictable turns to tease the other, equally wanting and needing and desperate for control as much as surrender.

189

Wes's fingers suddenly tighten, anchoring themselves onto the territory they're currently occupying. The possessive pull inward prompts a loud, body shaking moan outward that stumbles his mouth off mine.

Like a little lost fin bearing creature his mouth frenziedly searches for something to devour.

Something to sink its teeth into.

Light grazes across my cheek progress into nips that scatter along my jaw before evolving into bites that litter the length of my neck.

Glide across my throat.

Glissade up to my ear.

The lobe.

The shell.

Needy whimpers propel past my parted lips at the same time my hands greedily grab onto his jacket.

"*I know you hate me, little prey,*" Wes airily proclaims, "*but can you hate me while I'm deep inside of you?*"

Yanking him into me and me into him is mindlessly attached to my equally breathless answer, "*I'm willing to try.*"

Ferocious groans are instantly followed by a much more vicious bite.

Getting me out of the gown isn't a gentle feat, and I'm grateful.

The ripping and tearing of the material creates a salacious symphony around our penthouse bedroom that I haven't heard in a hot *Star Trek* binge session or two. Thuds and thumps are closely trailed by clashes and clangs as clothes are exiled to the very edges of the space where they cling onto things like our chaise lounge and floor lamp for dear life.

We don't bother pushing the rejected dresses to the ground or rearranging the pillows to be beneficial. We simply get lost in pouncing and pawing and preying on each other like insatiable creatures unexpectedly released back into the wild.

And wild is unquestionably what we become.

Chomping.

Clawing.

Colliding.

Recklessly jerking ourselves around to keep our lips locked and tongues furiously lashing.

Ending up with Wes flat on his back, leg spreads wide, with me facing away and mine dangling over his curled arms as my nails scratch at the mattress for stability while struggling to withstand the force of his frantic bucking isn't at all how I imagined our makeup session unfolding.

I arch myself forward into the frenetic fucking, body being bounced around as if I weigh practically nothing.

My inability to do very little, other than concede to having my pussy stretched further and further, leads to me squeezing my eyes shut.

Letting my head fall forward.

My jaw to my sweat covered lap.

Air relentlessly fights to find its way into my burning lungs but is repeatedly banished by barbaric blow after blow.

Hisses are continuously expelled during the heaving.

Growls around the savage thrusting.

Grunts when his strained arms flex to primitively pound harder.

Deeper.

Manically mold my helpless, contorted frame into a misshaped mess that belongs to him and only him.

"*Mine,*" is practically barked in between pants. "*Only. Mine.*"

It's impossible to answer as my tits pitilessly bounce and my pussy pleads for a moment of reprieve.

The tighter the sopping wet muscles grow the more determined my fiancé becomes not to allow it. "*Say it for me, baby.*"

His gruffly spoken words grate along my spine.

Send shivers through my sore legs and curled toes.

"Say you're mine."

I don't hesitate to do what I'm told, yet the turbulent thrusting hinders my capability.

"Say. It." Wes demands during additional pumps. *"Say what I wanna hear."*

Another attempt to cry out is ceased by a rough stroke.

One that causes my dripping wet pussy to anxiously constrict.

Threaten to come undone.

"Say what I need to hear, little prey," the man of heart purrs, untamed thrashes faltering. *"Say that you're still mine."* His dick swells in warning that he's also on the brink. *"Say you're still mine to fucking worship."*

Melting is effortless.

"Mine to fucking have."

There's no resisting the orgasmic tidal wave rolling in.

"Mine to fucking love."

"Yours," finally escapes in a whispered surrender during one last shudder. *"Always yours, Wes."*

Without further vacillation, we erupt into thousands of tiny, trembling, delirious pieces again and again and again, until we're left with no choice but to rhapsodically recreate something built from blistering bursts and unremitting pulsations.

Something rewritten in thick, white ink on soaking wet walls.

Something new.

Something unstoppable.

Something whole.

Chapter 21

Wes

"Are you sure about this?" I cautiously inquire, arm readjusting itself around Bryn's waist. "Are you sure *this* is what you want?"

"I'd say it in Klingon, but I don't think you'd understand."

"I might," leaves me prior to a warm chuckle.

Doubtful.

Learning *one* fucking phrase gave me a migraine and damn near ruined decades of friendship.

"Maybe I should try," is attached to a wide mouth grin.

"Maybe you should just give Valora your credit card."

Our wedding planner gives her long, recently blond highlighted strands an excited ruffle. "So, this is a yes?"

"It's a *fuck yes*," Bryn sassily counters over the sound of ocean waves crashing behind us. "I absolutely want a beach wedding."

"Perfect!" Her exclaiming occurs as I release Bryn and reach into my light khaki-colored pants. "This Frost Luxury Hotel beach venue is *phenomenal*. It's *always* at the top of beach wedding venue lists; however, it *rarely* tends to work out for them typically because of dates."

"October," I inform while retrieving my card. "Whatever day is available."

"And if there isn't one?"

The command delivered during the handing over of the object is fresh off the printer clear. "*Make one.*"

"And that is one of the *many, many* reasons why I love working with you, Weston."

"And the reason I love working *under him*," shamelessly flirts my fiancée.

Heat instantly coats my cheeks unnecessarily adding to the slight discomfort already being brought to them by the scorching sun.

One side of the page, I hate being outdoors like this.

I'm exposed.

Physically.

Mentally.

Emotionally.

Being out on this fairly public beach in South Haven in the middle of the morning in the lightest clothes I've owned in over a decade – an off-white polo and pair of khakis I had J.T.'s stylist specifically purchase for this trip – is me putting it all on the line for Bryn.

I'm in public.

My mutilated flesh is on display – which the press stalking us poorly in the distance is taking full advantage of.

She – who I can't believe is agreeing to not only marry me but marry me sooner – along with our wedding planner have my completely undivided attention.

Nothing else matters at this moment.

Not the weeks of disappointing Morgan Brand reports I'm still reviewing.

Not the charity events Evie wants me to choose from to make up for my noticeable absence during my psyche break.

Not even the share proposal from Hawthorne regarding what would be a reasonable amount for Monica to be offered based on where the company was when our father died.

No.

Being here with Bryn, *engaged* in this planning process, *present* for every little thing possible is where my focus is.

I can hardly believe she forgave me.

Or…shall I say *is forgiving* me.

194

That's the phrasing our relationship therapist Stella Yang encourages us to use, insisting that our word choices – particularly when it comes to our situation – highly matter.

Post our makeup session three nights ago – that lasted into the very early morning – we had several long talks, one of which included us seeking someone *outside of family* to assist in our romantic matters. Communication is a major problem and according to our therapist can become even more so once a child is brought into the equation. While there were several "more qualified" experts that specialize in working with highly influential and wealthy couples, Yang not only came recommended through Park – his sister is part of the same practice – she had the more flexible schedule we were looking for. Between our unpredictable hours as individuals and my currently rigid recovery program, we needed someone willing to be more accommodating hours wise and open to traveling to the estate.

I don't want photos of us coming in and out of her office.

I don't want new issues for public relations to have to battle, especially when they already have so many – particularly regarding our non-broken engagement – and are gearing up for even more post this parental revealing event.

I want our therapy sessions to be about *us*.

Making *us* better.

Making *our* family stronger.

I don't want the media's opinion interjected or hovering around what isn't meant to be *public*.

Yes, we *do* have quite a bit of ourselves out there for the masses to see and judge and invest in; however, we are still entitled to have a few things remain *private*.

"I'm gonna go put us on the books for October," Valora announces on a wave of my card, "and when I return, I want your color pallet choices. Express wedding means express decisions so no stalling," she shoots the love of my life a scolding scowl, *"Brynley."*

195

Her swift spinning away to march back up the sand barely precedes the woman at my side mumbling, "I don't stall."

It's my turn to present her with a playful glare.

"*What?*" Bryn less than innocently shrugs her bright yellow, thin strap bearing shoulders. "I sometimes just prefer to tread water."

"The human equivalent of stalling, little prey."

"Those with *capes* shouldn't judge those of us with *fins*."

"Is that what I'm doing?" Jovialness remains in my tone as I put my wallet away. "I thought I was encouraging those with fins to simply swim towards happily ever after a little faster." My fingers instantly find hers the second they're free again. "My mistake."

Having her fingers flex against mine causes her engagement band to gently scrape my skin, a sensation that undeniably swells my heart.

Hitches my breath.

"It's big of you to admit that, Mr. Wayne," giggles my fiancée prior to pulling me away to walk along the fairly vacant beach with security trailing a safe distance behind.

Small chuckles escape on a shake of the head.

DCknows, I've missed this.

Her.

No one has ever made me laugh like she does.

Or smile.

Or even *think* about smiling.

From the moment she arrived, I *knew* in a weird way she was my bat signal.

The light that could summon me from anywhere.

At any time.

Forgetting that for even a moment is a crime that should've gotten me years at Blackgate Penitentiary in Gotham Bay and several more at Arkham.

"And speaking of Mr. Wayne…" Bryn leads the conversation with an unexpected segue. "I want our wedding colors to be black, dark blue, and golden yellow."

There's no resisting the urge to cock my head in question.

"Dark Knight colors for *my* dark knight."

It's impossible to resist letting my shoulders sink in awe.

My body from drifting closer to hers.

Blushing.

"*However*," impishness remains in her voice, "this does mean I may opt in for wearing one of Catwoman's *many* leather costumes instead of the more traditional dress." Her bright crystal gaze glides over to latch onto my brown and blue. "*Or maybe I'll just save that for our honeymoon.*"

The low, hungry groans the image sparks are difficult to swallow. "What do you think about taking the boat down to South Haven Island for that?"

"You have a Batboat?!"

"Batman has a Batboat, Batstrike, or Batsub – depending on the Batverse you're in – while *Mr. Wayne* has a yacht."

"Which is what I'm assuming you have."

"*Correct.*" My unoccupied hand casually slips into my pocket. "What do you say to us getting married here on the sand, enjoying the wedding suite at the hotel that night, leaving by brunch, and sailing down to a private beach where you can swim naked for a week or two as I happily watch?" I don't bother fighting the crooked grin. "Any interest?"

"*All of the interest,*" she coos in return, her own smirk stretching the length of her face, "even though it's *clearly* your counter to flying anywhere tropical."

Anywhere at all, actually.

That's *not* changing.

And *that's* non-negotiable.

Rather than reply to her remark, I pull out my now buzzing device to see an important text.

"That time already?" Bryn cautiously inquires after seeing who it's from.

"Yes." Typing a response precedes tucking my cell back out of sight. "Sawyer says he's finishing up lunch now and to meet him poolside in about ten minutes." Our eyes lock once more. "Would you like to walk me to my session, Miss Kyle?"

A warm squeeze of her hand is attached to an even warmer cooing, "I'd love to, Mr. Wayne."

Pivoting in the sand to head the direction of the hotel where my psychiatrist is dining and our wedding planner is booking us a date effortlessly occurs in tandem with a subject change. "Hamilton recommended an increase in folic acid in *both* of our diets – you for the vital role it plays in pregnancy development, me for depression – which has led Lucky to taste testing new recipes on his fellow estate members. Apparently, tonight, our family meal will include cheddar roasted broccoli and Brussel sprouts."

"Is Puppet Boy coming?"

"Yes."

"Can I not then?"

Her good-natured goading prompts me to chuckle and shake my head. "Lucky is doing his best to make our new eating arrangements more than just tolerable."

"I know," she dramatically sighs. "Just like I know our real-life Bones is also doing everything he can for both of us." An unforeseen smile slips into place. "It's actually kinda cute how close in contact he insists on being with my OB/GYN."

"*He cares.*" I plant a small kiss on the back of her hand. "*We all care.*"

And I do mean *all* of us.

The round the clock ass chewing I've gotten about neglect proves it.

I had honestly never heard Lauren yell like that before.

I can say with certainty I never want to again.

"And I am grateful *you* are letting *me* care," lovingly leaves me. "I'm also grateful you're doing things like going with me to get my blood drawn this afternoon for the parental event. I know this transitional reconnecting period between us isn't easy."

Bryn mischievously waggles her eyebrows. "Parts of it are *really* easy."

More snickers escape as I relinquish the hold that I have on her hand to drop it around her shoulder in hopes of shielding her from some of the photos I wish weren't being taken. "They will continue to *be easy* as long as you want them to be." She looks up at me again. "I understand Dr. Yang advising that we *both* be in the mood for physical activities, but let's just ignore *that* tiny recommendation. You want me at any time, baby?" My mouth inches closer. "*You can have me.*"

We engage in a chaste kiss that she girlishly giggles after. "You just want me to touch your Batarang."

"You and J.T. have got to stop calling my cock that."

"But it's perfect!"

"My dick isn't pointed or crooked. *How* is it perfect?"

"Because it makes you so uncomfortable."

The twitch of a glare she's given gets her laughing again.

It also gets her wiggling.

Wiggling of course leads to squirming, an action that frees her to do the unexpected.

She takes off running.

Instinct of course insists I rush after her and our veering towards the water where our sandal covered feet can cool off simply aid in the spontaneous playfulness continuing.

Despite being pregnant, her body dodges and weaves and ducks out of reach quite impressively. Splashes of water are sporadically kicked in my direction along with damp sand, a combination that could easily frustrate me if we weren't having so much fun. Her athleticism repeatedly receives a shocked expression yet rather than concede to being outmatched I push myself to keep up.

Ignore the bit of tightening in my chest.

Burning in my calves.

I need this.

We need this.

A little bit of discomfort is a great time for growth.

Per one of the mental health professions.

Although, I can't recall which one.

"*You are so out of practice, Weston,*" Bryn teases, body finally migrating back to mine. "How do you expect to keep up with our pup?"

"I'll work on it," I mirthfully state while pulling her into me.

"Promise?"

It's impossible not to wind my arms tightly around her prior to resting my forehead gently against hers. "*Promise, little prey.*"

Chapter 22

Brynley

I just wanna leave an important note in today's Captain's log.

Getting mouth banged on the way to a mandatory gala for work absolutely defeats doing a word search in the pre-event time passing battle.

Especially when your future husband eats pussy like it's his last meal on earth before he takes flight in the morning.

Not that Wes flies.

Or is willing *to* fly.

Or is even willing to *discuss* the idea of flying.

Fuck, when that shit came up in therapy – all because Stella thought it was important that we approach our honeymoon with the same expectations – I thought he was going to fire the doc on the spot.

Turns out that it's a *really* not to be touched subject.

We're talking locked up in his comic book vault's vault's vault.

And unlike her – who gets paid to try to pick those types of brain locks – I simply surrendered.

Suggested he talks to Sawyer about it and pushed onward.

I don't wanna fight more than we already have to.

Unless it's the sexy type that ends with one or both of us naked eating chocolate covered strawberries in a warm, Epsom salt bath – since bubbles aren't allowed according to Hamilton.

Between him and the man I – *typically* – adore my "do not do while pregnant" list is growing nine times faster than my waist size.

Wes releases a throaty groan and grips the outside of my thighs noticeably harder.

The harsh vibrations add to the voracious lashings in such an irresistibly delicious nature that I'm left with no choice but to latch on tighter to the freshly tussled locks my recently manicured nails refuse to relinquish their hold over and feverishly grind into them, random strands of hair instantly coming loose from the nonstop pleasure-filled head whipping.

"*More,*" slips free between increasingly breathless pants. "*More, Weston.*"

Ravenous rolls are ceaselessly delivered around and around and around and around my clit, only momentarily breaking to indulge in short sucks that have my toes curling in my black lace up heels. The points on my stilettos savagely stab at his shoulders blade, barbarously carving my pleas to come into his black dress shirt; however, each scrape he receives sparks a brutish grunt.

And every grunt gets buried deeper between my thighs.

And the deeper they get buried the more determined he becomes to unearth them.

To free the sounds by frantically diving his tongue in, desperate to rescue them from the darkest depths where they're likely to fall off climax's cliff.

His feral determination and devotion and dynamism pushes him to transition away from torturous teasing to sheer, unmatched devouring.

Withstanding the unrelenting undulation swiftly spikes to impossible levels as my bare ass practically levitates off the limo seat, powerlessly being summoned upward into the carnal cloud of cries I can't stop creating.

The higher I get, the more furiously his tongue works.

And works.

And plunges, perpetually scribbling his signature on any, tiny orgasmic shiver that spreads throughout my system.

"*Wesssss!*" surges itself out of my mouth at the same time I throw my head back in pure ecstasy. "*Wesssss!*" Additional hollering is offered up in hopes of mercy. "*Wessss!*" Blissful pulsations continue without any indication of ending. "*Wessss!*" His incessant swiping and sucking and lapping persists in spite of my screeching. "*Icanttakeany-*"

"Wes," Lurch's voice floods through the speakers in an even tone, "we are two minutes out."

At that, my fiancé unlatches his mouth from my lower lips, leans back onto his hunches to meet my gaze, and wolfishly grumbles, "*I guess I'll have to finish my dessert later, little prey.*"

Finish?!

What the fuck does he mean finish?!

I'm pretty sure there's nothing left for him to have!

I'm practically kin to Clayface who was actually in the comic I was reading while Greta Blank, the hair and makeup stylist I often use for more high-class events, did a marvelous job that my soon to be husband has successfully *undone.*

Wes swipes away the taste of me on his lips prior to shooting me a shit eating grin.

Oooooo, he's *so* lucky this event is about *my job* and not his.

Otherwise?

I'd take him into one of the private bathrooms and do something for us to switch smug expressions.

Then again…we still might.

Getting my black and sequin, high slit, dress returned to its *appropriate* position takes about the same amount of time it does for Wes to use the selection of complimentary offerings to clean his face and freshen his breath.

Again, if this was one of the many, *many* events for Wilcox Enterprises rather than The Institute I'd say fuck it.

Let his breath smell like mint and a good time.

But it's not.

I mean…he technically is one of their highest donors and *was invited* as such; however, he's here *for me.*

To be *my* arm candy.

To assist me in kissing ass and belugas and whatever else it is my bitch of a boss demands I do to show allegiance to our organization.

You know I *love* what I do…but I don't love doing it under *her.*

She's like having to answer to The Borg Queen.

And I won't assimilate!

I don't care what she does to me.

I refuse to join her hivemind bullshit.

Seriously.

What kind of deep-sea monster wants to get rid of meaningful celebrations for our precious ocean babies?!

I'm not saying we need to throw a party every time a clown fish pops out of an egg, but what's wrong with honoring their rescue dates or giving them goodbye parties like we did for Steven?

Who I *deeply* miss.

I've gotten to see him once in person since his transfer; however, their lead shark biologist constantly sends me photos and swears he's happy.

Assisting in the care of our new baby hammerhead – that I affectionately named Bruce – has been helping me cope.

He's definitely not the same.

Has an entirely different personality.

But I can already tell he loves me the most in the whole building regardless of what Calen claims.

Inside the underwater themed event, Lurch lingers near the front doors – close to, yet not in interfering range of the already established security – while Wes and I politely conversationally swim around the patrons over to the bar to order ocean themed beverages.

"Mocktails," my fiancé grunts in an almost confused fashion. "I can honestly say this will be a first for me."

"I thought the princess was supposed to be the virgin in these fairy tales," I teasingly wink.

The sight of his cheeks growing a crimson shade instantly gets me giggling, a sound that prompts a wide mouth grin despite his obvious embarrassment.

Thank fuck, Evie isn't around tonight.

I would have to keep these top of the food chain quips to myself.

"I'm curious what the current profit margins are for mocktails as well as non-alcoholic beer." Wes's hand adoringly lands on the small of my back. "And now I'm even more curious as to what the trajectory for such might be in the coming decade." Our eyes lock about the time the bartender begins shaking around the container. "Perhaps investing in *non-alcoholic* spirits is the new business endeavor I didn't know I needed."

It's impossible to keep a smile off my face. "Never wonder what you bring to the Wilcox legacy, Weston."

"*Never doubt what you bring to me, Brynley.*"

A faint swoon slips free prior to our mouths gravitating towards one another.

Unfortunately, what would've been a sentimental kiss is interrupted by a surprising voice, "How are you late to your own event?"

Angling ourselves to face Puppet Boy occurs at the same time I snip, "I'm not late. The gala started at eight. It's only eight fifteen, which means I arrived within the allotted range of reasonable or dare I say *fashionable* in this gown."

"It's a great dress," he flatly compliments in hopes of avoiding his other best friend's wrathful grumbles, "however, you're still late."

"Eight fifteen is not late!"

"It's eight forty-two."

"Since when?!"

"Since eight forty-one left."

His snarky response sparks Wes to chortle under his breath, something he does his best to hide by gliding me over my blue ocean mocktail.

"Maybe the question shouldn't be why am I possibly tardy-"

"*Definitely tardy.*"

"-but why are you *punctual* for an event you weren't even invited to?"

"Except I *was* invited to it," Puppet Boy's clarification precedes a hand motion for the bartender to make him one of the drinks too. "Wilcox Enterprises is a major donor for The Bower and Powell Institute therefore physical representation of the company is *highly* encouraged by the PR department." Impishness invades his expression. "I feel like as an employee of one and on her way to being a shareholder of the other you should really know that."

"And I feel you only get this cheeky when your balls have been emptied in the last twenty-four hours."

Wes damn near chokes from abruptly swallowing his beverage.

"*Name?*" I interrogate on a swift retrieval of my glass.

"Fionna."

"Occupation?"

"Didn't ask."

"Didn't care?"

"Nope." His shrug is innocent and indifferent. "We both just wanted to get laid with no strings attached."

"Been there." My glass is tipped in his direction. "*Approve that.*"

Puppet Boy grabs his freshly made drink during his explanation, "Life's...kind of...*insane* at the moment. There's the merger, the app, the off-quarter sales figures...not to mention what we've got going on personally with the recovery, the family uniting episode next week, and the wedding." The beverage is given an adjustment in his grasp. "I don't have time or the capacity to *date* right now."

"Just to get your dick touched." An enthusiastic nod is attached to my exclaiming. "I get it."

Wes's frame presses itself against mine again. "You get it because you've lived it, I'm assuming."

"*One hundred percent.*"

Both men lightly chuckle, although Puppet Boy's is short-lived courtesy of his sudden gagging. "What's wrong with this drink?!"

"It's non-alcoholic," the bartender professionally informs from the other side of counter.

"*Why?!*"

"*Pregnant.*" I gesture inward to my well-hidden stomach and then outward to my fiancé. "*Recovering.*"

"*Supportive,*" adds the male whose signature blue shade is being worn only in the form of a pocket square this evening as he lifts the glass in a cheers fashion. "Perhaps we should look into the non-alcoholic beverage industry next year. I wonder if it's a lucrative avenue or if maybe one that *could be* more lucrative in the coming years."

"*See,*" I mockingly tease, "Batman and Robin really *do* share one mind."

"*Nightwing,*" Puppet Boy playfully bites. "I am Nightwing in the analogy."

"Who was originally Robin," Wes points out on an amused beam.

"Which makes me Captain Rightcard."

"Speaking of the best franchise to ever exist," he smoothly segues while motioning us to make room for others to order drinks, "they're auctioning off a pair of five-day, all-inclusive passes to Talk Trekky to Me, the annual *Star Trek* convention held on South Haven Island every summer."

My blue drink being housed in a martini glass is carelessly splashed around. "*What?!*"

"Yeah, I'm already bidding on it – because I *have* to bid on something for the company's sake-"

"*Do you?*" Wes effortlessly pokes.

"-but I need you to *swear,* Uhura, that when I win them, you'll go with me."

"Absolutely!"

"You mean *if,*" the man with his arm nestled around my lower back poorly tries to correct.

"No, I mean *when.*" Puppet Boy shoots him a wink. "Those passes are mine."

"*Ours.*"

He nods in agreement and tips his head at me. "*Ours.*"

"And does my opinion regarding you whisking what will be my wife away for a five-day romantic nerdy vacation hold any sort of weight?"

"Not really," I respond on J.T.'s behalf and swim ahead to the more important question. "Now, *who* do we need to be watching as far as outbidding goes?" My gaze cuts to the direction where the silent auction items are on display. "And please be aware, I am not above pretending said individual proposes a threat to me in my poor pregnant feeble state so that Lurch *has* to remove them from the area."

"This is the real reason why Batman and Catwoman are a *feared* couple rather than beloved," Wes light heartedly interjects.

"It's Wheeler "Wheels" Gentry...who is also *performing* tonight apparently."

"The boyband dude from One Voice?!"

"You liked boybands?!" Puppet Boy immediately jeers back.

"I was a teenage girl once upon a time." Stealing a small sip is quick. "Of course, I liked boybands and then boys *in* bands."

"Wow," airily croaks my partner in *Star Trek* crime.

208

"Those who hung posters of TLC and Gwen Stefani and ArKturus – known as the off brand Enya – *really* shouldn't judge those may have enjoyed watching groups of young guys sing together when they were younger." The love of my life presents him with an arrogant grin. "*Just saying.*"

"*Batman* is supposed to have *Nightwing's* back," Puppet boy aggressively scolds with a pointed finger.

"Yeah, but Batman also likes getting his Batarang touched, so he has to stand with pussy."

"*Cat,*" grunts Wes while guiding his drink up this mouth, "and I would really appreciate if *both* of you stopped referring to my cock that way."

"*Nah,*" the two of us chime in tandem before open mouth laughing.

More grumbles of unhappiness leave him, yet he secretly smiles.

Not so secretly relishes in the fact two of the most important people in his life love each other as well as him.

"Why don't you go bid on our dream bro bonding trip while *we,*" my free hand gestures between me and the man at my side, "go avoid my boss who is coming this direction by hiding in the jewelry section?"

Splitting in opposite directions is wordlessly done as is the beginning of what I can easily brand to be needless gem browsing.

I don't *need* anymore.

I have my airplane necklace, an array of Evie approved accessories, and my engagement ring.

I see no point in adding to the collection.

"I love that these are all made in labs rather than pilfered from the ocean." Our browsing of the pearl section is quick; however, the aquamarine one is much slower. "I *also* love that a portion of every purchase from this area tonight will go towards the ocean clean up department of our organization." Wes leads us to a complete stop. "Honestly? They kind of get shafted when it comes to budget."

His attention momentarily falls to me.

"I know we only have 'so much money' but they're *always* first to lose their funding. I swear they might as well just be called volunteers at this point."

"Let's change that, shall we?" Before I can ask questions, he taps his fingers near a pair of aquamarine cufflinks. "For J.T.?" Our eyes meet again. "They should pair well with…ninety percent of his closet contents, correct?"

There's no point in holding in my snickers.

"Why don't we also get something for Lauren?" The blonde woman in charge of this section across from us gasps in what I imagine to be excitement. "It can be gift to the mother of the bride."

"She gets gifts?!" my squawking causes him to chortle. "I have to buy *her* gifts?! I thought the whole point of getting married was so other people bought *us* gifts?!"

"That is not the *only* point to being married; however, it is an important one," an older, attractive, accented male unexpectedly chuckles from beside me. "And although I am not married, I am inclined to agree with you, Miss Winters." He flashes me an irresistible grin. "Other people most certainly *should* be bestowing upon you lavish gifts."

Amusement dances around my gaze as I ask, "Have we met?"

"Not in an official capacity, I'm afraid." The male extends an open palm in my direction. "Trenton Kenningston."

"As in *the* Kenningston?!" My voice squeaks while we shake. "As in the *K* in The K&T Aquatic Institute?!"

"*Technically*, I am both the K and the T." He indulges in a sip of champagne. "There is not an actual second founder. The T I use is for *Turner*. It is the last name of the woman I love but unfortunately lost due to my own selfish mistakes." Noticeable sadness coats his crystal gaze. "That woman is the entire reason I started K&T. The

210

institutes – both the one in South Haven and the one in Doctenn, my home country – are my *more therapeutically approved* way of coping with the heart wrenching agony of a life without her. She loved the ocean and every creature in it."

An almost whispered awe escapes as the man I know who understands his pain extends a kind hand in his direction. "Weston. Weston Wilcox."

"The billionaire."

Reluctantly, he nods at the label. "Yes."

"Your whiskey is the only one my family drinks."

"High praise to know that I'm up to *literal* royal standards."

"Royalty?!" escapes me prior to my better half pointing to box up the cufflinks. "I don't remember reading about you being royalty?!"

"I tend to have them leave that out of my bio section," he haughtily laughs on a casual shrug. "Brother of the king somewhat distracts from the cause I believe." At that, he motions a hand. "The cause in which I have heard you have done wonders for in R&R. *So* many wonders in fact, that I am tempted to see what it would take to get you to relocate *to* K&T permanently as opposed to simply working *with us* in the partnership the two institutes have."

"I would be tempted to consider it given that you now have a huge hunk of my heart in one of your tanks."

His head tilts in question. "Oh?"

"*Steven*," Wes replies for me after shaking his head the jewelry woman regarding a giftbag. "He's a young, scalloped hammerhead. You recently acquired him for breeding purposes." He places his glass down on the case. "And it broke my fiancée's heart not only having to say goodbye but to be unaware of *when* she can visit him in agreement with her busy schedule."

"An *easy* fix if you switch institutes."

"*Or*," begins the man whose grip on me tightens, "an easy fix if *you*, the head of the organization, simply gives me a number of his

211

choosing to donate – *yearly* – in order to grant my future wife unlimited access to visit her best – fin bearing – friend."

"And when you say unlimited access, you mean…?"

"It doesn't matter if it's two o'clock on a Tuesday or three A.M. on Christmas."

"*Wes,*" I whisper out in objection.

"That shark means everything to *her*, and she means everything to *me*." His statement is followed by a brief glance at the blonde in charge of jewelry. "Find me something for my mother-in-law. Simple. Not showy. Wrist or neck, not hand." The instant she nods in understanding he returns his focus back to the other male. "Paying for her to have an all-access pass while giving to a good cause seems like a better idea than installing our own personal shark tank on the estate grounds and *purchasing* Steven outright; however, if that is where this conversation ends then so be it."

"*You can't be serious,*" is hissed out in a hushed tone.

Can he?

Can he *actually* have a shark tank built on our property?!

Holy fuck, can he actually buy me a shark?!

Wait.

Should he?

Would that be a good idea?

I mean it would be for *me* but not the poor creature.

"Alright." Trenton's smile threatens to blind us in the dimly lit event. "Your fiancée can have full access anytime day or night to visit Steven."

"The cost?"

"A favor."

"I'm listening."

"My nephew, Kellan, has his own charity foundation that helps foster homeless children. Unfortunately, due to his decision to marry someone of a different ethnicity, his funding is enduring a bit of a financial snag. He will – most likely sooner rather than later – need an

212

additional backer who possesses a significant amount of *clout* to his name."

"Wilcox *does* possess such clout." A warm-hearted smile slides into the conversation. "Regardless of him *needing* my clout or not, it would be an honor to support a worthy cause. I'm always in search of places where I can actually see the funding making a difference to the organization versus those who run it."

The member of the royal family tips his glass towards him. "*Cheers to that.*"

New waves of awe wash over me to the point I'm left speechless.

Literally.

Speechless.

Of all the things he could've said or done to *show* that he's not only sorry but understands *me*, understands what really lights up my life, this isn't one that would've ever crossed my mind.

"*Ohgod, not that,*" Trenton abruptly criticizes the piece of jewelry the woman is presenting. "My deceased mother wouldn't dare wear that on her wrist even in her grave."

His blunt refusal receives warm laughs from us. Afterward, we resume shopping alongside casually chit chatting, the two of them mostly ironing out paperwork and timing details while I pick out something appropriate for my mom.

And Vanessa.

And Calen.

Calen who, to my surprise, I haven't seen yet.

I wonder if his ass is shoveling back sushi in private knowing I can't have any.

Post purchasing presents – that they'll hold until we return ready to leave the event – we ditch our empty mocktail glasses and relocate to the "Trench of Treats", the hallway like area where various food vendors are offering bite size samples of their seafood specialties.

213

Too many of which I can't fucking have!

Wes pointing to seaweed based dishes has me repeatedly gagging – an action he does his best to apologize to each of the vendors about during our passing – however the second I sprint away to fuss at Calen, he abandons his efforts of kindness to maintain his position at my side.

"*How. Dare. You.*" The sharp finger wag he receives is executed in tandem with an unforgiving glare. "*You're over here shoveling back Tuna Tataki with jalapenos like a fucking whale shark while the most I can have is seaweed wrapped avocado?!*"

My best friend guilty swallows the contents of his mouth. "I-"

"*Betrayal!*"

"I-"

"*Absolute. Betrayal.*"

"I wasn't the one who knocked you up," he playfully jeers back between wiping his fingers clean with his napkin. "You wanna be pissy at someone about you not being able to eat fish the way you want?" Calen kicks his chin at Wes. "*Be mad at him.*"

"Oh, she is," my fiancé jovially jabs. "*Livid* almost every meal we have."

"No one should have to eat this many vegetables!"

"Stop yelling," chuckles the man I haven't seen in a couple days courtesy of him prepping for his return to school. "We're at a nice event *for work*, not in the back room *at work*."

A second glare is quickly shot in his direction and more laughter can't be helped.

And here's another reason why I could never leave our institute for K&T.

I couldn't make it without him.

I wouldn't *want* to make it without him.

He's been there for anything and everything I needed, especially during the rocky time with Wes.

Giving him up would suck worse than giving up Steven.

And that shit sucked like a Starfleet exam I have to pass or risk flunking out of the academy.

"Date?" I casually investigate around enjoying the delicious fragrance of the food I can't consume.

"Stone," he announces on a defeated shrug. "Trying to get school shit setup sort of took priority over finding someone to come with me." Calen tosses the crumpled napkin into the nearby garbage. "It's all good though. He gets good press, and I get a gold star for bringing a celebrity guest."

"Who's Stone?" Wes quickly inquires.

"Levi Stone." Calen meets his stare. "He's an actor."

"*And super fucking hot,*" is less than quietly murmured.

"And you're *super fucking engaged,*" the male across from me warmly laughs.

"Yes." Leaning into his hold is absentmindedly done. "Yes, you are."

A playful eye roll precedes me announcing, "Since we're on the subject of shackling-"

"I do not approve of that language."

"-and pregnancy brain fog comes and goes, I can't remember if you got my text about the date and venue changes."

He casually nods and struggles not to twitch a glare at Wes.

Can't blame him.

Calen wiped away a lot of tears and fed me even more sandwiches.

"*Thank you,*" unexpectedly leaves the very person that makes him want to glower.

His twitched brow isn't a surprise. "*Excuse me?*"

"*Thank you,*" he repeats without vacilation. "For being there for Bryn, *especially* when I wasn't."

Nodding barely precedes him blunting stating, "She deserves better than you."

"*Dude!*"

215

"I agree."

My mouth twitches yet isn't given a chance to let sound escape. "Break her heart again, and I'll break my board over your head."

"*Bro!*"

"*Understood.*" Wes extends a hand towards him. "*Completely.*"

"Good." Their shaking occurs despite my objection. "Now, please take our Little Grrrmaid elsewhere. I wanna eat my weight in Smoked Trout Roulades and not feel like I'm being watched by the judgmental child who got separated from her tour group just in time to disapprovingly watch the shark's daily feeding."

One word is attached to his crooked grin. "Descriptive."

"*Accurate.*" Calen shifts his stare over to me. "I can no longer fuckin' chew cinnamon gum at work."

"Forgive me for not wanting to smell spicy fish ass all day."

A mirth-filled hand gesture precedes him muttering, "I rest my case, Mega Millions."

"*Billions,*" is the only word I manage to get out thanks to Wes leading me back towards the main area for dancing.

Or at least what I *hope* is dancing.

The idea of standing *near* the DJ but not moving to the music isn't appealing.

We can pretty much do that *anywhere* around the room.

Dancing should be done closest to the music.

And hopefully Wheels plays "Wheel Woman" because that song was *so* my song when I was in college.

Easy listening jazz like tunes flow out of the speakers surrounding the dance floor and rather than complain or request a change, we decide to just go with it.

Enjoy the random change in our personal music scape.

Shockingly, my typically reserved partner is nowhere to be found.

The man spinning and twirling and dipping me when he's not executing shimmies and sultry hip thrusts is *not* the same one, I've been to almost a hundred of these things with.

No.

This one couldn't care less about who is watching or taking our picture.

He can't even seem to spark up a fuck to give about what others might say regarding his hand occasionally on my ass or his tongue repeatedly in my mouth.

GeordiLaForgehavemercy, do men get weird hormone spikes during this pregnancy thing too?!

Or is this all...just part of him keeping his promise to keep showing up *for me* like he claims I've always shown up *for him*?

Wes slyly slips his leg in between mine that are slightly parted to allow a closer grinding motion; however, before it can really get good – and by good, I mean result in that bathroom bang I'm now thinking about again – we're joined by someone who is more interested in my moves than his in the sex aspect.

"Hate to be a tendy here," Jenni awkwardly interjects, "but I think we've got a problem."

"Why are you here?" I less than warmly ask. "Who sent you? Was it Evie? Did she tell you that we couldn't be trusted unsupervised?"

"*Ohnonono*," brushes off the energetic, young woman, "she doesn't even know I'm here."

"Then *why* are you here, Miss Cohen?" Wes unhappily grumbles. "Disrupting my fiancée's mandatory appearance?"

"Technically, I'm here to *support* The Institute. My brother was invited by one his teammates – although I, personally, think they're secretly dating – who is a *huge* fan of P&B, having grown up in the area and taken like *so many* school fields trips to it, and he himself donates and them being here is great PR for the club – and they need it, the Dragons suck so bad in every department – and since

217

he's in *my town*, he thought it'd be a good idea for me to tag along with them, so here I am popping champers and shrimp cocktail pretending I'm not excited to hear Wheels sing even though I so totally am."

An all-knowing wink is shot at Wes.

"And now the reason you're *here* interrupting us instead of fangirling in secret elsewhere?"

"*Right!*" Her long fingers deliver a tiny tap to the middle of her forehead. "Okay, so cas' look to the left and find the tiny blond in the short silk dress. She's gonna be past the woman with one sleeve puffy shit, but if you've spotted the woman with the fish head sticking out of her drink you've gone too far-"

"*Whythefuckdoesshehaveafishinherdrink?!*"

"Found," Wes announces, prompting me to abandon boarding the train of curiosity for whatever one Jenni is requesting.

"The blonde that's talking to my boss?" I nonchalantly investigate. "What about her?"

"That's Monica's assistant." We cut our glares to Jenni in tandem. "As in *the* Monica Simmons." An uncomfortable cringe is quickly flashed. "As in the woman who seems to have an *inside source* on all things Bryn, Wes, and Wilcox drama related... I recognize her from the day they came to the office to confront you about your lineage. Monica instructed her to wait at the coffee shop across the street rather than go *with her* to the meeting."

"*Holyshit,*" doesn't finish leaving my lips before I'm jetting off in the direction with them on my heels.

"*Uh...Bryn?*" Jenni poorly attempts to stop me. "*Um...don't you think-*"

"This Gamma Quadrant, female changeling cunt, is the one leaking information about us to the media?!"

Jenni fumbles out another effort to intervene, "*Maybe we should-*"

218

"You Bajoran Wormhole using bitch!" One hard push on the back of Raquel's shoulder stumbles her around. "You've been selling my personal shit to the fucking press!"

Her expression pales at the same time her mouth drops to lie. *"It's not what you-"*

"Of course it's what I fucking think!" I loudly huff prompting the female she was talking with try to bail. *"Ohnoyoufuckingdon't."* A harsh finger is thrown at her. "Move another goddamn inch, and I will rip out every strand of your extensions like a fucking bull shark frenzied by chum."

The unidentified blonde squeaks, yet completely freezes.

"You're the leak?" Wes questions in a calmly eerie tone. *"You're* the source that's spoon-feeding information not meant for the general public *to* the public?"

Raquel immediately croaks, *"I'm-"*

"It would be wise of you not to waste my time with lies, Ms. Lane, as the longer you lie, the *worse* this situation will play out for you," he leans menacingly forward, *"indefinitely."*

While moaning over his power flex is my first instinct, it's momentarily suppressed by the new level of irateness coursing through my veins.

"You have one chance," my future husband practically growls, entire body straining to stay in place. *"Use it."*

Her red stained lip gets pinned harshly between her teeth.

"Now."

"Monica said it wasn't a breach of contract," Raquel rushes to explain. "That the NDA I signed didn't cover second handed conversations I had *or* conclusions I came to based on information I gathered."

"Like finding my pregnancy test in the fucking trash?!"

A small sigh of surrender precedes her whispered confession. "Yes."

"Sonofawhore!" The frustrated lunge I make in her direction is barely stopped by the man beside me. *"How could you fucking do this to me?!"* Wes tightens his hold around my waist to keep beside him. *"How could you betray me?! How could you break the trust of your employee?!"* All of a sudden, something else hits me like a brick of whale sharks. *"Is that why you've put me on desk duty in the office closest to yours?!"* Additional outrage has my voice rising once more. *"So that you can literally hear my conversations through the fucking wall?!"*

"Mr. Wilcox," Lurch's voice forcefully intrudes. "Is there a problem here?"

"There is," he replies, voice sinking to an alarming, low tone. "Please alert Park that we have *two* level one situations we need handled."

"Yes, Sir," the large male responds prior to touching the device in his ear.

"And unless you would like that situation to end with you raising your child via video chat from a foreign country, I suggest you explain to me *why* you breeched your contract."

"Monica said-"

"Monica lied!" I shriek garnering more attention.

"She didn't *lie*," her assistant tries to inject into the conversation. "She simply manipulated the definition of the truth."

There's no stopping me from stomping my foot. "That's a lie!"

"That makes *you* liable for buying into it. *And* the loopholes, Monica has led you to believe she legally circumvented, my team will undoubtedly prove were actually still breeched." Wes states, reclaiming the conversation. "The cost of betrayal is most certainly high financially speaking."

"That's why I did it!" my boss hopelessly professes. "I've got a shitty ex-husband that doesn't pay *shit* to help his dying fucking daughter that's in the hospital waiting for a transplant! That shit isn't free! Keeping her alive isn't free! Trying to figure out how to fucking

220

live not knowing if she's going to make it another day or seven or thirty-seven is exhausting and costly and I…I…I…did the only thing I thought I could do to help the situation! I did what I thought was best for my daughter!"

"*You put my family in jeopardy to save yours,*" my fiancé coldly claims on a chilling step forward. "*That was a deadly mistake.*"

Chapter 23

Wes

The last time I was this sick to my stomach I was coming off quite an awful bender.

This time it's because I'm about to confess to the entire world – on a *live* streaming event – my family's deep, dark, dirty little secret they had successfully kept hidden for literal decades.

Why wouldn't I feel like I'm about to fucking vomit everything I've consumed since the last time I felt this way?

"*Stop it*," Evie hisses from her position directly in front of me in our Frost Luxury Hotel suite living room area. "*You're going to start sweating again.*" She less than gently dabs at my forehead. "Hair and makeup *just* fixed you."

I poorly swallow my grumbles and glance to the left where I catch Bryn finally ending her call on a polite note. "I'll be in touch." She carelessly tosses the device on the nearby bar counter, flicks a messy loose strand away from her blue mascara coated eyelashes, and exasperatedly sighs, "Gotta admit. That shit went better for me than it did when Kirk faced the Academy Board."

Leaning into the urge to smile isn't resisted. "It should've considering *you* weren't the one who cheated in this scenario."

"Uh, I'm with Kirk on that one. You creating a 'no-win' test is cheating."

"I'm with Spock," I effortlessly counter. "He missed the point the test was trying to make."

"Is this heaven's lobby?" J.T. interjects from beside me around light chuckles. "Are we really *all* engaging in a highbrow *Star Trek* debate?"

"Not all of us," Evie sneers.

Grateful for the distraction, I redirect the conversation back to Bryn, "What happened?"

"Well, after Renee Drake, the *head* of the entire board, felt reassured that I wasn't going to sue the organization, which would practically bankrupt them-"

"Wouldn't it just be Wilcox money either way?" my best friend ponders out at the same time he crosses one, navy blue covered pant leg over the other.

"-she offered me Raquel's job." A small tug at the belt of her bright yellow, floor length, gathered shirtdress is given. "And *educationally* I'm *beyond* qualified to do it. Experiencely-"

"Not a word."

"-on the other fin, I'm not so sure. Running an *entire* department is vastly different than running a rescue team."

"Vastly might be an oversell, little prey."

Her quirked eyebrow indicates she's listening.

"To effectively run a department, you *are* running a team. It may be bigger, there may be more on the line, and there will ultimately be larger scale consequences as well as rewards; however, the fundamentals are the same. The skills that make you great at R&R are what will make you fantastic as head of the department. You know the employees. You know the animals. You know the handbook *and* the aquatic governing laws you must abide by."

"That was the *least* amount of fun I've ever had playing trivia," J.T. announces on an adjustment of his rolled pant leg. "*Just FYI.*"

I hate that I wasn't a part of that preparation.

I hate that I wasn't around to help her study.

Focus.

Build her confidence.

I hate that my own blindness prevented me from being involved in such a crucial transition for her.

And I hate that my own ego almost fucking impeded me from another.

There won't be a third.

That's my word.

"You want the job?" I bluntly question.

"I don't know that I want the paperwork," she sassily teases. "Then again, I could just hire an assistant to handle all that shit right. That's all Zaidee does for you, isn't it?"

"*Incorrect.*"

Laughter bounces between us prior to her professing, "Honest to Spock? *I do want it.*"

There's no use in hiding my proud beam.

"And it makes sense *for me* – career wise – with Calen changing over to veterinary in the coming weeks as well as not being able to be – *legally* – in the field until our little pup is born."

"Is pup gonna be my niece or nephew's nickname?"

"*Nephew,*" Bryn firmly declares despite not knowing that to be true, "and probably not. It's just our placeholder until we start looking at names."

"I understand child names are completely up to you two, but are *uncle* nicknames up for debate?"

"Calen asked me the same shit."

Our son or daughter is lucking out in that department.

Relatively speaking.

While I *plan* to do everything I possibly can to warmly welcome Monica into the Wilcox family, she hasn't exactly made it easy.

Baiting me into this public haranguing.

Bribing my future wife's boss into regurgitating private and personal incriminating information.

Belittling each fucking decision my brand has made in *every* aspect of business.

The woman is a menace.

224

However, through therapy exercises and fatherly advice from Clark – who is currently helping Lauren prepare a get to know you meal for us all at their home – I am going to persist in trying to develop a relationship with her if that's what she wants.

In her mind…she's been rejected her entire existence.

I just happen to be the only one alive for her to seek penance from.

Would it be great if my son or daughter got to refer to her as *Aunt Monica*?

Sure.

Do I think that's likely?

Not at all.

Which is quite alright.

Vanessa will play the role fantastically.

She's already shopping for "tamer" playing at the park clothing.

And as for uncles, J.T. and Calen absolutely have that covered.

Taking into account the allegiance and dedication Calen provided my fiancée in my absence, it's safe to assume, he's trustworthy, and once you add in the not so ideal threat, he made to me at this past Thursday, I have no doubts that he has what it takes to *protect* his future niece or nephew from whatever the world throws at them.

I may not *love* their relationship, but I respect it.

Them.

Him.

I owe the guy more than I had the opportunity to express at the event, so I'm hoping after his educational program sends him an email to confirm his entire tuition has been paid in full that he understands my deep gratitude.

If that doesn't do it, perhaps getting an alert that he's now completely debt free might.

"I've got a week to consider my options," Bryn announces at the same time she snatches up a package I don't recognize. "So...*for now*...let's focus on *you*. And *our* family."

She's flashed a small smile.

"Starting with these." The opening of her box is theatrical. "They're chocolate peanut butter stuffed hunks of foodgasms." She waits until I've grabbed one to dangle it in front of J.T. "They're from Yasmine's Yummies who *will* be catering our wedding." Post him grabbing one, she offers them to Evie – who declines – and Jenni – who doesn't. "The owner, Yasmine, is a total baking badass, by the way." I watch her saunter across the room to deliver one to Holmes and Hill. "She told me her specialty is *non-traditional* treats, so we could pretty much request whatever we want, no questions asked. We want it? She'll figure out how to fucking make it."

Pleased that my other half has not only returned to planning our wedding but genuinely seems excited about it, prompts me to smile.

Wide.

Bryn's mouth begins to move again yet is unfortunately interrupted by a knock on the door beside her.

Holmes gestures her away with his cookie bearing hand and cautiously checks the peephole. "*Name?*"

"Joel." The timid voice from the other side of the door announces. "*Joel Righetti.*" A short pause presents itself. "One of the filming assistants with today's event."

My stomach instantly drops.

Returns to its previous unsettled state.

"*Badge?*" Holmes demands, face still smushed against the blockade.

Post another brief lull, my security guard grants him access inside, making sure to snag a bite of the cookie in his possession prior to ushering the young man my direction.

"It's time to get you mic'ed, Mr. Wilcox."

I nervously nod and prepare to rise to my feet when my wife to be sternly points. *"Eat your cookie."*

The loving scolding has me bobbing my head in agreement. Indulging.

As much as I would rather have a shot of alcohol to steady my nerves a rush of sugar beats the shit out of nothing.

Together, me and my entire entourage relocate to the area where numerous cameras are waiting to hit record.

To plaster my face all over screens worldwide.

My team positions themselves on the side wall near the door to be out of the way of the cameras; however, before I can join Monica in the presentation space she's created, the love of my life abruptly winds both arms around my neck and knocks her mouth into mine.

Our lips spread just enough to allow a brief brushing of our tongues, but it's enough.

Enough to reassure me everything will be fine.

Enough to remind me that unlike what I had convinced myself earlier in this journey to be the truth, I'm not alone.

I'll never *be* alone.

When Bryn pulls back, she adoringly whispers, *"I love you, Mr. Wayne."*

Warmth spreading throughout my chest has me cooing, *"And I love you, Miss Kyle."*

One affectionate squeeze of shoulders from her along with one supportive nod from J.T. propels me to the area where Monica is adjusting her blouse. She doesn't even bother looking up when she comments on my wardrobe, "How nice of you to wear black *and* a touch of white, Wes." The bright lighting around us is moved around a smidge. "It will help emphasize the transparency your family lacks." At that, she lets her gaze find mine. *"I mean our family."*

Instead of giving into the instinct to glare and gripe about how ridiculous she's being, I merely straighten my spine and push my shoulders back.

Lift my chin.

Inhale a deep breath and remember that hiding her from the world was *our father's choice.*

Not mine.

I don't speak for him.

I speak for me.

The man I am.

The one he raised me to be.

The one I have taught myself to become.

"Ooooo, silent and brooding," mocks Monica while angling her crossed legs in my direction. "Saving it all for the cameras." She brushes her dark locks over her shoulder. "*Love it.*"

And I will love when this is over.

There isn't much of a delay between her last statement and the first she makes into the cameras, "Hello, everyone. I'm Monica Simmons with Global Laundry and am fortunate enough to be sitting here with the recently engaged, billionaire, philanthropist, Weston Wilcox of Wilcox Enterprises to conduct an *exclusive* interview regarding some striking accusations that have been made regarding his lineage."

I keep my increasingly sweaty palms on my black casual pants as I politely greet, "Hello, Monica."

"You are known for being the *sole heir* to the extensive Wilcox fortune, correct?"

"Yes."

"However, *recently*, there's been documentation presented to you regarding the *possibility* that that fact, isn't a fact after all, correct?"

Additional tightening occurs in my chest during my answering, "Yes."

"And how did you *respond* when you first received the news?"

Like a recalcitrant child with easy access to alcohol.

"I struggled to process the idea," slips past my lips in the open, honest tone Evie coached me into showcasing. "I had been led to believe my entire life that I was an only child, so the notion of that not being true, the concept that those who loved me could keep something like that to themselves, hurt." My stare stays locked onto hers. "*Deeply.*"

Against her own volition sympathy is flashed in her stare. "I completely understand."

Yes, Batman's greatest foes often have the most tragic backstories themselves.

"Since receiving the claim, would you say you and your team have been provided with adequate time to review it?"

Adequate is a bit of a fucking stretch.

"Yes."

"And now that you have, how do you feel in comparison to your initial feelings?"

"*Informed.*"

My response receives a curious twitch of her brow. "Oh?"

"Analyzing and exploring and investigating the allegations brought new insight to who my parents were, who they surrounded themselves with, and the lengths they felt were necessary to go to in order to do what *they* believed to be right for *them, their marriage,* and *the brand* at the time."

"Do you agree with their decisions?"

"It is not my place to agree or disagree. To judge or condemn." One hard swallow is abruptly stolen. "And I cannot and *will not* be held accountable for *their* decisions, simply my own."

The response seems to displease her by the tightening of her mouth. "*Which are?*"

"I agreed to a *non-bias,* 3rd party DNA test to confirm the individual in question is indeed a blood relative. Once the information is verified, I will provide them documentation that gives them their rightful shares – *from my existing shares* – that should've been theirs

229

upon our shared parent's death compensating them financially and welcoming them into the brand." My fingers fold together between proclamations. "*And* me, my fiancée, my best friend – also known as the face of the company – as well as a few other important people in my personal life will be inviting this person over for an early dinner this evening. If the test proves that we are related, we look forward to getting to know all about them."

Her mouth stumbles in what I am assuming is shock. "*You're just going to welcome them with open arms?*"

"Yes." Maintaining eye contact isn't difficult. "Because that is one of *my choices*, which are the only ones I am to be held responsible for."

Monica sucks in a deep breath, nods, and resumes her media stoic presence to the cameras. "For those watching, I'm sure you're wondering about the aforementioned person. Who they are. What they do. Where they came from." Her nude pump bearing ankles cross. "Well, the potential long, lost heir, is *me*." She pauses for what I'm sure she's envisioning to be a sea of gasps from those watching. "My mother Marzia Simmons passed away late last year after a lengthy battle with pancreatic cancer."

According to what I read, it was brutal.

For them both.

I used to wonder what was worse.

The abrupt, unexpected death of losing a loved one, or the slower, longer agony of watching them go.

On one page, they're basically here one moment and gone the next, leaving you with questions and what ifs, yet only memories of their life, while on the other page, when it's paced out, you may be left with all the answers, no missed opportunities of time with them, but a haunting, hard to shake mental picture of their final days.

Truthfully, I don't believe either side is harder than the other.

I believe both sides are difficult and painful.

Just different types.

"On her deathbed, she revealed to me a relationship with a man named Will Cox that she had kept hidden for my entire life. She explained how he was the most important man she'd ever had in her life and after her death – like a good journalist – I went in search of him and answers. That search is what led to me discovering that Will Cox was an alias used by billionaire, William Willard Wilcox." Another opportunity is given for the audience to react. "Upon this finding, I extended my exploration and when the time was best, reached out to Wes to collaborate my deductions only to uncover he had no idea."

Of course, she's going to paint herself as the fucking saint instead of a snake in this scenario.

"We agreed to him and his team conducting their own investigation as well as the DNA test that was mentioned, which we will *now* be reading the results of." Her hand lifts to make a summoning motion. "My assistant is now presenting me with the *sealed* information."

The blonde from the other night wordlessly delivers her the envelope doing her best not to make eye contact with me.

That's wise.

I haven't quite decided her fate yet.

Raquel not only has *multiple* restraining orders against her regarding my family – and extended family – she's lost her job and has been blackballed to the point that minimum wage won't simply be a starting point but *the only point* she reaches for decades to come.

Based on the amount of pain and misery she caused me – and more importantly *the love of my life* – she should consider herself grateful I didn't sentence her to death, a thought that did cross my mind until I realized I would be hurting an innocent child in the process.

Taking away their only real parent.

Practically orphaning them.

Abruptly.

231

Like I was.

The choice to let her live was certainly merciful and said mercy continued when a charity stepped in to help cover the cost of her daughter's hefty medical bills – in their entirety – as well as provide cost-of-living funds to her for a few months.

Charities can be wonderful like that.

Particularly the ones I donate to.

She nods to the young woman in a dismal fashion prior to meeting my gaze. "You ready?"

As ready as I can be to have my family's legacy destroyed in the press.

A cordial grin is forced onto my face. "Whenever you are."

Monica victoriously smirks, slides her finger along the edge to open it, and smoothly slides out the results. "Antecedentcorp – out of Vlasta, Wisconsin – was contracted to provide a more *objective* test and testing facility given its location." Her attention drops to the paperwork. "According to the highly accredited organization, Weston William Wilcox and me, Monica Leigh Simmons, are not genetically related."

It's impossible to stop myself from leaning forward, certain I misheard her. *"Excuse me?"*

"The test says..." her jaw bobs in bewilderment, "that...we're...*not* genetically...related." My brow pulls together in blatant confusion as her watery stare shifts to mine. "I am *not* your half-sister."

Chapter 24

Brynley

There are miracles.

And then there are *miracles*.

Kirk not dying on that ice planet in the *Star Trek* movie...miracle.

Kirk running into old Spock, getting over to the outpost, and then beamed back onto a moving Enterprise?

Miracle.

The difference is noticeable.

And significant.

And life altering.

Just like this is.

"You know these episodes of *Maury* are a lot less fun when no one flips over a chair in excitement," I juvenilely joke between bites of my chocolate, peanut butter cookie. "Or frustration. Or sadness. Or really just at all." Another nibble is taken as I lean back onto the couch I'm occupying. "Our life needs more chair flips in it."

Evie covers the receiver to her phone and hisses at me, "No, it doesn't."

"You're biased."

"You're a headache."

"But a beautiful one, especially in yellow," Jenni compliments prior to ushering me and Wes's personal publicist to the other side of the room to resume PR damage control.

You know, you'd think finding out he *doesn't* secretly have a sibling would be a dream come true for her, yet it isn't.

Apparently, it's just a new nightmare she wasn't prepared for.

And she *hates* not being prepared for shit.

The woman is basically a doomsday prepper for public relations.

This was not on her approved disaster list.

She's pissed.

But my future husband?

He seems…perplexed.

Perhaps even a little disheartened.

Puppet Boy drops down onto the seat cushion beside me at the same time he asks, "Wanna talk about it?"

Wes abruptly ceases his pacing to meet his best friend's stare and reply, "Yes."

The two of us brace ourselves for listening.

"*But not with you.*"

"Ouch?" J.T. retorts, clearly confused regarding the right response to have.

"I think we need to go talk to Monica."

"I don't think so!" Evie screeches in the background.

Ignoring her is fairly easy considering how often I do it. "When you say we do you happen to mean like the *royal* we?"

"No." His hands casually slide into his pockets. "I mean the *actual* we. As in you and me."

"As in you, Wes, and me, Bryn?"

"Say it in an octave lower and that shit would sound like Tarzan porn," Puppet Boy impishly points out under his breath.

My mouth twitches a smirk when the man standing definitely states, "*Yes.* We as in the two of us. Together. United." Wes lets his head angle slightly to the side. "I want you there with me." He briefly presses his lips together before correcting. "*I need you there with me.*"

"For an alilie?"

"*Alibi,*" corrects the male beside me.

"Depends on what he plans to do to her once we're inside her room."

"*Talk.*"

234

Pursing my lips together in disgust can't be helped.

"Look, putting aside the test results-"

"We should *not* put those aside," I swiftly interject while shaking my head. "We should definitely *focus* on those. On the fact you are *not* related. That that fucking head hunting Hirogen *isn't* going to be an aunt to our unborn child."

"*Ooph,*" mumbles Puppet Boy. "She brought out *Voyager.* That's a new level of hatred, dude."

Wes struggles not to smirk at the comment prior to sighing, "I understand where you're coming from, little prey-"

"Then this conversation should be over."

"*However-*"

"I hate that word almost more than that show."

"*However*...Monica and I are still connected."

"A restraining order will take care of that."

"Despite those test results, my father *did* have an affair with *her* mother."

Chomping on my cookie is the only rebuttal I can make.

"My father *was* around for *her* birth."

Another harsh bite is executed.

"And he cared enough about the two of them to go to extreme lengths to ensure they were well taken care of, *literally* until her dying day."

Slowly chewing what remains in its entirety becomes my wordless surrender.

"She's most likely hurting, Bryn." The sight of his shoulders falling prompts my own to do the same. "She has no one else in her life. She most likely feels abandoned. Helpless. Hopeless. Isolated. Like the only thing she has left in this world is work." Undeniable sympathy invades his stare. "*I know exactly what that's like.*"

Loud, theatrical moans and groans and grumbles precede my huffed proclamation. "And let this serve as another example of why the sexy, leather clad jewel thief was hesitant to hook up with the superhero in the comics."

"Because he was a better person than she was?" Puppet Boy teases at the same time he stretches his arm along the back of the couch.

"*Obviously,*" I sassily snip, rise to my feet, and cross over to the man I know I'd cross galaxies for. The second I'm within reach, his hands circle around my waist prompting me to playfully whisper, "Being first officer on this mission is going to cost you, Captain."

"Expected." He doesn't hesitate to smirk. "Name your price."

"A trip to see Steven tomorrow after couple's therapy."

"Fine print?"

"We spend the night with him."

"And?"

"And…you…arrange for me to do his feeding the next day."

I'm given another crooked grin. "*We have a deal, Brynley.*"

"*Pleasure doing business with you, Weston.*"

Our agreement is sealed with a soft kiss that encourages Puppet Boy to grouse, "You two make me hate being single."

"Remember," my fingers lovingly fold with Wes's, "Number One found love."

"Eventually."

"Eventually is better than not at all, Riker."

J.T. gives me a half-hearted shrug. "I suppose."

A friendly wink is shot in his direction prior to allowing my fiancé to lead us out of the suite with Holmes for protection against all of Evie's objections.

If I didn't know any better, I'd think my capeless vigilante is actually enjoying watching her panic.

Maybe I've rubbed off on him more than I realized.

I definitely enjoy rubbing him off more than *he* realizes.

Then again…he might have an idea after this morning's rub and tug in the shower.

Our journey several floors down to Monica's room occurs in silence.

Assuming Wes is using the time to properly collect his thoughts is what keeps me quiet, yet my own urges to unleash my inner bull shark for the shit she put *me* through threaten to have me nulling this arrangement.

Just because you're hurting doesn't give you the right to make others hurt.

Or unhappy.

Or fucking miserable.

Which...is exactly what Wes did to me over the Penny situation.

And again with this one.

Huh.

Perhaps he *is* exactly the person she needs to talk to.

The ghost of Christmas Future that convinces her to stop making it fucking snow discontent.

Wes's first knock on her door is expectedly ignored.

As is the second.

And third.

But by his fourth, understanding in me begins to waiver.

His fifth?

Patience is sent to med bay leaving outrage to control my emotional ship.

Furious, heavy pounding is attached to a far from idle threat, "You open this door right now to talk to my fiancé or I will march my pregnant ass down to the lobby where I know there are at least a handful of tiger sharks hoping for chum and give it to them in the form of revealing your ugly bribing and blackmailing ways that have destroyed the lives of many, *many* people."

It's no surprise to me when we hear heavy stomping almost immediately.

I flash the men around me a smug smile and fold my arms firmly across my chest.

You know what?

I think I'm gonna take that job.

I *know* I can get shit done.

Real shit.

More shit than Species 8472 ever did.

Monica aggressively opens the door revealing her puffy, makeup smeared face alongside her severely disheveled hair. "*What can I do for you Wilcoxes?*" A loud sniffle is stolen. "You want a public apology? She tucks strands behind her ear. "A copy of my resignation letter?" Her hand falls defeatedly onto her dark green pants. "For me to relocate at least fifty miles away from your family to save you the trouble of having a restraining order drafted and filed?"

"Yes," instantly leaves me. "*To all of that.*"

"*Bryn,*" Wes hisses in disapproval forcing me to seal my lips shut.

Oops.

Didn't realize they were rhetorical questions.

"May we come in?" he politely asks.

"Why?"

"To talk."

"You mean to gloat?"

It's damn near impossible to bite my tongue, yet I do.

For his sake.

"I mean what I say," Wes emotionlessly announces. "I understand that you're accustomed to having to manipulate speech in order to collect information or achieve the desired results you seek; however, this is not an investigation or an interrogation, Monica."

"Then what is it?"

238

"Simply a request to speak candidly between one another." His expression tightens at the same time he leans slightly forward. "*Completely. Off. The. Record.*"

At that, she slightly nods, steps back, and wordlessly ushers us inside, leaving Holmes on the outside to do his job.

My fiancé waits until his non-sister has flopped onto the edge of her mattress to sincerely state, "I offer my deepest apologies that the test results were not favorable to you."

Her eyebrows pull together in obvious puzzlement. "*What?*"

"Obsessing over this…over you…over our parents…it almost ruined my entire life, and I only had to deal with it for a few weeks. I can easily see how having to deal with it for *months…alone on top of it all…*could drive you insane."

She barely nods as she crosses her ankles.

"I understand the agony of having more questions than answers. Of having more accusations than those to hold accountable. Of feeling completely alone because the person you had been counting on in your life died before you were truly ready."

New tears begin to line the rims of her lids.

"I also understand the anger…that…*deep seated rage…*the one that you swear won't be sated until someone else…*hell, everyone else…*is experiencing the same pain that you are."

"*Your life just seemed so fucking perfect.*" A single tear falls in tandem with her whispering, "*And I hated you for it.*"

"My life Monica, has never been perfect." An almost amused beam is delivered. "Money doesn't make it perfect. It never has. I learned that from a *very* early age."

"Same," slips free from me.

"You just…you seemed to have this magical, fairy tale life, with the world's greatest father, who could do no wrong, who had never done anything wrong – according to everything my mother ever said or wrote – and I couldn't accept that. I wanted him to fall from grace. I couldn't accept that this man…this *perfect* man…that the

239

entire world claimed to love…refused to openly be there for *both* of his children. To keep one a dirty secret. I couldn't accept that the man my mother claimed to be the most important one to ever be in her life could just…abandon one child over the other for the sake of his legacy." She slowly shakes her head before defeatedly shrugging. "But he didn't. Because I was never really his. I was just…*there.*"

"You meant more to him than you think," Wes unexpectedly claims. "He paid for all of your education – *including college* – through a shell corporation hidden so well that I had no idea it even existed until you brought their…affair to my doorstep."

It's her turn to look shocked. "*He* did that?"

"That same shell corporation was also used to fund you both with top dollar medical care *and* covered the cost of operations and taxes for the ranch you grew up on."

"I didn't find any record of that."

"My father was *clever.*" An almost admirable expression graces his face. "*Resourceful.*"

Her jaw lowers a smidge further.

"*And I. Am. His. Son.*" The proclamation is filled with so much notable pride and adoration that I can't resist wrapping my arm around his lower back. "Which is why I'm going to have Park arrange a meeting for you with Nedi Fernadez, a highly recommended investigator that specializes in locating and reconnecting separated relatives."

The wide mouth look remains.

"I'll cover the costs for you up to a year while you *reevaluate* your life." His arm drapes around my shoulder as he continues. "I suggest redirecting your impressive journalism skills to do something perhaps more positively productive *behind* the camera like highlighting injustices or hidden dangers in certain industries rather than destructive in front of it as you agreed to retire from." My thumb gently strokes his side in additional support. "I also *highly suggest* grief counseling or talk therapy to explore some of your unresolved resentment regarding me, my father, and the absence of yours."

"*Why?*" Monica brushes away another tear prior to further investigating, "Why are you being so kind to me in spite of what I put you through?" Her gaze latches onto mine. "What I put you *both* through?"

"Because despite the way you've spent your time portraying my fiancé, he's actually *not* a monster." Our grips tighten in tandem. "He's kind. And generous. And maybe a little overprotective at times but just the right amount at others."

"I learned those things from my father," Wes warmly compliments, "and my godfather. They're the same things I hope my son – or daughter – learns from me."

Beaming up at him is attached to a loving coo, "They will."

"I'm sorry," she abruptly fumbles out, tone still stricken with thick tears. "*To both of you.*"

"Hurt people, hurt people my psychiatrist often reminds me," compassionately escapes the man I can't wait to spend forever with. "And healing people…have the power to help heal people." An off-kilter grin grows on his face. "I'm choosing to use my power for good, Ms. Simmons. I hope one day you choose to do the same."

Chapter 25

Wes

"I don't think that live event unfolded the way *anyone* foresaw it," Clark casually claims at the same time he places a dish full of couscous in the middle of their kitchen table. "Self-included."

"You honestly had no idea that Monica wasn't his sister?" J.T. investigates from the other side of the table. "Like...*none*?"

"That's not what he said," Lauren reprimands while placing a tray of lemon roasted broccoli with pine nuts close to the center.

My best friend's eyebrows instantly dart down in consternation. "Is it not?"

"How have your listening skills gotten *worse* over time?" Clark scolds, playfulness dancing through his tone.

"I'm inclined to blame Uhura," he swiftly sells out the woman at my side.

"And I'm inclined to kick you off my ship."

"Your *mom's* ship." His taunting gets us both laughing. "You are not the captain here."

"Like I've said before," Lauren sweetly interjects, the brown sugar glazed plate of salmon joining the other food on the table, "it's best that I only had one."

"Because one was just enough."

"Or more than enough," pokes J.T. around another laugh.

"You are *this close*," Bryn demonstrates on her fingers, "to getting a shitty uncle nickname."

More snickers reverberate around their rustic cottage home prior to Clark placing a kind hand on my shoulder. "How are you doing with everything?"

The temptation to lie is short courtesy of a stern stare I know better than to disregard. "I'm ambivalent."

He shifts his body into the head of the table seat to my right. "Why?"

"Part of me is grateful to know that my father *didn't* hide my actual sibling from me, yet the other part of me hates that in a way he still did. That he hid so much from us both. That *both* of our parents – Monica's mom and my father – weren't *honest*." Bryn's hand lands on my thigh and mine drops to cradle it. "I think we have a weird Batman and Joker like camaraderie built from not knowing of their relationship when they were alive and not having enough answers to satisfy our curiosities; however, I feel guilty for still wanting more information. For hating that there are unfilled gaps that will probably never be filled."

"Weston," my mother-in-law in the making unexpectedly calls out as she settles into her seat opposite her husband, "do you know what a parable is?"

"A made-up story to teach a moral lesson."

"I told them often to you when you were a boy," Clark fondly chimes in.

"Bryn was never a fan of *listening* to me tell a story-"

"Not when *Star Trek* did it better," mumbles my fiancée between scoops of side dishes.

"However, I am hoping now that I'm going to be a grandma-"

"Have we *settled* on grandma?" she asks on a casual point. "Have we considered g-ma? Or Gigi? Or Gam Gam? Or maybe even something way off script like Roz?"

"Homage to Helena Rozhenko?" J.T. asks without missing a beat. "Worf's mom? The saint of a woman who raised a Klingon child?"

"*Exactly!*" exclaims Bryn, accidentally flinging tiny pieces everywhere.

"Okay, no," Lauren denies with an open palm, "we won't be calling me that."

It's impossible to bat away my smirk when the woman at my side dramatically rolls her entire head.

"Like I was saying…" finding my gaze occurs again, "now that I'm going to be a grandma, I hope that I finally get the opportunity to weave such tales."

Touched by the idea, I softly smile. "I have no doubt that you will."

"There's one in particular that I think *you* might like to hear."

A small twitch of befuddlement is presented.

"And it's one I know Clark would love to help me *tell*."

Additional confusion cuts through my glare.

"Once upon a time, there was a noble and mighty king, beloved by many, who had been bitten by the Golden Bug very early in his life…" he begins, clearly having planned this entire moment. "The bite was big and nasty and often turned him into a cold, cruel, and uncaring king."

"Like an anti-Spiderman," J.T. interjects.

"A king that sought ruthless ways to acquire riches upon riches and conquer kingdoms upon kingdoms," emphasizes Lauren.

"Like a dick," my better half murmurs under her breath before sliding a salmon fillet onto my plate.

"This king wanted an heir. In fact, he told his queen, that it was the only thing he *really* wanted, that all the riches in the world would be dull in comparison, that they wouldn't matter nearly as much as they did once he had one, yet after she bore him his son, his greedy ways still continued," Clark proceeds, attention fixated on me.

"So, a dick *and* a liar," grumbles Bryn between sucks of her sticky fingers.

"The king spent ludicrous amounts on extravagant clothing for the queen that she did not want. The king also insisted every night be

244

accompanied with the most expensive food and music and alcohol that he could find," Lauren illustrates further.

"His drinking made all of his Golden Bug symptoms *worse*. Much, much worse." Clark's eyebrows soar to the ceiling, and I thoughtlessly sink into my seat. "Most of the kingdom – outside his queen and his faithful royal adviser – had no idea about the ongoing war he faced with the bottle, but it was *real*. It was as strong if not stronger than any adversary he had sent his men to face in battle."

Bryn and J.T. join me in leaning closer to him.

Into the tale.

"As the young prince began to grow up," my Head of Household shifts the reins back to her, "the beautiful queen often feared for his life *because* of the Golden Bug bitten king's drinking. And then one dark and stormy night, her worst fear came true."

"*How?*" whispers her daughter.

"During dinner, the king grabbed the young prince's wrist so roughly for refusing to eat his peas that it almost snapped."

Gasps from the other guests aren't surprising.

And what's even *less* surprising is vaguely remembering that moment.

Or something *like* that moment.

Was it peas?

Why is there a niggling in the back of mind that it was a different vegetable?

Asparagus, maybe?

"The queen knew – *she knew* – she had to do whatever it took to protect her only son," Lauren proceeds, "so, she gave the dreaded king a no-win choice before bed."

"A Kobayashi Maru!" squawk the *Star Trek* twins at the table.

"When morning came, he could leave or she would," finishes the woman I have no doubt knows more about parts of my upbringing than I do.

They gasp again, yet I let my gaze drift to Clark.

245

Focus on what he's going to say.

"The next day the heartbroken king made the sober decision *not* to rip his child and wife away from the palace so long as *she promised* that after enough time had passed, they would talk. Attempt to reconcile. He didn't wanna lose her forever." A wistful glance in the distance is taken. "The queen *reluctantly* agreed and off he went."

"I get it," Bryn quietly concurs on a mouthful of couscous.

She does.

And I *hate* that she does.

I also hate how much my father and I have in common.

It's haunting.

"Thankfully, it didn't take the sad king long to realize how sick he truly was, nor did it take him long to set off on a magical quest for a cure." Clark mindlessly fiddles with the fork beside his plate. "That quest led him to buy a small home in a very poor village where he knew he could completely heal. He went to extreme lengths to keep the kingdom from knowing why he had momentarily stepped away from his throne and continued pretending that everything was as perfect as ever. The very sick king knew that he couldn't defeat the poison in his system all alone and hired *help*, which included a young, homeless woman who had recently become pregnant."

"*Oh, shit,*" escapes without my consent.

"The two quickly built a beautiful friendship," Lauren exclaims, voice flooded with hope and cheer. "She helped keep him sober and far, far away from the poison that made his bug bite worse, and he helped keep her healthy. He had the local doctor tend to her pregnancy in private as to not start new rumors about her in the village. He kept her fed. Loved. And in return she reminded him of the man he was *before* he had been bitten by the Golden Bug."

"Eventually, their relationship turned into something more than just friendship." My father's best friend tilts his head pensively to one side. "However, shortly after the village woman gave birth to

246

her beautiful baby girl, the king realized something very important. He longed for his *own* child. The one who bared *his name*."

"The one he had with the queen. *His. Queen.*"

"The one he had big dreams of ruling the kingdom with passion and purpose." He leans himself back in his seat. "It was at that moment that he realized it wasn't the young village woman he was in love with, but *the queen*. He came to the conclusion that the woman he had spent months caring for, who had spent months helping him get past the sickness from the Golden Bug and other poisons, was nothing more than an angel sent to assist him in finding his way home."

"So," Lauren excitedly takes over yet again, "the king left the angel with promises to thank her however he could. Upon his return to the palace and reconciliation with the queen – who had missed him more than words could say – there was a royal decree for the household to *never* speak about that time or what they knew."

That's the legal document Clark signed.

"The king and the queen also came to an agreement to give the young angel – that they both felt indebted to for bringing them back together – all the riches she could ever want or need for her and her child for what remained of her life. Her thanks to them was her life-long *silence* about the king's difficult journey back to his queen and keeping them informed of whenever someone went searching for answers that were not theirs to have."

Monica's mother didn't *have* to stay silent?

She actively *chose* to be?

To hide their relationship?

To contribute to having that whole town erase the evidence?

"I *love* that all the women in this story are badass," Bryn announces on a bite of fish. "*That's* my kind of women empowerment shit."

"After the king and the queen were together again, the entire kingdom changed," Clark resumes speaking. "The king spent more

247

time with his heir and his queen. He allowed for his riches to continue to grow plentiful yet made it *his mission* to give back to the towns he reigned over. He became known as a great and *kind* king, loved and adored by many rather than simply feared. He along with his trusted royal adviser and the queen, went to great lengths to protect the young heir from ever getting bitten by the Golden Bug. The king – in particular – didn't want him to suffer through the same fate he had endured." He braces his bent arms on the table. Leans forward. "He wanted *more* for his son, but not in the financial aspect. The king didn't want greed or alcohol to lead the heir astray as it had once led him. He wanted the prince to be a *better man* than he was. He wanted him to keep his eyes on making the kingdom *better for all* rather than getting wrapped up in keeping it better for just *himself*."

"And the young heir did just that," Lauren lovingly adds, finally dragging over the tray of vegetables. "He created a wonderful kingdom for all those in his realm, fell in love with a strong – albeit mouthy – princess, and lived happily ever after, which is all the king and queen truly wanted for their only child."

"There's nothing wrong with a princess speaking her mind," Bryn sasses at her mom. "*We both know that.*"

Laughter circles the table alongside the containers of food as the truth of the tale properly settles in.

I *am* the king's heir.

I *am* following in his footsteps.

I *am* living the life he wanted me to lead in spite of his absence.

No.

He wasn't perfect.

He made mistakes.

Many of the same mistakes that I've now made; however, he pushed on.

For himself.

For my mother.

For me.

I, too, will progress forward.

For me.

For them.

For Bryn.

And for my own heir that I can't wait to meet.

***

Thank you for reading Public: The Extended Edition (The Private Series #2)! I hope you loved this contemporary, redemption, billionaire romance!

Want a BONUS scene from their wedding? Grab it EXCLUSIVELY here:

https://bit.ly/PublicTheExtendedEditionBonusScene

Get ready to follow this couple's relationship into their next phase of life in Personal: The Extended Edition (The Private Series #3)

https://mybook.to/JhUK7

(You can check out a SNEAK PEEK on the next page)

Be sure to check out my other book, Duched (The Duched Series #1) where you will find another powerful public figure forced to deal with secrets, lies, and surprises!

https://mybook.to/6BcHQ

***

Keep reading for a SNEAK PEEK at Personal: The Extended Edition (The Private Series #3)!

(Personal: The Extended Edition Private Series #3)

Chapter 1

Wes

There are several notable things I love about my downtown office here in Highland.

The first being its location.

This is the perfect point between our penthouse, Brynley's job at The Bower and Powell Institute, and the private academy that our two and half year-old son, Wyland Wayne Wilcox, attends.

Next?

The view.

Awe-inspiring is an under sell.

Having the ability to randomly take a moment to admire the remarkable architecture that creates our city is most certainly a pro for being in the building rather than a con.

And most importantly?

Impeccable privacy due to the soundproofing I had installed during our honeymoon.

I can have my wife under my desk or over my desk or on my couch, moaning and groaning and screaming like she's Harvey Dent, having half her face burned off by acid.

Interestingly enough, Little Prey is still quite vocal despite having a son with Superhero level hearing.

I swear the kid can hear the second my zipper lowers from across the fucking property in one of the guesthouses we sneak away to for a little "alone time" while he's with his grandparents.

Hamilton believes I'm exaggerating; however, he did his job and provided me with the best otolaryngologists in our area to further investigate if necessary.

Which I just may.

My family's health is not a subject matter I take lightly.

It's not one I've ever taken lightly.

It's not one to ever be taken lightly.

Especially when it comes to my son.

***

Find out exactly what happens next with his family in this contemporary, romantic suspense, billionaire romance trilogy here:
https://mybook.to/kBPXh

Did you enjoy reading Public: The Extended Edition (The Private Series #2)? I would appreciate you leaving a review if you did!
https://mybook.to/BJhaiaP

OTHER WORKS

Do you love EASTER EGGS in books? Well, mine are often full of them and this one is no exception.

Here are links to other stories/places/people that were mentioned/referenced in the book!
Did you catch all of these?

Dalvegan Dragons (The Owner)
https://amzn.to/3IImDpx

The Frost Luxury Hotel (Free-Form: The Extended Edition)
https://www.amazon.com/dp/B0C5RXHJBG

Cliffsworth, Fire & Ash (The Bros Series)
https://www.amazon.com/dp/B07H9KLC2M

Roscoe's Wheels & Waffles (The Love Duet)
https://www.amazon.com/dp/B09VK1R3C8

South Haven Island (Redneck Romeo)
https://amzn.to/2vYuPhM

Little Soup of Horrors (Compassion: The Extended Edition)
https://amzn.to/3zI6GdI

Vlasta (The Hockey Gods Series)
https://amzn.to/38HYH0z

Haworth Enterprises (Haworth Enterprises Series)
https://amzn.to/3FHw8nr

Pierce Wyatt (Already Written)
https://www.amazon.com/dp/B01EGR3BV2

Cooper Copeland (Cowboy Casanova)
https://amzn.to/2sxwqGT

Ann Arbor (Waiting)
https://amzn.to/3QwTXBa

Lawson Brothers (Eden)
https://amzn.to/3mumx98

Bennett Enterprise (The Bennett Duet)
https://amzn.to/3z5oEWl

Doctenn, Trenton Kenningston (The Duched Series)
https://mybook.to/6BcHQ

Gwendolyn Kincaid (Walking Away)
https://www.amazon.com/dp/B07981Z4X2

South Haven (Already Designed)
https://www.amazon.com/dp/B07B46JNJC

Yasmine's Yummies (Hike, Hike, Baby)
https://www.amazon.com/dp/B07VPC5WBH

Applecourt (Aleatory)
https://amzn.to/3xKJQ2L

Middlebrook (Horseback Hero)
https://amzn.to/2BhT91r

Misfit bikers (Camelot Misfits Series)
https://amzn.to/2TTnNCI

Torrez (The Shatter & Shock Duet)
https://www.amazon.com/dp/B0C1CNS58X

Sunshine Bend (Baby Got Pack)
https://www.amazon.com/dp/B09VKBRJKK

Runt's Beer (Must Love Hogs)
https://www.amazon.com/dp/B074HX1VK2

Mistletoe, Montana (Sleighbride)
https://www.amazon.com/dp/B08MWQJ3BL

Charming Chef (The Chef)
https://www.amazon.com/dp/B07HPFNZ76

Nedi Fernadez (The Veteran)
https://www.amazon.com/dp/B0CSPQ2MNC

GRATITUDE:

The list of people who assist in this entire process is truly too many to name. So rather than run the risk of forgetting anyone, I want to just say thank you to EVERYONE. Readers, bloggers, book influencers (new and old), friends, family, reviewers, and street teamers...you have allowed me to have a great career in PUBLIC and showcase my stories there. Thank you for supporting me and making every good time and hard time in this journey filled with love and laughter as well as for believing in my vision.

Until next time...

FOLLOW ME!!!

Website (Signed Paperback Purchases Available)
https://www.xavierneal.com/

Facebook
https://www.facebook.com/XavierNealAuthorPage

Facebook Group
https://www.facebook.com/groups/1471618443081356

Twitter (Now known as X)
@XavierNeal87

Instagram
@authorxavierneal

Pinterest
https://www.pinterest.com/xavierneal/

Bookbub
https://www.bookbub.com/authors/xavier-neal

Goodreads
https://www.goodreads.com/author/show/4990135.Xavier_Neal

New Release Alerts
https://www.xavierneal.com/newsletter

Tik Tok
https://www.tiktok.com/@authorxavierneal

Spotify
http://bit.ly/XNSpotifyProfile

Store Front
http://tee.pub/lic/authorxavierneal

FULL List of My Works

Standalones

Cinderfella (YA Contemporary) - https://amzn.to/2pBHZff
The Gamble (Romantic Comedy) - https://amzn.to/2uf4ZFw
Part of The List (Contemporary Romance) -
https://amzn.to/2udYwuz
Walking Away (Contemporary Ménage Romance) -
https://amzn.to/2pAOEGf
Can't Match This (Romantic Comedy) - https://amzn.to/2XapsVw
Hike, Hike Baby (Romantic Comedy) - https://amzn.to/2PNj456
(Available in Audio)
Baewatch (Romantic Comedy) – https://amzn.to/3izNvaG
Sleigh Bride (Holiday Romantic Comedy) -
https://amzn.to/2J0Qk8D
Aleatory (Contemporary Age-Gap Romance) -
https://amzn.to/3xKJQ2L (Available in Audio)
Picnic Perfect (Romantic Comedy) - https://amzn.to/2UZdgeN
Eden (Dark, Taboo Romance) - https://amzn.to/3mumx98
Baby Got Pack (Romantic Comedy) - https://amzn.to/3rsQpoO
Waiting (Contemporary Age-Gap Romance) –
https://amzn.to/3QwTXBa (Available in Audio)

Senses Series
(Sports Romance/ Romantic Comedy) (Complete Series)

Vital (Prequel Novella)- FREE ON ALL PLATFORMS
https://amzn.to/2ueL5KJ
Blind- https://amzn.to/2GmEMcO
Deaf- https://amzn.to/2IK71Rf
Numb- https://amzn.to/2pAOYVt

Hush- https://amzn.to/2pzV2gS
Savor- https://amzn.to/2HZsVP1
Callous- https://amzn.to/2pAPmTV
Agonize- https://amzn.to/2ILLaZw
Suffocate - https://amzn.to/2GjLU9T
Mollify- https://amzn.to/2GgRJoJ
Blur- https://amzn.to/2pD1rrK
Blear - https://amzn.to/2DQGb6a
Blare- https://amzn.to/33nnqV8
Senses Box Set (Books 1-5) – https://amzn.to/2Gkxruw

Adrenaline Series
(Romance/ Romantic Suspense)
Classic (FREE ON MOST PLATFORMS) -
https://amzn.to/2I0wd4D
Vintage- https://amzn.to/2HXksMw
Masterpiece- https://amzn.to/2G0tWKj
Unmask- https://amzn.to/2Gn2tBK
Error- https://amzn.to/2pBakC6
Iconic- https://amzn.to/2G1Q8Ua
Box Set (Books 1-3) - https://amzn.to/2IP7GRe

Prince of Tease Series
(Romance/ Romantic Comedy)
Prince Arik- https://amzn.to/2pAuhbF
Prince Hunter- https://amzn.to/2IKzuGu
Prince Brock- https://amzn.to/2ufmghN
Prince Chance- https://amzn.to/2LuclMw
Prince Zane- TBA

Hollywood Exchange Series
(Romance/ Romantic Comedy)
Already Written - https://amzn.to/2G0F2ix

Already Secure- TBA
Already Designed (The South Haven Crew #1) -
https://amzn.to/2G8A0fP
Already Scripted (The South Haven Crew #2) - TBA
Already Legal (The South Haven Crew #3) - TBA
Already Driven (The South Haven Crew #4) - TBA
Already Cast (The South Haven Crew #5) – TBA

The Just Series
(Second Chance Romance)
Just Out of Reach- https://amzn.to/2ubzfBe
Just So Far Away- https://amzn.to/2DR57KM

Private Series
(Romantic Suspense) (Complete Series)
Private: The Extended Edition - https://amzn.to/2IN7P7R
Public: The Extended Edition - https://mybook.to/1Brfw
Personal: The Extended Edition - https://mybook.to/eu0GLoW
Priority (A Private Series Holiday Novella) -
https://mybook.to/ObKJ8r
Popular (A Private Series Standalone) - https://mybook.to/T8bytB

Duched Series
(Romantic Comedy) (Complete Series)
Duched- https://amzn.to/2G4Xlim
Royally Duched- https://amzn.to/2pAnvDh
Royally Duched Up- https://amzn.to/2G089SP
Duched Deleted (FREE Novella ON ALL PLATOFRMS)-
https://amzn.to/2GlOQTy

The Bros Series
(Erotic Romance) (Complete)
The Substitute- https://amzn.to/2ub9CAc

The Hacker- https://amzn.to/2FZFxJr
The Suit- https://amzn.to/2poTcyX
The Chef- https://amzn.to/2Dgi7MR

Must Love Series
(Sweet, Romantic Comedy)
Must Love Hogs- https://amzn.to/2IMmmkg
Must Love Jogs- https://amzn.to/2pBIiqp
Must Love Pogs- https://amzn.to/2ueUUIu
Must Love Logs- https://amzn.to/2IFGrL7
Must Love Flogs- TBA

The Culture Blind Series
(Contemporary Romance)
Redneck Romeo- https://amzn.to/2vYuPhM
Cowboy Casanova- https://amzn.to/2sxwqGT
Horseback Hero- https://amzn.to/2BhT91r
Blue Jean Bachelor- TBA

Camelot Misfits MC Series
(MC Romance/ Romantic Suspense)
King's Return - https://amzn.to/2TTnNCI (Available in Audio)
King's Conquest - https://amzn.to/2IaYZo8 (Available in Audio)
King's Legacy – https://amzn.to/2YfvY1i (Available in Audio)
Wiz's Remedy – https://amzn.to/2PMmJDK (Available in Audio)
Locke's (Currently Untitled) Novel - TBA
Trick's (Currently Untitled) Novel – TBA

Synful Syndicate Series
(Dark Romance)
Unleashed- https://amzn.to/2VVhcfT
Unleashed Syn- https://www.amazon.com/dp/B0BZQRYT72
Unchained - TBA

The Bennett Duet
(Dark, Mafia/Mob Romance) (Complete)
Dark Ruler – https://amzn.to/3z5oEW1 (Available in Audio)
Dark Reign - https://amzn.to/3H9v3SO (Available in Audio)

Haworth Enterprises Series
(Romantic Suspense
Bulletproof - https://amzn.to/3FHw8nr (Available in Audio)
Shatterproof – https://www.amazon.com/dp/B0C1CNS58X
(Available in Audio)
Shockproof – https://www.amazon.com/dp/B0CG6NS3FH
Sleighproof – https://www.amazon.com/dp/B0CNDBFCMT

The Hockey Gods Series
(Sports Romance/Romantic Comedy)
Can't Block My Love – https://amzn.to/38HYH0z
My Fair Puck Bunny – https://amzn.to/33t2nSw
The Forward Must Cry – https://amzn.to/3ijTfpm
Defenseman No. 9 – https://amzn.to/3sqAgiJ
Taming of The Crew - https://amzn.to/3jo5gwR

The Draak Legacy
(PNR Romance)

Saving Silver – https://amzn.to/3J5jG06 (Available in Audio)
Getting Gold - https://amzn.to/3ejkdNW (Coming to Audio)
Pleasing Platinum – https://amzn.to/3rsCQ9g (Coming to Audio)

The Love Duet
(Contemporary/Second Chance Romance)
First Love – https://amzn.to/3xrUnlt
Last Love – https://amzn.to/36hyjit

Complete Boxset (w/bonus material) – https://amzn.to/37RNpeK

The Debt Tales
(Dark Fairy Tale Retellings)

Twisted Debt – https://amzn.to/3c2eyhM
Savage Debt - https://amzn.to/3E08QrX

Compassion Series
(Slow Burn Contemporary Romance)

Compassion: The Extended Edition: https://amzn.to/3zI6GdI
Silent Knight: https://amzn.to/3FGIqfT

Dalvegan Dragons Series
(Sports Romance, Romantic Comedy)
The Owner – https://amzn.to/3IImDpx (Available in Audio)
The Veteran – https://www.amazon.com/dp/B0CSPQ2MNC
The Stud – https://www.amazon.com/dp/B0CW39SB3B

The Free Series
(Opposites-Attract, Romantic Comedy)
Free-Form: The Extended Edition –
https://www.amazon.com/dp/B0C5RXHJBG
Free-Spirit – https://www.amazon.com/dp/B0C5RWB63Y

The Hunted Series
(Dark MMF Romance)
Hunted (Season 1) – https://www.amazon.com/dp/B0CY35XZQZ

Made in the USA
Middletown, DE
25 January 2025

70137988R00148